ALSO BY FREIDA MCFADDEN

The Intruder

The Tenant

The Crash

The Boyfriend

The Teacher

The Coworker

Ward D

Never Lie

The Inmate

The Housemaid

The Housemaid's Secret

The Housemaid Is Watching

Do You Remember?

Do Not Disturb

The Locked Door

Want to Know a Secret?

One by One

The Wife Upstairs

The Perfect Son

The Ex

The Surrogate Mother

Brain Damage

Dead Med

DEAR DEBBIE

FREIDA McFADDEN

Poisoned Pen
PRESS

Published by Poisoned Pen Press, an imprint of Sourcebooks
1935 Brookdale RD, Naperville, IL 60563-2773
(630) 961-3900
sourcebooks.com

Cataloging-in-Publication Data is on file with the Library of Congress.

Printed and bound in the United States of America.
MA 10 9 8 7 6 5 4 3 2 1

For my mother,
Who loves nothing better than a good revenge story

AUTHOR'S NOTE

Even though my books are thrillers, a genre that traditionally has dark elements, I do my best to keep them as family friendly as I possibly can. You're not going to come across any graphic scenes of violence or S-E-X. (Mostly because I know my family members will be reading!)

However, people have emotional responses to different things, and some of my books delve into more controversial topics. So for this reason, I created a list of content warnings for all my thrillers, which can be found linked off the top of my website:

freidamcfadden.com

This is a resource that can be used by readers who need to protect their mental health as well as for adults whose kids are reading my books. Please also keep in mind that in a few cases, these content warnings are major spoilers for twists that take place in the book.

With that in mind, I hope you safely enjoy this journey into my imagination!

CHAPTER 1

FROM *DEAR DEBBIE* DRAFTS FILE

Dear Debbie,

You always tell us in your fabulous column that breakfast is the most important meal of the day, and I believe you! But is my family ever willing to sit down and eat it? Not a chance.

Every morning it's the same circus. My kids are searching for missing shoes or homework assignments that vanished overnight, and my husband can't find his keys or reading glasses. Nobody is interested in taking five minutes to sit down at the kitchen table to enjoy the perfectly good breakfast that I just spent the last fifteen minutes cooking up.

I've tried everything! Quick meals, grab-and-go options, bribery (don't ask!), but no matter what I do, my family always leaves the house with empty bellies!

How on earth am I supposed to get my family to take a few minutes to eat a nutritious breakfast before they dash out the door without so much as a goodbye? Help me, Debbie!

Hungry in Hingham

Dear Hungry in Hingham,

Indeed, breakfast is the most important meal of the day. It boosts your energy levels and alertness, and if you don't get a healthy breakfast, you can feel sluggish all day long. In children and adolescents, a nutritious breakfast can improve recall and focus for school.

If your family isn't interested in having breakfast, try to probe to see what sorts of foods might tempt them to take those crucial extra 15 minutes in the morning. Some people prefer a bowl of cereal, others might want pancakes, and others might want a full breakfast with eggs and bacon and whole grain toast. Find out what your family likes best, and cater to those desires!

And if that doesn't work, I would recommend installing a padlock on the front and back door of your house. First thing in the morning, lock both doors from the inside, and keep the key in your pocket. Let everyone know that they will not be leaving the house until they have consumed a healthy breakfast. If they seem hesitant, a simple threat to swallow the key unless they sit down and eat will surely move things along.

I have no doubt you will soon be enjoying a wonderful daily breakfast with your family!

Debbie

CHAPTER 2

DEBBIE

I have been forbidden to speak to my daughter Lexi in the morning.

Lexi imposed this rule around when she started high school, and now that she is a senior, it remains rigidly in place. The rule was implemented when Lexi decided she didn't like it when I dared to ask her "How are you?" first thing in the morning, and she simply didn't "feel like talking right now, my *God*, Mom."

So midway through freshman year, Lexi officially announced that I was no longer permitted to speak to her during early morning hours. And if I attempt any form of communication—verbal or nonverbal—she will snap at me and say, "What did I tell you?" Or possibly worse, glare at me with *that look*.

You know what look I mean. At least if you have teenagers, you know.

So when Lexi marches into our kitchen on this Wednesday morning, I don't say a word. I just keep eating my bowl of cornflakes—the kind with extra fiber. (Now that I'm in my forties, anything that has a lot of fiber is an auto buy.) It's easy to remember not to talk to Lexi, because she has a pair of giant headphones covering her ears. She's always wearing those headphones. It's possible they have fused with the temporal bones of her skull.

Lexi has her hair in a messy ponytail that looks as though she tied it last night or perhaps even several days ago and hasn't gotten around to adjusting it. She's wearing an oversize hoodie, which looks like something one might sleep in, and that impression is not helped by the fact that she's wearing plaid pajama pants. It's not pajama day at school or anything. This is what kids wear now. I find it distasteful, but on the other hand, I'm also jealous. I wish I could wear pajama pants every day.

Between my two kids, Lexi is the one who looks like me—a fact I'm sure is terribly embarrassing to her. She has the same delicate bone structure in her face and a similar dark shade to her slightly wavy hair. Like me, schoolwork comes easy to her, which is why she's taking four AP classes this year and a number theory class because she already took AP Calculus BC last year.

Like me, she might be a little too smart for her own good.

Lexi doesn't so much as glance at me as she makes a beeline for the refrigerator, although she casts a derisive look at the cans I have stacked on the kitchen counter for the canned food drive. Everything I do is a combination of embarrassing and aggravating. However, my most unforgivable crime of all was naming her Alexa. In my defense, how was I supposed to know Alexa would become a *thing*?

Lexi casts a look over her shoulder and does a double

4

take when she sees me. She's itching to comment, but that would break her eternal vow of silence. The internal struggle is real.

Finally, I break her. It's the lipstick—I never wear lipstick.

"What are you so dressed up for, Mom?" she wants to know.

I take another bite of my fiber cereal, then dab my lips with a napkin. I'm more of a T-shirt-and-yoga-pants kind of mom, so it surprises her to see me in a dress and full makeup. I even blow-dried my hair instead of leaving it damp in a ponytail.

"The photographers from *Home Gardening* are coming today," I remind her. "They're taking pictures of the yard."

It was an honor to be chosen by the magazine for this particular spread. As a stay-at-home mother to two girls, there have been times when my life has felt a bit... well, empty. I'm proud of my daughters, but I wanted to be proud of something that was all my own. This photo shoot gave me a nice boost to my confidence. I work hard on my garden.

There have been times when I felt that if I didn't have my flowers, I wouldn't even be able to get out of bed in the morning.

"I didn't know that," Lexi says, even though I mentioned it dozens of times. I don't point out the irony that if I had forgotten something she told me only yesterday, she would be lambasting me at this very moment. "Well, good luck."

That was a nice thing to say. And another miracle has occurred: my seventeen-year-old is now *speaking to me in the morning*. It feels like some sort of wacky, wonderful

5

dream. Dare I hope the difficult teenage years might be coming to a close?

"Thank you," I say cautiously, not wanting to do anything to disturb the peace.

Then Lexi wrinkles her nose. "You're not really going to bring all these cans to our school today, are you? You're going to look like a garbage woman."

Okay, maybe the difficult years aren't behind us *quite yet*.

Before I can come up with a suitable response to my daughter's criticism of me collecting food for those who need it, my other daughter, Isabel, pops into the kitchen. It's probably for the best, because she wouldn't have liked whatever I said.

Izzy is a sophomore at Hingham Prep, two years below her sister. While Lexi reminds me disturbingly of myself, Izzy is much more like her father. She has his lighter brown hair, earnest grin, and solid build. And like him, she's happy-go-lucky.

Unlike me and Lexi, Izzy has always been very athletic. I have hypothesized the endorphins might make her more pleasant than her sister. That's my running theory anyway. If I didn't force myself to go to the gym several times a week, I would murder everyone on my block.

"Hey, Mom." Izzy grabs an apple from the bowl on the kitchen counter. "Gotta run. The bus will be here in a minute."

"That's all you're eating for breakfast?" I protest.

"Mom, I gotta *go*."

In life and motherhood, *especially* motherhood of teenagers, you have to pick your battles. "Okay, I love you," I call out. "I'll pick you up after soccer."

Izzy hesitates, her high ponytail swinging slightly behind her head as she stands there, seeming to debate her next words. She stuffs the apple into the pocket of her hoodie. "That's okay," she finally says. "I'll take the bus home."

"But wait." As I rise quickly to my feet, my bowl of cereal tips over enough that some milk splashes on the kitchen table. It doesn't spill on my dress at least. "The school bus won't be around after soccer is over. I can get you."

Izzy doesn't reply.

"It's no problem at all!" I assure her, trying not to think of the days when I'd pick Izzy up at day care and she'd run to me so fast and hard that she'd nearly knock me off my feet.

I'm not sure how long Izzy would have stood there staring at me with her hands shoved into her pockets if Lexi hadn't blurted out, "For God's sake, just *tell* her, Iz."

I look between both girls. I hate it when they share secrets, although it's better than when they're fighting. "Tell me *what*?"

Izzy still doesn't say anything.

Lexi lets out an exaggerated sigh and says, "She got kicked off the soccer team."

"Lexi!" Izzy hisses, her face turning pink.

"*What?*"

Okay, this is flat out ridiculous. Izzy has been playing soccer since she was in kindergarten. She could dribble that soccer ball in her sleep. How could she have gotten kicked off the team? She's one of the best sophomores they have. Hell, she's one of the best *players* they have.

"I don't understand," I say. "Why were you kicked off the team?"

7

Izzy won't meet my eyes. "Mom…"

This has got to be some sort of mistake. There's no other explanation. "I'm going to give Coach Pike a call."

"Mom, *no.*" Her eyes widen in panic. "I have to go now. Don't call Coach Pike."

"Izzy…"

"Please don't call him." Her eyes are full of desperation. "Promise me you won't call him, Mom."

I don't want her to miss the bus. I can't afford to drive her right now, since I need to be here for the photo shoot. But she's not going to budge until I agree, so I finally spit out, "I promise."

I promise I won't *call* him. But I didn't promise I won't go to his office and ask him what the hell he was thinking when he cut my daughter from the team.

Izzy gives me one last look, and then she dashes out the door. That girl is always running. She's an *amazing* soccer player. I don't know what happened to get her kicked off the team, but I'm determined to get to the bottom of it.

I turn my attention to my older daughter, who has picked up a can of creamed corn and is reading the label with a sour expression on her face, like the ingredients have personally offended her.

"Do you know what happened?" I ask Lexi.

"Oh my God, Mom, *no,* I *don't.*" Lexi grunts. "Can you please stop asking, like, a million times?"

This is the first time I asked her, but whatever. "You haven't heard anything at all?"

"*No.*" Lexi gives me a seething look but then adds, "She's better off ditching the team anyway. Coach Pike is such a perv."

"A perv?"

She rolls her eyes, irritated that she has to take the time to explain every little thing to me. "My friend Mira was on the soccer team, and she said he was always, like, 'accidentally' walking into the locker room when the girls were changing. He'd say sorry and leave right away, but... well, that doesn't sound like an accident to me."

He did *what*?

The cereal sticks in my throat as I contemplate this new revelation. Izzy never said anything like that, but I know Lexi's friend Mira, and she's not the type of girl who makes up stories. Is it possible that it's true? And if it is, do I even *want* Izzy on the soccer team?

"Ugh, could you quit it, Mom?" Lexi says irritably.

I force myself to swallow the mouthful of cereal. "Quit what?"

"Chewing," she says.

"Chewing?" I repeat incredulously.

"The way you chew...it's so loud. Like, nobody else in the world chews that loudly. Trust me—it's super weird. They can probably hear it next door."

Nobody has ever criticized the volume of my mastication before. For a moment, I'm at a loss. "Sorry. I'll try to chew more *quietly*."

"It's so *loud*," she reiterates. "You're always chewing, and it's, like, *so* annoying."

I am momentarily distracted from my thoughts of Coach Pike by the more immediate issue of what on earth happened to my relationship with my firstborn. I remember a time when I used to make pancakes for Lexi in the morning. I would go all out. I formed a smiley face on each individual one using blueberries or, if it was a special

9

day, chocolate chips. When Lexi saw those smiley face pancakes (especially the chocolate chip ones), her eyes would light up. She would eat all the blueberries or chocolate chips first, and then she would smother the stack in maple syrup. After a few bites, she would look up at me with a sticky, happy smile. *You make the bestest pancakes in the world, Mommy!*

I take another bite of my cereal, wondering if there's any activity I could suggest we do together. Maybe a shopping trip. Lexi has always loved to go shopping, even when she was little, and now she still loves clothes. Finding the clothes she likes might be a challenge though.

Maybe I could offer to take her to a pajama store. Is there such a thing? If there isn't, they should make one. It's a million-dollar idea.

A car horn blasts from outside the house, loud enough that both of us startle. I can't make my daughter smile anymore, but that horn does the job. It's her boyfriend, Zane, who recently turned eighteen and got his full license and now can drive her to school every single day.

He never comes inside the house though. He only blasts that damn horn loud enough to let everybody in the neighboring towns know that he has arrived. It might even be a little louder than my chewing.

"Gotta go," Lexi chirps.

My daughter grabs her backpack off the floor, which is heavy enough that when she's wearing it, she walks with a slight backward tilt. She opens her mouth as if to tell me goodbye, but then she remembers her rule about not speaking to me in the morning, so she instead darts out the door without another word.

I've only finished about half my cereal, but I don't have

much of an appetite anyway. I follow the path through the living room that Lexi took to the front door, knowing she didn't bother to lock it on her way out. Why should she, since I always lock it behind her.

I am always here for my family. Always.

I peek out the window at the broken-down red Kia that is pulling out of my driveway. Whenever I see that car, I think to myself that he should just drive it straight to the town dump and leave it there. I'm not thrilled about the fact that my oldest child is being transported to high school in that piece of junk, but I recognize that I don't have much of a say in the matter.

My thoughts about the boy driving the piece of junk are even less charitable.

I catch a glimpse of Zane as he pulls onto the road in front of my house. He has long, shaggy hair and is skinny as a rail, even though the times he has been in my house, he has devoured a small truckload of food. If half of my refrigerator has been emptied, it means Zane has been by for a visit. Especially if the refrigerator has been left slightly ajar and the toilet seat is up. Not to mention the fact that I'm pretty sure he vapes. I don't even entirely know what vaping is, but I know I don't want my daughter dating a boy who does it. Not that I have a choice.

But most of all, I don't like the way he looks at Lexi. There's something in his expression that makes me uneasy. It's something I've seen before—a memory that I can't ever block out.

Lexi and Zane have been dating for about four months, and I was ready for it to be over three and a half months ago.

But I can't forbid her to date him. She is seventeen

years old, and that won't go well. If I tell her not to see him, she'll only see him…harder. No, the smart thing to do is to wait this out. She's a smart girl, and she'll wise up. Eventually, Zane will be gone.

And if not, well, I intend to protect my daughter. Both of them. Whether they like it or not.

I am about to return to the kitchen but stop when I notice another flash of movement out the window. It's my neighbor Brett Carlson, walking down the driveway that separates our houses. Actually, he's not so much walking as *stomping*. He's making his way toward our front door. In another minute, he's going to be pounding on it.

This day is about to get interesting.

CHAPTER 3

E ven though I'm standing only a few feet away from the door, I don't open it right away. I give Brett a chance to ring the doorbell. Repeatedly. Then, as predicted, the pounding starts.

"Open up!" he shouts as he slams his fists uselessly against our door. "Right this minute!"

What a drama queen.

Brett Carlson moved into our neighborhood about a year ago. I know most of our neighbors fairly well, but I barely know Brett. All I know is that he works in finance, drives a sports car much too fast, and blasts music in his home office while he's working, loud enough to bother the whole neighborhood. He always seems to manage to turn it down just before the police arrive for noise complaints.

Taking my time, I open the door. But before I do, I snatch the box cutter that we keep in a cabinet in the foyer and slip it into the small pocket in the skirt of my dress. Just in case.

Brett is standing on my front porch, his hands balled into fists, his whole face a deep scarlet. He's glaring at me with menacing eyes. I keep the fingers of my right hand wrapped around the box cutter I've tucked away.

"Good morning, Brett!" I say cheerfully. "How can I help you?"

"I know what you did," he hisses at me. "I know what you did, Debbie! And you're not going to get away with it!"

I blink at him. "I don't know what you're talking about. What on earth do you think I did?"

"I know it was you!" All the veins in Brett's neck are standing out. "You think after all those noise complaints, I wouldn't figure it out?"

"Honestly," I say, "I don't know what you mean, Brett."

"My fuse box," he clarifies. "You went into my basement and snapped off the switch for my office. I've got *no power* in that room. This is going to cost me thousands of dollars to fix!"

I clasp a hand to my chest. "Oh my!"

"*Oh my*," Brett repeats mockingly. "You are so full of shit. You hate how loud I play my music, so you cut the power." He narrows his eyes at me. "I know you're the one who did it. And you're going to pay for it, one way or another."

He looks like he is attempting to shoulder his way inside the house to continue the conversation. I block his entrance, ready to pull out that box cutter if I need to. It won't come to that though. Brett is all talk.

"I'm *so* sorry about what happened to your fuse box, Brett." I furrow my brow. "But I swear it wasn't me. I barely even know how to use our own! All that wiring

14

stuff...it's just a big mystery to me. Ask Cooper. He always resets the breakers."

Brett is still glaring at me, unconvinced. "I know it was you."

"Do you have any proof?"

"Proof?"

I smile politely. "It's a simple question, Brett."

"I don't need proof," he snaps. "I know it was you."

I laugh, which only seems to infuriate him. "This is so preposterous. How would I even get into your basement?"

He pauses for only a split second to consider this. "I had a key hidden under the lantern in the backyard. You must've figured out it was there."

It's true that there are certain naive people who hide the keys to their front door in an easily found location: under a rock, in a flowerpot, or even under the welcome mat. It's like sending an engraved invitation to burglars. When we visit friends, Cooper and I play a little game where I have to guess where the spare key is hidden before we reach the front door. It always makes him laugh. When we recently visited one of his coworkers for dinner, I informed him their spare key was hidden under a garden gnome by the door. When we lifted it up, sure enough, there it was. I have a knack for these kinds of things.

"So you're saying," I begin, "that I found this key that you hid in your backyard, and then I broke into your house in the middle of the night and somehow snapped a switch in your fuse box? I'm just a housewife, Brett. You really think I did all that?"

For the first time since Brett showed up, there's a twinge of uncertainty on his face.

"You know," I say, "it was probably some teenagers. I

saw some surly-looking boys hanging around on the street yesterday evening. I wouldn't be surprised if they got it in their heads to stir up some trouble."

That's not entirely a lie. Zane is always hanging around here, and he's about as surly as they come.

"I still think it was you." Brett glares at me from the front porch, although some of the conviction behind his words has subsided. "I might not have any proof, but I'm putting up a camera as soon as I get this fixed."

"Wonderful idea!" I chirp. "Security cameras are an excellent way to keep your home safe."

Brett looks like he wants to strangle me with his bare hands. I nearly reach for the box cutter again, but then I stop myself. Instead, I smile up at my neighbor.

"I sure hope they catch the hooligan who did this to you," I say.

"Yeah," he mutters, "I'm sure you do."

With those words, he turns around and storms down the porch steps, casting seething looks over his shoulder the entire time.

CHAPTER 4

My phone is ringing in the kitchen.

Despite the fact that I frequently scold the children for having their phones out at the dinner table, my phone is admittedly never far from me either. It is, in fact, right next to my cereal bowl on the kitchen table. At first, I assume it's the magazine with some last-minute instructions for the photo shoot. But as I return to the kitchen, I see the name Garrett Meers flashing on the screen.

My boss.

Although I sometimes refer to myself as a stay-at-home mother, I actually do work part-time at a local family-oriented newspaper called the *Hingham Household*, writing an advice column called Dear Debbie. It's sort of like Dear Abby, except I wrote it, so it's Debbie instead of Abby. Get it? People from all over Hingham send in questions, seeking the fruits of my wisdom. I do my best.

People tell me they love my column, and even though

it doesn't pay that much, I enjoy it. Of course, when I started college at MIT nearly thirty years ago, majoring in computer science, I would never have believed my primary employment would be as a newspaper advice columnist. My high school computer science teacher told me I'd be the next Bill Gates.

Suffice it to say, I'm not the next Bill Gates. Far from it. In fact, I dropped out of MIT during the second semester of my sophomore year.

I still tinker in programming though. I've actually created some apps for the smartphone, although nobody uses them except for our immediate family. The one I'm most proud of is an app called Findly, which is a highly accurate tracker of friends and family. Izzy and Lexi both have Findly installed on their phones, which means that not only do I know where they are, but I'm also able to download a history of their prior locations. My children are safer when I know where they are.

I've got a tracker on my husband's phone too. With his permission, of course.

My phone is still ringing, so I snatch it off the kitchen table, swiping to take the call. The photographers won't be here for nearly an hour, and Garrett never wants to talk for very long. As he always says, he's "a busy man."

"Hello, Debbie," he says. "I'm so glad I caught you."

"Uh-huh." I settle back down in my seat. Garrett took over the paper two years ago, and he's not my favorite person in the world. I avoid him as much as possible. "What's up?"

"Actually," he says, "do you think you could stop by the office today?"

I frown at his unusual request. I usually email him my

articles, and my paychecks are direct deposited. "Today? What time?"

"As soon as possible."

I get an uneasy feeling in the pit of my stomach. I'm feeling anxious over this photo shoot already, and a mystery meeting with my boss is the last thing I need to think about. "Sure. I'll come this afternoon. Around two?"

"Sounds good, Debbie. I'll see you then."

Before I can probe further, Garrett disconnects the call. Now what was *that* all about?

My stomach still has that queasy feeling. I've got half a mind to head over there right now to get to the bottom of this, but there's no way. The photographers will be here soon, and right after, I've got a lunchtime book club meeting with some women in the neighborhood. If I skip the book club, I will never hear the end of it.

I look down at my phone. Should I call Garrett back to get more information? I'm tempted, but at that moment, Cooper wanders into the kitchen. He's always the last member of the family to arrive downstairs in the morning, since he doesn't have to be at his accounting firm until a leisurely nine o'clock. He likes to sleep in, and I enjoy having those few quiet moments with my husband.

Cooper is wearing a white dress shirt with light blue stripes, and his gray tie is hanging loose around his neck. He's freshly shaved, and there's a tiny piece of toilet paper stuck to a cut on his smooth lower jaw. He smells like his minty aftershave, and he smiles at me with a row of straight, even, almost white teeth.

I rise from my seat, grabbing my bowl of soggy cereal. If it ever tasted good, that time has passed. I might as well throw it away.

"Can I make you a bowl of cereal?" I offer.

"I can make it."

"It's no trouble." I wink at him. "I like to take care of you."

He laughs a bit self-consciously. Cooper was raised well, which means he's happy to do chores. He was shocked when we first got married and I offered to do his laundry for him going forward. But it made sense, since he was working and I wasn't. If I could make his life easier, why not? It's not like I had anything better to do.

Cooper slides into one of the seats at the kitchen table and sits there, watching me get his breakfast. While I'm pouring milk in the bowl, his phone starts ringing, and he pulls it out of his pocket. His phone isn't the latest model or even the model before the latest model. Cooper gets a new phone when his is so old that the software won't update anymore. He didn't even get a smartphone until everyone else we knew already had one, and I told him I was confiscating his flip phone. Unlike me, he has an aversion to technology. He avoids all social media, and he doesn't even like to text unless forced. *What's wrong with a phone call?* he often grumbles.

It's one of the things I love about him. He's the opposite of what I used to be.

Cooper glances down at the screen of his phone and frowns. His gaze flickers up at me for a millisecond, and I can't help but notice the way he angles the phone so I can't see the screen. He silences the call and shoves the phone back in his pocket.

I place Cooper's cereal on the kitchen table. It's not exactly a gourmet breakfast, but unlike our children, at least he's eating something before he leaves the house. But

20

instead of digging into his breakfast, he's fumbling with his tie. He doesn't usually wear a tie, but today is an important day for him.

"Let me help you with that," I say.

"I got it."

"No, let me. This is painful to watch."

Cooper obligingly stands up. He looks nice today, in his freshly ironed shirt, his hair still slightly damp from the shower. He's in his midforties like me—actually, he's in his *late* forties, if we're being completely pedantic about it. But even though his hair is a little thinner than it used to be, he still looks good. He doesn't even look that much different than he did when we first met in our early twenties, although maybe that's just because I look at him every day, so I don't notice the more gradual changes. He doesn't turn heads, but then again, he never did. He's good looking in that cute, boy-next-door sort of way, sort of like I'm pretty in that cute, girl-next-door sort of way.

Or at least I was once upon a time.

I cinch the tie around his neck, and that's when Cooper's gaze drops to my dress, which is white with red uneven shapes on it. I swear, it looked great in the store, but when I look down at the pattern now, the red blotches sort of look like...well, like bloodstains.

Shoot. Maybe I should change.

"Hey," he says, "you look *great*."

He appears to mean it. "Thanks."

"Your photo shoot is today, right?"

He remembers. Cooper might be the only person in my household who actually listens to the words coming out of my mouth. "That's right. They're coming at ten."

"This is *so* cool." He wraps his arms around my body,

drawing me close to him. "Our garden is going to be in a *magazine*. We'll be famous!"

I think Cooper is vastly overestimating the reach of *Home Gardening* magazine. "Not really."

"Don't sell yourself short." He lowers his lips to peck mine. Cooper is the perfect height for kisses while standing up. "I always tell everyone that you're the best gardener in town."

"Hmm."

"I have the most talented wife in the whole neighborhood." He kisses me again, more deeply this time. His next words are whispered in my ear. "And the sexiest."

Cooper and I have been married for close to twenty years now, and even after all that time, he always makes me feel like I'm just as attractive as the day we met. He acts like I'm still that same receptionist in my early twenties, going over the company's books with him, while he tried to pretend he wasn't looking at my legs.

When he asked me out, I almost said no automatically. I was so close to shutting him down. I wasn't dating back then, but there was something in his eyes that changed my mind. Now, all these years later, I have no regrets—not about him anyway.

I wonder if he feels the same way.

I finally break away from the kiss with a twinge of regret. As much as I'm anticipating this photo shoot, a quickie with Cooper wouldn't be a bad thing either. He always seems up for it in the morning, but neither of us have the time.

"You're wearing my lipstick," I tease him, gesturing at the smear of red that rubbed off my lips onto his.

He chuckles and grabs a napkin from the table to wipe

it away. "Ken would frown on me showing up to work with lipstick on."

That's not saying much. His boss frowns on *everything*.

"So," I say, "is today the day you're talking to him about…you know?"

Cooper flinches. He has been working for Ken Bryant for a decade now, and he's not getting paid nearly what he deserves. Cooper Mullen has many good qualities: he's a good husband, a good father, and a damn good accountant. But his fatal flaw is that he's not ambitious. He doesn't want to strike out on his own, even though it would be more lucrative. He's been feeling Ken out about the idea of a partner share in the accounting firm, and they're supposed to have a meeting about it today. Hence the tie that he can't figure out how to tie.

"Supposed to," Cooper mumbles, not meeting my eyes. So much for feeling amorous.

I snatch the little piece of toilet paper off the nick on his chin, and he winces. "He won't want to lose you. You're amazing at what you do. Just tell him what you want, and I bet he'll be happy to make you a partner."

"He won't be happy," Cooper says, which is probably true.

"Still. Just make your case, and hold your ground."

Cooper is saying something else, but I'm not listening, distracted by a glimpse of a truck driving by the side of the house. It looks like an electrician has arrived to help poor Brett. I sure hope the damage to his fuse box isn't far worse than he thought.

CHAPTER 5

COOPER

Debbie ties a perfect knot.

I've tied dozens of ties—no, hundreds—but whenever I do it, it looks like the handiwork of a small child. I don't know what's wrong with me; my dexterity is just lacking. But Debbie does it perfectly every time. It's one of her superpowers, along with all those brightly colored flowers in the backyard that seem to appear out of thin air.

And that's only the tip of the iceberg. My wife is good at everything she tries. She's a genius: she's created multiple apps for our phones that actually work. She writes them herself. I can barely figure out how to use most of the crap on my phone, and here she is, creating apps out of nothing.

Honestly, I wonder sometimes how she ended up in this life, married to a schlub like me.

"Just remember." Debbie tilts her face up to look at me. I'd almost forgotten how hot she looks with makeup on. "Don't *ask* for what you want. *Tell him* what you want."

She's talking about the partnership at the firm. She's more confident than I am, which is because she's never even met Ken Bryant. My boss has a very firm policy about separating home life and work life. We don't have elaborate Christmas parties at the firm where spouses and children are invited and one of us dresses up as Santa. Ken gets upset if you even put up a *photo* of your family in your own private office. The guy smiles maybe two times per year—tops.

So no, I'm not confident about this meeting. Not by a long shot.

I can't admit to Debbie that this meeting almost certainly isn't going to go the way she hopes. The mortgage on our house is depressingly high, and the cost of living in our town is through the roof. Debbie makes some money at the paper, but I am the primary breadwinner. We need this boost in salary—badly.

But maybe she's right. Maybe Ken will go along with it. He doesn't want to lose me after all.

"Confidence," Debbie reminds me. "Now eat your cereal."

I grin at her. "Yes, ma'am. But only because you said it with *confidence*."

I settle down into the seat across from her to dig in. It's this terrible fiber cereal she started buying a while back. I shove it down my throat, even though I hate it. I keep meaning to tell her to buy something that doesn't taste like the cardboard box it was packed in, but at least it's healthy. Judging by the way it tastes, it's got to be.

While I eat, I rest my hand protectively over my pocket where my phone is nestled. I tried not to let on, but that unexpected phone call threw me off my game. How could she call me when she knows I'm still home, likely in the middle of breakfast. If Debbie had seen…

I don't want to think about that.

I shove a few more mouthfuls of cardboard flakes into my mouth, and that's about all I can stand. I wipe my mouth with the back of my hand and get to my feet. "I better get going. I don't want to be late today. Let me just grab my lunch."

"Actually…" Debbie scrambles to her feet anxiously. "I didn't have a chance to make you lunch yet. I can make it now though. Would you like a sandwich?"

Debbie *always* packs me lunch. I never asked her to do it, but as soon as we got married, she declared that to be one of her responsibilities. I couldn't say no, since whatever she made was always a hell of a lot better than what I'd get from the food cart or some drive-through.

This is the first time in our marriage that she hasn't had anything packed for me. It leaves me feeling strangely off-kilter.

"That's okay." I don't want to let on how hurt I feel that my wife forgot to make me lunch. I'm a grown man, and it seems ridiculous to say it out loud. "I'll grab something at the strip mall near the office."

I round the table to give Debbie a kiss. I don't think I've ever left the house without kissing her goodbye, and that's one ritual we *won't* be forgetting today. I press my lips against hers as I lower my hand to her back, feeling the curve of her delicate rib cage through the soft fabric of her dress.

As our lips separate, Debbie looks into my eyes. "Good luck with Ken."

Yeah, I'll need it.

I parked in the driveway yesterday, so I leave through the front door to get to my car. I lock the door behind me, which is a reflex drilled into me by Debbie. We live in a safe neighborhood, but she always says that an unlocked front door is just asking for trouble.

"Mullen!"

I pull my key out of the lock in time to see my neighbor, Brett Carlson, standing on our front lawn, his boots crushing the green grass that my wife has spent so much time keeping lush and healthy. I don't know how Debbie does it. She's some kind of plant genius.

"What's up, Brett?" I say, stifling my irritation about the grass.

That's when I notice the way Brett's teeth are clenched together. A muscle under his right eye twitches as he takes a menacing step toward me. He looks *pissed*. I've never been in a fistfight before, but I'm worried it's going to happen for the first time today. Right now.

"The electrician is here," he spits out at me. "She didn't just snap off the switch. She destroyed the wiring too."

What the hell is he talking about? "Wiring?"

"My fuse box," Brett clarifies. "Your wife snuck into my basement last night and wrecked it."

At first, I think he's got to be joking, so I laugh. But the furious expression on his face quickly makes the smile drop off my face.

"What are you talking about?" I shake my head. "Debbie didn't do anything to your fuse box."

"Bullshit. She's the one always complaining to the cops about my music."

It's possible that's true, but still. The accusation is

27

outrageous. I'd think Brett has been drinking, but I don't smell it on him. "You're wrong."

"I'm not wrong," he says, "and let me tell you, Cooper: you better keep a close eye on that wife of yours."

I roll my eyes before I remember how much I hate it when Lexi does that. "Oh yeah?"

"Yeah." He levels his gaze at me. "She's *dangerous.*"

I don't know what to say to that.

So I keep my mouth shut. Debbie always says you can't reason someone out of a mindset they didn't reason themselves into. Thankfully, the electrician comes out of Brett's house and calls him over, so I'm off the hook. Still, my shoulders don't relax until Brett is back in his house with the door closed behind him.

For a moment, I wonder if I should warn Debbie about Brett being on the warpath. But that seems unnecessary. His accusation is so outlandish, I'm sure he'll soon realize that he made a terrible mistake.

CHAPTER 6

FROM *DEAR DEBBIE* DRAFTS FILE

Dear Debbie,

Let me tell you, I just love me some jazz. Nothing beats flipping on the radio and hearing something from Kind of Blue. But bless his heart, my husband won't let me listen to it! He's all into folk music, which just ain't my cup of sweet tea.

But here's the kicker: If we're in his car, he says that since he's driving, he should get to choose the music. Fair enough, I say. But when we're in my car and I'm driving, he says that since he earns more money than I do, it's technically his car, so he should get to choose the music then too! Tell me that ain't the biggest load of hogwash you've ever heard!

I don't mind listening to what he wants, but it seems like I should get to choose the music at least once in a blue moon! What should I do?

Frustrated with Folk Music

Dear Frustrated with Folk Music,

Believe me, you're not the first couple that has gone to battle over the soundtrack of a car ride! But marriage is all about compromise, so this is a good place to start. Before your next long drive, try to think of a few artists that you both like to listen to, and make a playlist featuring those artists. That way, you can both enjoy the music!

If your husband is not agreeable to this compromise, it's time to get out that sewing kit! Slip an over-the-counter antihistamine into his wine at night, and while he is sleeping, you can make a hole in his eardrum using the needle from the kit (they're so handy!). When you've completed the first ear, move on to the second. It can be a little tedious, but it's a fairly simple procedure!

After that, he definitely won't mind what you listen to in the car anymore!

Debbie

CHAPTER 7

DEBBIE

The cameras will be here in fifteen minutes.

I take one last glance at my garden to make sure it looks perfect. I know roses are very popular, like the ones in Jo Dolan's garden down the road, but I have a beautiful mix of vivid pink, red, and violet flowers. When the journalist asked me what type of flowers they were, I said they were windflowers because that's what they look like, but they're not really.

If I told them what the flowers really were, I wouldn't be in the magazine. Even Cooper doesn't know.

The garden looks perfect, so I take another look down at my dress, smoothing out any creases. The red splotches do look a lot like bloodstains, but I don't know if it's worth changing. I'm not even certain that they'll photograph me at all, and if they do, it may just be a headshot.

I glance down at my watch—still ten more minutes. Time seems to be moving in slow motion. It suddenly occurs to me that they'll want coffee, so I get a pot brewing using the state-of-the-art coffee machine we received as a housewarming gift, which Cooper immediately deemed "too complicated." He now gets his coffee at work. But it's hardly nuclear physics (which is actually nowhere near as difficult as my advanced database systems class in college). I pour the coffee grounds into the machine and press a button that makes the machine spring to life. There. The coffee is now forthcoming.

I am too restless to sit in the kitchen, so instead, I head to the front door. I peek out the window to see if they might have arrived early and are waiting until ten just to be polite. But there are no unfamiliar cars parked in front of my house. I do, however, spy Bev Petrie, who lives right across from me, on her hands and knees in the dirt, and before I can stop myself, I'm rushing out my front door.

"Bev!" I call out. "Bev, are you okay?"

Bev is eighty-seven years old and lives all alone in the small one-story house a stone's throw away from mine. Her brain is sharp as a tack, but she's frail enough that I worry one big gust of wind could blow her away. I've taken to rushing over to her house to see if there's anything she needs help with—usually taking out her garbage and hauling it to the curb, picking up a giant bag of kibble for her dog that's as old as she is (in dog years), and of course, lawn-related tasks. I worry that a bad tumble could send her to the hospital with a broken hip, and I hope that's not in the cards for today.

"Bev!" I say again when I get closer, because her hearing isn't what it used to be. "What's going on? Did you fall?"

Bev raises her slightly bleary blue eyes, and a smile

creases her face. She doesn't appear to be seriously injured and is, in fact, *gardening.* "Debbie! Good morning!"

I hold out a hand to help her back to her feet—I'm concerned it might not have been possible without my help. I make a note to myself to check on her more frequently.

"I was just trying to pull a few weeds." She gives her garden a glowering look. "Damn crabgrass is everywhere. Jo Dolan was commenting that I've got more weeds than flowers."

"Bev, I can take care of your weeds for you this weekend," I tell her.

Her eyes brighten. "You can?"

"Sure. It's easy."

People often write to Dear Debbie to ask for help killing weeds without harming their other plants. I usually recommend a solution of vinegar, salt, and soap. However, my absolute favorite way to kill weeds is to take a pot of boiling water and scald the little devils.

Bev looks me up and down. "Don't you look lovely this morning! Is your photo shoot today?"

I nod. "It is. I better get back to the house."

It's just about ten, and although it's clear the photographer has not arrived, it wouldn't look right if I weren't even home when they came.

"Good luck, dear," Bev says. "Jo is going to be so jealous! I can't wait to see her face!"

I shrug and act like I couldn't care less, but I'd be lying if I said that it won't give me a little bit of joy to stick it to my neighbor from down the block who's always putting me down. Jo thinks she has the best lawn on the block, and she'll tell anyone who will listen.

I bid Bev goodbye and walk back across the street to my own house. It's now several minutes after ten, and there's still no sign of the people from the magazine. They must be running late. Nobody is on time for anything in the real world. The only thing you must be on time for is the school bus, because that waits for nobody.

As I walk into the kitchen, the coffee machine lets out a loud hiss, and a slow and steady stream of brown liquid starts to drip into the pot. Perfect. Now I have coffee. I'm all set for when they show up.

I check my watch again. I do have a phone number for the magazine, but I hate to be that person. *Your photographer is fifteen minutes late. Where are you?* I'm sure they'll be here eventually. *Home Gardening* wouldn't just ghost me.

Would they?

I sit at the kitchen table, tapping my foot as I listen to the coffee slowly dripping into the coffeepot. Every few minutes, I check my watch, and every few minutes, it's a few minutes later, but the photographer still isn't here. I even check my email to confirm that this was the day and time we had agreed on.

At ten twenty-five, I crack. I check the phone number, which is in an email from Nita Geisler, the journalist who contacted me about the photos. She came to my house and gushed about the beautiful garden, and we set up this photo shoot for today. September 26 at ten in the morning.

I punch the number into my phone with slightly trembling fingers. I have spent the last week anticipating this photo shoot, and somehow I must have screwed something up. After all, this has to be my fault. Maybe I didn't confirm the day and time like I was supposed to? A legit magazine wouldn't just not show up this way.

"Home Gardening," a peppy female voice chirps on the other end of the line.

Great. I was hoping the number was a private line for Nita, but apparently I have to deal with a gatekeeper. "Um, hi," I say. "This is Debra Mullen. I'm trying to reach Nita Geisler."

"Sure! And what is this regarding?"

"Well..." I toy with a lock of my hair, but then I end up tugging it so hard that my scalp hurts. "She was supposed to come here this morning with the photographer at ten, but she's not here."

"Hmm." Keys tap on the other end of the line. "I don't see any appointments in Nita's schedule for today."

"Well, she emailed me that we were meeting this morning." I pause. "I have the email..."

"That is so strange!" the receptionist says again, like she's been tasked to solve a particularly difficult mystery. "Let me investigate! Hold please!"

The hold music is a Taylor Swift song. I generally like Taylor Swift music, but I am *not* in the mood right now. Also, the longer I sit here, twiddling my thumbs, the more I'm starting to get the implicit message that I'm the problem, it's me.

Just when I am about to hang up, the girl's voice pipes up, "Mrs. Miller?"

"Mullen," I correct her.

"Mrs. Muller," she repeats, making an admirable attempt to get it correct on her second try. "I have Nita Geisler on the other line. Can you please hold?"

I suppress an eye roll worthy of Lexi, not understanding why she couldn't just transfer me directly to Nita, given that I was already on hold. I feel like I'm trying to reach the *president* or something. Nita is just a journalist at a dinky gardening magazine. "Sure."

I have to listen to another fifteen seconds of hold music before Nita's throaty voice comes on the other end of the line. "Hello?" she says.

"Hi!" I exclaim, pathetically grateful that I'm talking to a human instead of listening to music. "This is Debbie… Debra Mullen? We… I mean, I thought the camera crew was coming here this morning. To photograph my garden, you know? That's what it said in the email. Did I… Did I get the date wrong?"

"Oh, Debbie," Nita sighs. "I am *so* sorry. I thought my assistant called you to cancel, but apparently not."

Fantastic. I have been waiting here all morning in my bloodstained dress for nothing. Well, at least I can decide on something less gory to wear before the actual photo shoot. Now that I know this isn't going to happen, I'm a tiny bit relieved. "So should we reschedule?"

"Actually," Nita says, "we decided to go in another direction."

The relief I felt a second ago vanishes, replaced with a sick feeling in the pit of my stomach. "Another direction?"

"Well," she says, "when we were leaving your house, we ran into your neighbor, Josephine Dolan. We saw her rose garden, and roses are just so classic. I thought it would be a nice throwback look for the photo spread."

My jaw drops. I am absolutely stunned. Jo *stole* my photo shoot?

"I really thought my assistant told you," Nita says. "I'm *so* sorry. I hope you didn't go to too much trouble."

"No," I say numbly. "Not at all. But… I mean, you

can't photograph both of our gardens? It's just one or the other?"

She laughs. "We can't very well do two gardens on the same block. That would be ridiculous."

Yes, of course.

"Again, I'm so sorry about this, Debbie," she says. "As an apology, we would be happy to sign you up for three months of a free subscription to *Home Gardening*. We would need your credit card, of course, but you could cancel it anytime after the free trial. Although most people love their subscription and continue it for years."

I don't know what to say to that. I don't want a magazine arriving at my house with a big spread showing Jo's garden.

"So," Nita says, "can I transfer you back to my receptionist so she can take your information?"

"Sure," I manage.

But then the second Taylor Swift starts up again, I hang up the phone.

I sit there at the kitchen table, staring at the now full coffeepot. I'll have to pour it down the sink. Jo and I have had a healthy rivalry over our gardens for years, but I never thought she'd stoop so low. I want to believe there's an explanation that doesn't involve her stealing my magazine spread right out from under my nose.

The aroma of brewed coffee fills the room, but the only thing that might make me feel better right now isn't coffee. I need a stiff drink.

I'm not much of a drinker, and neither is Cooper, but I still have a bottle of expensive pinot grigio that my neighbor Rochelle gave me for Christmas last year, knowing that whatever I gave her wouldn't be as nice. I haven't managed to crack it open yet, but this seems like a good opportunity.

We keep the bottle of wine in the cabinet over the refrigerator. I have to stand on my tippy-toes to nudge it open, and I grasp the bottle in my right hand. I'm not a huge fan of wine, and I recognize that chugging wine in the middle of the morning is a slippery slope, but I try not to think about it. It will numb the pain of the phone conversation I just had.

The first thing I notice about the bottle of wine is that the cork has been dislodged. That's not *so* strange though. Maybe Cooper had a glass at some point. Although when I hold it up, the bottle looks completely full. Did someone open the bottle, then fail to drink anything?

I pop out the cork and don't even bother with a glass. I swig the wine straight from the bottle, not taking time to swish it around my mouth and savor the fruity undertones or whatever. I just want the pleasant numbing buzz.

Except when I take a swallow of the wine, I get a big surprise. There are no fruity undertones or pleasant numbing buzz. There's nothing.

It tastes like water.

I stare at the bottle in confusion. Did I somehow read the label wrong, and it's actually sparkling water? But this doesn't taste like sparkling water. It tastes like something out of the tap.

I shift over to the sink and tip the mouth of the bottle until the contents pour out. I would have expected a pale straw-colored liquid to flow into my sink, but instead, the contents of the bottle are mostly clear. Someone drank my wine, then replaced it with water so I wouldn't know.

Who would've done something like that?

With the jolt of 100 percent certainty, I know who it must have been. Zane. Lexi's boyfriend.

I already knew that kid was bad news, and now that little creep is actually *drinking our alcohol* on top of everything else. Of course, if I say anything to Lexi, she'll deny it. She thinks her boyfriend walks on water. All I can do is make sure there's no other alcohol in the house for him to steal.

I had been anticipating the pleasant buzz of being slightly drunk. But now that possibility is off the table, and I can't stop fuming about what just happened to me. My garden was supposed to be in a magazine spread. It was all booked, and somehow, my neighbor stole it from me.

Well, she's not going to get away with it. I'm going over there right now.

CHAPTER 8

Jo Dolan and I live on the same block, but she is on one
end, and I am on the other. The ground slopes upward,
so if you considered our block to be a hill, I would be at
the top of the hill, and she would be at the bottom. Jo
says she doesn't walk that well anymore, which is why she
doesn't often come up the hill to my end of the block.

Looks like she made an exception when Nita Geisler
was here.

I don't bother to change out of my dress, but I do kick
off the uncomfortable heels I've been wearing and trade
them out for a pair of ballet flats that I bought on sale, two
for the price of one. I tried to give the other pair to Lexi,
but she looked at me like I was offering her poison, so I
ended up keeping them both.

And then I walk the block down the road to Jo's house.

Her house is nothing special. Like a lot of the prop-
erties around here, including my own, it's old. It was
likely built in the late 1800s but renovated on the inside,

although not very recently. The outside is painted a dull gray color with the trim painted a slightly different shade of gray. It's the sort of house you could walk by a hundred times without noticing it.

Except for the spectacular rose garden.

It's beautiful. I have to give her that. She's got roses that are yellow, red, light pink, and white. They line the edges of her yard, sprouting vividly colored flowers that I can see from halfway down the block. She works hard on those roses, but that said, it's a rose garden. Of *course* they're going to be beautiful.

Jo brags that her house still has the original door that it was built with. Hingham has a long colonial history, and a lot of the houses were built back in the nineteenth century, although more recently renovated to include luxuries like electrical outlets. My own house is about the same age as Jo's, but much of the original woodwork has been replaced, including the doors. I can't say I've shed any tears over not having a two hundred-year-old door, but this one does have a large ornate bronze knocker. I opt for the doorbell.

Jo takes her sweet time coming to answer the door—long enough that I feel compelled to ring a second time. After that second chime, a voice from behind the door barks, "Okay, okay, hold your horses! I'm coming!"

Jo is wearing a dress like me, although hers is the sort of billowy dress that you can't really wear if you're going anywhere outside your own backyard or possibly the grocery store, because it looks like you're running around town in a nightgown. It would be impolite to ask how old she is, but based on her close-cropped gray hair and the lines on her face, I've guessed late sixties. She's never married or had children, and she doesn't have any pets either—she yells at anyone who so much as walks their dog past her house. I get the sense that she doesn't really enjoy any species from Kingdom Animalia very much. But she likes roses.

Either way, I'm absolutely positive that she doesn't like me.

"Oh." Jo seems visibly disappointed to find me at her front door. "What do *you* want?"

"I just got off the phone with *Home Gardening*."

That particular revelation puts a smile on Jo's face. "Oh?"

"They told me that you talked them into photographing your garden instead of mine." My hands ball into such tight fists that my fingernails bite into my palms. "I can't believe you'd do that."

Jo is several inches shorter than me, and when she raises her eyes to meet mine, there isn't the slightest bit of remorse. "I didn't talk them into anything. I saw them here, looking at your pathetic little garden, and I asked them if they wanted to see a *real* garden. Whatever happened after that was entirely *their* decision."

"I called them about my garden," I point out. "I already had an arrangement with them. This was *my* article. You stole it from me, Jo."

"I did no such thing!" Jo insists. "Honestly, you should be thanking me. I saved you the embarrassment of having your pitiful excuse for a garden in a magazine." She looks me up and down, a smirk on her lips. "Apparently, I also saved you the embarrassment of being in a magazine looking like you were just butchering livestock."

I should have predicted this would happen. What did I

think? That Jo was going to fall to her knees, begging me for forgiveness? I should have guessed she would defend everything she's done.

I feel a sudden buzzing in the back of my head. Like a fly is trapped inside my skull and trying to get free. I wonder what that's all about. Does it mean I'm having a stroke? Am I going to drop dead now, right on Jo's front porch, in front of the original door her house was built with?

"I'll tell you what," Jo says. "When the article comes out, I'd be happy to give you a copy. I'll stick it in your mailbox. That way, you'll have the thrill of telling people that your very own neighborhood is in a magazine."

The buzzing gets louder. I close my eyes for a moment, trying to calm myself. When I open them, Jo is still standing there in her housedress, a smug expression on her mean little face.

"There's such a thing as karma, you know," I say.

She waves a hand. "I don't care about that hippie nonsense."

"Do you know what karma means?"

"No, and I don't care."

My jaw tightens. "It means what goes around comes around."

Jo actually laughs in my face, and the sound is like nails on a chalkboard. I've never liked Jo Dolan, but at this moment, I hate her.

"Whatever you say, Debbie," she snickers. "But that sounds like loser talk to me."

Loser. I've been feeling like a loser a lot lately. I can't control my kids, we're strapped for cash because my husband won't ask for a raise, and I can't even get a second-rate magazine to photograph my garden. I've never felt like more of a loser in my entire life. Jo clearly noticed that I was weak and went in for the kill.

"Karma," I repeat.

Jo just shakes her head. "I'll send you the article, Debbie."

Then she slams the door in my face.

CHAPTER 9

Since getting drunk doesn't seem to be an easy option, I do the next best thing: hit the gym.

I joined a local gym called Titan Fitness about six months ago. Cooper was already a member, so we got a family discount. I never enjoyed exercising in the past, but I've been pushing myself. I'm tired of being weak and out of shape. And I've become hooked on the rush of adrenaline I feel as I push my body to the limit on the treadmill.

It's better than any antidepressant. And I should know—I've been on all of them at one time or another.

Before I head to the gym, I make a pit stop at the nursery where I buy supplies for my garden. I don't need anything for my garden today, but there is a related purchase I need to make. I hope they have it.

The nursery is surprisingly busy for a Wednesday morning. I pass through the glass enclosed area containing a variety of plants into the heart of the store. I suspect what I need will be in the main store, but I'm not entirely sure since I've never purchased anything for pest control here before.

Fortunately, I spot Lou, an elderly man who owns the nursery with his wife, Louise (I know—how cute). He knows just about everything when it comes to plants, and he'll certainly be able to help me find what I need, even if I can't find it here. He's stocking one of the shelves with a fresh supply of clay pots and is so focused that I have to clear my throat repeatedly to get his attention.

"Debbie!" His face creases in pleasure when he finally realizes I'm standing next to him. "How can I help you this morning, my dear?"

"I'm looking for Japanese beetle traps."

Lou tilts his head to the side. "Japanese beetle traps? Are you growing roses?"

"No." I hesitate, reluctant to say too much. "I'm picking them up for a friend."

He nods thoughtfully. "Sure, we have them. Those things are a scourge, aren't they? Probably the most common lawn pest we see around these parts."

"So I've heard."

Lou leads me down an aisle labeled "pest removal." Between a spray bottle for mite control and one to kill gnats, there are several neon green boxes labeled "Japanese beetle traps." Right next to them, there's also a supply of trap refills. I reach for a handful of the refill boxes.

"Those are just refills," Lou points out to me. "They won't trap the beetles."

"Yes, I know." I smile at him. "That's all I need for my friend."

I wonder if three of the refills will be enough. I suppose I could always come back for more of them if I need to.

With the three packages in my arms, I head over to the checkout line, where there's a line of five people waiting for Louise, whose two checkout speeds are slow and slower. I check my watch and let out an exaggerated sigh that reminds me of Lexi. My book club meeting is at twelve thirty, and it's now eleven, which means that I'll barely have time to work out, as long as I shower and change at the gym.

That awful Jo—this is all her fault.

The line moves forward agonizingly slowly. Louise is negotiating a customer attempting to pay with a check. She's peering through her reading glasses at the check, holding it up to the overhead light. It might be twelve thirty before I even get to the front of this line.

Finally—*finally!*—I am at the front of the line with only one person ahead of me at the cashier. When I am next in line, a slim woman in her sixties who reminds me a lot of Jo Dolan elbows her way in front of me. She's gripping a small bag of seeds, which she holds up as if in explanation.

I freeze for a moment, stunned that this woman just cut to the front of the line after I've been waiting for twenty minutes. The move sets off the same buzzing sensation in the back of my head that I had when I was talking to Jo Dolan. I stare at the back of the woman's head for a few seconds, then clear my throat.

"Excuse me," I say.

The woman ignores me.

"Excuse me," I say again, "but the line is back there, behind me."

The woman gives a half turn this time. She sees me standing there and seems astonished that I said anything.

"Yes, but I was here earlier," the woman says as if this is a completely reasonable explanation. "And all I've got is just this one thing. I'll only be a minute."

The buzzing in my head gets louder. What *is* that? Am I dying?

I shake my head. "It doesn't matter how many items you have. You can't cut the line. We've all been waiting."

The woman blinks at me as if personally offended that I am questioning the fact that she cut ahead of, like, five people to the front of the line.

"I'm not cutting," she insists. "I was here *earlier*."

Is she kidding me? I don't understand how some people believe they can do anything they want. Like they are completely above all the rules.

"I don't care if you've been here all week," I retort. "The back of the line is *behind me*. Now are you going to go there on your own, or do I have to *make* you?"

The woman looks like she's going to protest, but then our eyes meet, and she changes her mind. She takes a step back, a flicker of fear in her eyes as she hugs the bag of seeds to her chest.

"Psychopath," she mutters under her breath.

Nobody else hears her though, and there's actually a smattering of applause as she trudges to the back of the line. And that's when I notice that the buzzing has completely vanished.

CHAPTER 10

I have read that if a gym is more than a fifteen-minute drive from your home, you'll never end up working out. Titan Fitness is a small gym that's a ten-minute drive from my house, and I have managed to go there a respectable three times per week since joining. I hadn't planned on going today because of the photo shoot, but my morning has unexpectedly cleared.

Titan's welcome desk is run by a woman named Cindy, whose shiny blond hair curls around her ears. She's a good ten years older than me, and her level of strength and endurance gave me hope when I first joined. During those first few weeks, I couldn't run for more than five minutes without getting out of breath, but my endurance has improved a lot. I'm becoming stronger, just like I hoped I would.

"Hi, Debbie!" Cindy glances at the clock overhead as I scan the gym ID that grants me access to their two rooms of equipment. "You're here a bit late in the morning."

The last thing I want to do is unload onto poor Cindy about my awful day. Besides, I've already wasted enough time buying those beetle traps. So I just shrug and force a smile. "Just squeezing in a quick workout before lunch."

"Good for you!" Cindy says, which actually does make me feel better about the whole thing.

I had already changed into workout clothes before leaving the house, and my purse is locked up safely in my car, so I head right into the equipment area with my water bottle to stretch out before hopping onto the elliptical. I definitely feel like I need some cardio today.

"Hey, Debbie! You're never here on Wednesdays!"

I take a break from stretching my hamstrings when I hear the voice of Harley Sibbern, one of the trainers at Titan, who also teaches spin class and kickboxing. I met her last month when she came over to correct my form while I was lifting weights. I thought she was trying to pick up another personal trainer client, but she didn't offer her services. We got to talking about fitness, then moved on to other topics, and I found that I actually enjoyed talking to her.

Since then, Harley and I have had coffee a few times at the café next door to the gym. Even though she's ten years younger than I am, we have strangely hit it off. I have friends whose children go to my kids' school and friends who live in my neighborhood, but it feels like Harley is the first friend I've had who is just for me. And she's the first friend I've had in a long time who doesn't have children, which I count as a major plus. She has a lot more free time, plus we're allowed to talk about other things besides... well, kids. It's *refreshing*.

Plus, Harley is *cool*. I feel like I'm about as old as my

kids when I say that, but in my forty-plus years of friendships, I've never had a friend like Harley. She's got multiple piercings in each ear, and there's a pink streak laced through her blond hair. I always assumed anybody that hip wouldn't want to spend time with me. When I was younger, I was a massive nerd—obsessed with computers and studying nonstop. And now... Well, at my age, if I ever had a chance to be cool, those years are long behind me.

"I wanted to squeeze in a quick workout before the book club," I say. "You're still coming, right?"

I'm still feeling out the book club etiquette. I wasn't sure if I should invite Harley, because it would be mixing universes. But I also desperately need reinforcements during these book club meetings. One of my favorite things is discussing complex books with other adults, but I've come to realize I'm not very fond of any of the women at my book club. When Harley mentioned she had already read the book, *Velvet Moon*, I decided to risk the invitation.

"Of course I am," Harley says. "Are you sure I can't bring anything? You said it was potluck."

"No, it's fine." I wave a hand. "We always have much too much food. Rochelle puts out a massive spread. Don't worry about it."

She raises her eyebrows. "Are you sure?"

I don't know why she's so anxious. Why would someone as cool and self-assured as Harley be worried about what a bunch of middle-aged book club attendees think of her? But I suppose everyone has their insecurities.

"Definitely," I say. "Now, remind me. You said you have an allergy to..."

"Avocados," she says. "It's not lethal or anything, but I break out in a rash from even a bite. I know it's everyone's favorite healthy fat, so it's a bummer for me."

"No avocados," I say. "Got it."

Harley tugs at the Lycra of her workout pants. Even if I spent every moment in this gym between now and eternity, I wouldn't have a body like hers—not after two pregnancies and fifteen extra years of living. Working out won't get rid of stretch marks or the parts of my body that used to be firm but now sag.

I remind myself that I earned every single imperfection in my body, and I have no regrets. I sure wouldn't give up Lexi and Izzy to have a tighter tummy and perkier boobs. And my husband doesn't seem to have any complaints.

Harley grins at me, oblivious to the way I'm ogling her thighs. "I'm really looking forward to this. I've never been in a book club before."

"Oh, it's really fun."

Except that's a lie. I'm sure there are book clubs out there that are actually enjoyable, but the one I have been attending in my neighborhood is not the slightest bit fun. But if I say that to Harley, she might decide not to come.

"So I'll see you at 12:30?" I say. "Meet at my house?"

She winks at me. "I'll see you there."

After Harley walks away, I climb up on the elliptical for a workout. It might not be a bottle of pinot grigio, but it will help me forget my problems for a little while.

CHAPTER 11

COOPER

S ome people are friends with their bosses. Some people have dinner with their bosses or head to the golf course together. Maybe they share a couple of drinks at the local bar after a long workday.

My boss prefers that I speak to him as little as humanly possible.

No, Ken Bryant is not a warm and fuzzy boss. He doesn't want to know how my weekend went come Monday. He doesn't give a shit if I went to the beach over the summer with my family. He doesn't want to chitchat. He just wants me to get my damn work done on time, which I'm usually excellent at doing.

Ken wasn't thrilled when I requested a meeting with him earlier in the week. When he asked me what it was about and I said, "my future at the company," he looked even less thrilled.

Right now, I am psyching myself up for the meeting in my shoebox of an office. In about five minutes, I will explain to Ken why he should—nay, *must*—make me a partner at the firm. I can't anticipate it going well. But I have to try. When I get home, Debbie is going to ask me how it went, and I can't just tell her I chickened out, can I?

She deserves better than me. For more reasons than she even knows.

"Coop? You okay?"

I look up at the sound of the voice at my door. Jesse joined the firm about a year ago, and now I finally have a colleague that I want to spend time with outside work. He and I have had dinner together, I've met his wife, and he's met Debbie. He even convinced me to join a local gym, and I no longer get out of breath when I climb the steps from the first to second floor of my house.

"Fine," I say quickly. "I'm just... I'm going to have that talk with Ken now, and..."

I confided in Jesse about the meeting, and he agreed with Debbie that I deserve a piece of the firm. He didn't seem to think it was as big a pie in the sky as I did. I have been here for ten years after all.

If my boss were anyone else but Ken, I'd agree with him. But every time I envision this conversation, I can't see how it will go my way.

"Don't worry." Jesse winks at me. "By this time tomorrow, you're going to be my boss."

"Maybe..." I rub my fingertips against my temples. I've never had a migraine before, but I feel one coming on. "If it were anyone besides Ken..."

Jesse leans against the doorframe of my office. He can't come inside, because there quite literally is no room. The office is big enough for my desk and the chair that I sit in, but nobody else can comfortably fit inside. Even if

Ken miraculously agrees to the partnership, I won't get a bigger office.

"Look," Jesse says, "you're a damn good accountant, Cooper. Ken would be screwed if you left, and he knows it. You're in a really good position. Give yourself some credit, okay?"

"Okay."

"Also…" Jesse squints at me across the room. "What's going on with your tie? It usually looks so perfect, but today it looks like you had one of your kids knot it for you."

I fiddle with my tie, which I had to retie when I got here. I didn't realize it at the time, but Debbie tied it crooked this morning. She's never done that before. I guess she had a lot on her mind with that photo shoot and all. But it doesn't look like I did a much better job.

"Debbie usually does it," I explain as I attempt to repair the damage. "Is it really that bad?"

"Nah, it's fine." He looks down at his watch. "Just get in there and make sure you don't come out until he gives you what you deserve."

What I deserve? I already have more than I deserve. When I was in college, my whole life was going down the toilet, but I somehow turned it around, and then I met Debbie. Jesse has met Debbie a handful of times, but he barely knows her, and he doesn't realize she's way too good for me. He doesn't know I've done a lot of things in our marriage that have proven that she deserves better. I only want this promotion so I can live up to that impossible standard. I *need* this—for her.

Shit, now I'm freaking out even more.

Ken is the only one of us who has a secretary. Her name

is Mrs. McCauley, and we're not allowed to call her anything but Mrs. McCauley. Mrs. McCauley has been with Ken as long as I've been working here and possibly since the beginning of time. Despite the fact that I'm certain Mrs. McCauley knows that I have an appointment now, and she most certainly *knows my name* since I've worked with her for ten years, she gives me a blank expression when I approach the desk she occupies right outside Ken's office.

"Can I help you?" she asks.

"I have an appointment with Ken," I say through my teeth. She's not making this easier, which I suppose is the point.

Mrs. McCauley peers up at me through her horn-rimmed glasses that hang from a beaded chain that encircles her neck. "Is he expecting you?"

"Yes. That's why it's an appointment."

I swear, I'm not usually a smart-ass, but something in Mrs. McCauley brings it out in me.

"Let me check with him." Mrs. McCauley picks up the phone at her desk, even though she is within shouting distance of her boss. Hell, he's probably listening to this entire conversation. But she goes through the motion of dialing his extension. "Hello? Mr. Bryant? This is Mrs. McCauley." She pauses, waiting for his response. "Yes, I have Mr. Mullen here to see you."

I stand there, waiting for Ken to allow me to enter his office.

After what feels like an interminable pause, Mrs. McCauley nods. She smiles up at me. "You can go inside, Mr. Mullen."

Even though I have been given permission to enter, Mrs. McCauley jumps up to get ahead of me, and she knocks on the door one final time, waiting for Ken to grant us permission before she opens the door for me. Ken is sitting behind his desk, a stack of papers in front of him, in roughly the same exact position he was in the last time I was in his office several months ago.

I only wear a tie on occasions when I know I'll be interacting with Ken, but he always wears one, in addition to a suit jacket. I'd always thought that if I started losing my hair, I'd shave my head like a lot of men my age do, but Ken has been balding the whole time I've known him, and he has not gone that route. The entire top of his head is shiny and free of hair, but there are still remnants of his gray hair along the crown of his head. It makes him look far older than his fiftysomething years.

"Mullen," he says. "What's this about?"

His office isn't huge, but it's at least big enough for a couple of chairs in front of his desk. However, he doesn't offer me the opportunity to sit, and I don't take it. This will be easier standing anyway.

"Ken," I begin, wiping the sweat from my palms onto the legs of my pants. They are damp enough to leave a stain. "I've been working here for ten years now. Almost eleven. And…I've been thinking a lot about my future at this firm."

Ken narrows his eyes as he folds his arms across his suit jacket. He leans back in his chair, an unreadable expression on his face. "Is that so?"

Remember, you are a valuable part of this company. He won't want to lose you.

"I like working here," I say, plowing forward, my voice wobbling, "but when I first started here, you mentioned the possibility of partnership sometime in the future."

Ken's expression gives nothing away. "That was a long time ago."

"Maybe," I say, "but if anything, the company is bigger than it was back then. I've been a loyal member of the firm, and I could be an asset to you as a partner." After a pause, I add, "Sir."

Ken rubs his chin. "No," he says. "I don't see it."

What? It feels like the wind was suddenly knocked out of me.

"Ex…excuse me?" I stammer.

"You do well enough as a worker bee," he says thoughtfully. "But a leader? No, definitely not. Certainly not a partner."

Until this moment, I hadn't realized how much I wanted this partnership. I deserve this partnership. I've worked my ass off for this firm, and I don't deserve to be treated as a worker drone. Plus, I can't imagine going home to Debbie and telling her about this conversation. If Debbie were here, she would tell me that I deserve this promotion, and I should *demand* it.

"Listen," I say with courage I didn't know I possessed, "if you can't consider me for a partnership, then maybe I should look for opportunities elsewhere."

Ken snorts. "You think you'll find a better job than this?"

"I'd rather not," I hedge. "But if you're telling me there's no opportunity for advancement here, then…well, you can consider this my two weeks' notice."

Ken's eyebrows shoot up. My legs have turned to liquid, but I keep my chin high in the air. Ken needs me, and he knows it. There's no way he's going to call me on my bluff.

"If that's how you feel," he says, "then I accept your resignation."

It feels like the world has just dropped out from under me. I had imagined this conversation going a lot of different ways, but I never imagined it ending with my resignation. I can't believe he's willing to just let me walk out the door. I'm one of his busiest accountants—I have more clients than anyone else. And I *never* make mistakes. This place would fall apart without me.

"Ken," I choke out. Maybe I can fix this. "I…I really value this company, and I'd prefer to stay…"

"You're not getting a partnership, Mullen." His eyes flick to the screen of his computer, as if he's already tired of this conversation. "If you'd like to leave sooner than two weeks, be my guest."

I open my mouth, but no sound comes out. What would I say anyway? Ken has already made up his mind. And I'd like to think I have too much dignity to ask for my job back five seconds after quitting.

"I'll stay for the two weeks," I murmur.

Ken nods, no longer looking at me at all. This conversation is over.

My head is spinning as I stumble out of Ken's office. What just happened in there? Did I really just quit my job? How am I going to pay for my kids to go to college? What are we going to do about our mortgage? Our health insurance?

Oh Christ, what am I going to tell Debbie? She's going to be *furious*.

CHAPTER 12

DEBBIE

I'm running a few minutes late for my book club.

I decided to run home to shower and change clothes, and it all took just a little bit longer than I expected. On top of that, Harley is meeting me at my house, because she felt uncomfortable showing up alone at a book club where she didn't know anyone. So when I get out of my house, a tray of sandwiches balanced in one hand and a paperback copy of *Velvet Moon* in my other hand, I find Harley leaning against her blue Ford.

"Can I help you carry anything?" Harley regards my tinfoil-wrapped tray. "It looks like you're doing a balancing act."

I smile gratefully, handing her my book. "Here, take this."

Harley takes the paperback so I'm able to hold the tray with both hands, significantly decreasing the chances that it will fly out of them, landing face down on the sidewalk. We're already running late, so I don't want to dawdle. I start in the direction of Rochelle's house, but Harley—frustratingly—is lagging behind.

"Gosh, Debbie," she says, "your house is gorgeous."

"Thank you."

It's a compliment I don't hear very often. My house is nice enough—another old house that's been renovated on the inside so that we have electricity and running water. The outside is sorely in need of a paint job, but we've been putting it off until Cooper gets that promotion. The front cement steps always crumble during the winter snowstorms, and Cooper has to repair them every summer. Eventually, I'd love to hire someone to fix them in a way that they won't need to be redone every year.

Compared to some of the other houses in Hingham, it's particularly modest. A lot of the houses here are over the top. It's a wealthy town, and the reason we chose to live here—even though it's a bit out of our price range—was because of the excellent public schools. Being in a good school district was a top priority when we were buying.

She looks around appreciatively. "A house must've cost a fortune in a neighborhood like this."

"It did," I admit. "More than we can afford, honestly."

"You should see the dump where I live." She sighs. "Titan pays crap. It must be nice having a man to take care of you."

I don't comment on that. I had never wanted to be in a position where I had to rely on a man to support me. That's why I worked so hard in school and went to a top college. But she's exactly right—Cooper is the breadwinner in our family. Unfortunately, Cooper's income is nothing to brag about. Money has always been tight in our family, although I strongly suspect that will change in the very near future.

"Anyway, we better get going," I say. "Rochelle hates it when people are late."

That's an understatement. I can 100 percent guarantee there will be a comment from Rochelle on our arrival time when we show up at her door.

We cross the street and walk down the block to Rochelle's house. If Harley thought mine was impressive, Rochelle's must look like a castle. I don't think I've ever been over to her house without her feeling the need to point out that she has twice as many bedrooms and bathrooms as I have. You wouldn't think she could work it into the conversation so easily, but somehow she manages. Every time.

"Whoa," Harley comments when we make our way up the walkway to Rochelle's front door. "Now this chick is *really* rich."

"She sure is."

Rochelle's husband is some sort of soulless corporate lawyer. Obviously, she doesn't need to work. Not even as a lowly advice columnist. She spends her days doing charity and PTA work. I suppose that's admirable in theory, but in practice, it's horrible to be bossed around by Rochelle during a school bake sale.

No, Rochelle and her friends are not my favorite people in the world. But I *love* to read, and I've been desperate to discuss the books I've read with other real-life adults. So when Rochelle extended the invitation to join her book club, I jumped at the chance.

And every month, I consider quitting.

Rochelle opens the front door for us, wearing a sleek

pantsuit that's nicer than anything I have in my closet. Certainly nicer than my bloodstained dress, which I was smart enough to change out of. Her black hair is so shiny that I can almost see my reflection in it.

"Debbie." She beams at me, and then we do the hug and cheek-touching thing. "So good of you to come."

"This must be…Harlow?"

"Harley," Harley corrects her with a wry smile.

Rochelle raises an eyebrow at me, probably a reaction to Harley's pink hair. "And I *love* your dress, Debbie." Her gaze rakes over the yellow dress I put on to replace the bloody one. "It makes you look older." When she notices the look on my face, she quickly adds, "But in a *good* way." While I'm trying to work out in my brain how telling a middle-aged woman she looks older could ever be construed as a compliment (spoiler: it can't), her eyes fall on the tray in my hands. "Oh, and you brought sandwiches! How *cute*."

Rochelle leads us into her house, down the endless foyer into her living room. Harley's jaw looks like it's about to unhinge. Rochelle takes us into her newly renovated living room, where every piece of furniture is made out of the most expensive Italian leather (including the television, I think). The two other members of our book club, Tabitha and Sloane, are both already on the sofa.

"I told you that Debbie would be here *eventually*," Rochelle announces to the other two women.

Tabitha giggles. "We took bets on what time you would finally show up, Debbie."

Harley looks at me in confusion, because we're only two minutes late. Somehow, my lateness has become a running joke, even though I'm usually quite prompt.

"Please excuse the mess," Rochelle says to me and Harley, even though her house is spotless except for the row of champagne bottles lined neatly on a side table in the living room. "We are preparing for an incredibly important party tonight. Did I mention to you that Gerard is going to announce his candidacy for the state senate seat tonight?"

"Yes, I believe you did," I murmur.

"Anyway, tonight is going to be so crucial," she says. "Even the mayor is going to be making an appearance to endorse him."

"The mayor?" Harley repeats in amazement.

Rochelle nods solemnly. "It's going to be quite the event. Esmerelda came this morning to clean the entire house, and it took forever." She gives me a knowing look. "You're so lucky you have so few bedrooms, Debbie. A house like mine takes forever to clean. But it has to be perfect."

"Don't worry, Rochelle," Sloane says. "Tabby and I will be right at your side to support you tonight."

Of course, I won't be at Rochelle's side, because I have not been invited to the party. There was a brief explanation from Rochelle about the guest list being "limited." Not that I want to go to her stupid mayor party anyway.

But it would have been nice to be invited.

I set my tray down on Rochelle's antique coffee table and remove the tinfoil from on top of the sandwiches. As soon as I take the foil off, Tabitha and Sloane both simultaneously dissolve into giggles.

"Did you make the sandwiches yourself?" Rochelle asks me, stifling a giggle of her own.

"I did." I'm trying to keep the defensive edge out of

my voice, but it's hard when I'm talking to Rochelle. "It's turkey and avocado with a sun-dried tomato spread."

"How *cute!*" Sloane exclaims.

Harley frowns at me. "Debbie, didn't I mention that I'm allergic to avocados?"

I clasp a hand over my mouth. "Oh my God, you *did.* I can't believe I forgot. I am *so* sorry, Harley."

"Debbie is the most forgetful person I know," Rochelle comments, even though I can't recall ever forgetting anything in the past. "But don't worry, Harley. Our cook threw together a charcuterie board."

It is quite the elaborate charcuterie board. There isn't one piece of meat on it that hasn't been formed into the shape of a flower. And I can count no less than eight types of cheese.

"I hope you'll try my sandwiches though," I say to Rochelle.

"Of course I will!" Rochelle picks up a triangular slice of one of the sandwiches that I painstakingly put together after I got back from the gym. "Like I said, they're adorable. You can just tell that they're homemade."

She nibbles on the edge, which encourages the other women to take a piece too. I'm so pleased they're trying my sandwiches. I certainly wouldn't want all that hard work to go to waste.

CHAPTER 13

HARLEY

R ich bitches.

That's what I keep calling these women in my head. I've been chanting it over and over again, especially when Rochelle starts pontificating about this stupid boring book that I didn't actually manage to read.

Rich bitches, rich bitches, rich bitches.

It helps that the words rhyme.

"I just think *Velvet Moon* is so clearly a takeoff on *King Lear*," Rochelle says. "There is the elderly father and the three daughters vying for his favor. It's such an obvious retelling."

Rich bitches, rich bitches, rich bitches, rich bitches.

"I mean," Rochelle continues, "I don't even know how you can appreciate it without having read the play."

Sloane and Tabitha nod in solemn agreement. It's only Debbie who says stoutly, "I liked the book, and I never read *King Lear*."

"Well, of course not," Rochelle says. "You never went

to college, and that's the sort of book that you need to read on a *collegiate* level."

Debbie's face turns slightly pink. I don't even know why she is at this book club, because she doesn't seem to like any of these women very much. Unlike the three of them, Debbie is actually nice. Sometimes it seems like she doesn't have much going on upstairs, but she tries her best.

And her house isn't as big as this one, but it's still beautiful. The sort of house I've always wanted. The sort of house I *will* have one day.

I still don't know how she forgot about my avocado allergy though, considering we talked about it only a couple of hours ago. Even though the charcuterie board is something else, Debbie's sandwiches look really good, and I wish I could have one. Debbie is flighty, but this is next level.

"It feels like this one might have gone over your head a bit." Rochelle flashes Debbie a sympathetic look. "It *was* a very complicated book, and the writing was very literary. And I imagine it was a *bit* long for some readers."

A *bit* long? *Velvet Moon* was nearly six hundred pages, and I had to read every sentence twice before it made sense. If I ever come back to book club, I wouldn't mind a book that isn't written for people who have doctoral degrees. I told Debbie that I read *Velvet Moon*, but there was no way that was going to happen. It felt like I was back in high school again, struggling through an impossible book assigned by the teacher.

But I still wanted to come. So I did what I did in high school—I bought the CliffsNotes version of *Velvet Moon*. Those things are incredible, you know. They summarize every chapter and then interpret it. It even mentioned the thing about *King Lear*, although it said that it was a common *mis*interpretation.

Anyway, there's nothing wrong with CliffsNotes. I wouldn't have gotten through high school without them, although it's slightly mortifying to need to cheat for a *book club*. But nobody has to know.

Debbie actually read the book though. Not only that, but she genuinely *enjoyed* it, and based on the comments she's made so far, she seemed to understand it better than any of these other women. But now she just sits there, like she's not quite sure what to say.

"I wouldn't mind reading something...shorter," I speak up. I don't want to admit that the book was much too hard to get through, risking Rochelle's snide comments being directed at me instead of Debbie. "More like...three hundred pages."

"But five hundred and eighty-nine pages go by in a flash with a brilliant author like Barbara Fanning!" Sloane protests. "It's like drinking a *fine wine*. And if you can't make it through six hundred pages, you won't be able to get through three hundred pages either."

I may not have been much better in math than I was in English, but that one doesn't quite add up for me. I have to admit though, I'm not sure I could have made it through even twenty pages of *Velvet Moon*.

"I just think it's not worth discussing any book that hasn't won a Pulitzer," Sloane continues. "We shouldn't have to dumb down our book choices for the people with less education. If Debbie can't participate, we can meet separately."

"I can participate," Debbie protests weakly.

At that comment, the three women exchange

meaningful looks. I know what that look means. These three women are gearing up to kick Debbie out of their little club. I shift uncomfortably on the sofa, wishing I could make up an excuse and get out of here.

"Debbie," Rochelle begins in an authoritative voice, "I just think that this book club might not be right for..." She stops speaking abruptly, as if her train of thought was interrupted by something. Her long, dark eyelashes flutter, and she takes a deep breath. "Is it *hot* in here?"

That ass kisser Tabitha looks like she's about to protest that the temperature is a perfect seventy-four degrees, but then something changes in her expression. "Yes. It *is* a bit hot."

"I don't feel hot," Debbie says helpfully.

"Maybe it's menopause?" I suggest.

Rochelle shoots me a look, but there isn't much conviction behind it. She looks very pale all of a sudden. I mean, she did have perfect alabaster skin, but it's changed color in the last few minutes. It looks...

Actually, she looks a bit green.

Abruptly, Rochelle clamps a hand over her mouth. She makes a mad dash out of the room, bumping the side table in her haste to get to the bathroom. Multiple bottles of champagne tip over like pins in a bowling alley, shattering as they crash to the floor. The champagne that spills out of the bottle is probably worth more than my car, but Rochelle is past caring. The sound of her retching echoes through the entire first floor of the house.

Sloane and Tabitha exchange looks, and that's when I notice that the two of them look a bit green as well. "I think I might head out," Tabitha murmurs. "I...I'm not feeling that hot."

"I've heard there's a bug going around," Debbie says sympathetically, although she doesn't look green in the slightest. In fact, she's got a big smile on her face.

Tabitha and Sloane seem quite eager to get out of the house. Sloane makes it entirely down the walkway, but Tabitha isn't so lucky. As we exit Rochelle's property, I catch a glimpse of her vomiting in the pristine front yard. Debbie doesn't so much as pause to make sure her friend is okay.

"As you can see, there's a bad bug going around," she tells me as we head down the block back to her own house. "I hope Rochelle doesn't have to cancel her lovely party tonight with the mayor."

"Debbie," I say quietly. "It seems like they have…you know, food poisoning…"

She blinks at me, her wide-eyed stare completely blank. "Gee," she says, "you think so?"

I almost ask if there's any chance it could have been something in the sandwiches she made. I didn't eat any, and I didn't get sick, and I happened to notice Debbie didn't have one either. Then again, it would be rude to imply to my friend that something she made with her own two hands caused three women to go into fits of vomiting, even if it could be true.

I'm just grateful Debbie forgot about my avocado allergy. Things could've been much worse.

CHAPTER 14

FROM *DEAR DEBBIE* DRAFTS FILE

Dear Debbie,

I have been married for over 20 years now, and although in many ways it is a happy marriage, there are certain aspects that I am unhappy with. I'm hoping you could give me some advice.

When we first got married, my husband was adamant that he didn't want me to work. I thought this was very sweet, and when my children were young, it made sense. I loved how he provided for us. But it could also be frustrating. For example, he set up our credit card so that he had to approve every purchase. When I wanted to buy something, I would have to call him about it and get his verbal approval beforehand, or else the card would be declined.

Similarly, we only have one joint bank account, and it only has a small amount of money that is my "allowance." Since I am the one who buys groceries, most of the money must be spent on that, and if I want any other purchases, I have to ask him to add money to the account. He insists that I "save" the money from my tiny allowance, so if my shoes wear out and I need a new pair, I have to save for months to buy them.

He feels that I'm not responsible with my spending, and he has a point. I'm not the one earning the money. For that reason, now that our children are older, I suggested the possibility of getting a job so I could have my own money. I thought this was the perfect solution, but when I mentioned it, he became furious and said that if I got a job, it would mean that I don't trust him to support me.

I am just frustrated because even though we are well off, I have been living on a shoestring budget for my entire marriage. How can I convince my husband to let me work and become more financially independent?

Rich But Broke

Dear Rich But Broke,

What you are describing is financial abuse. Your husband is using money as a way to control you ~~and he deserves to suffer~~. You don't need his permission to get a job. You don't need his permission for anything! My advice is that you should ~~slip poison into his wine at dinner~~ speak to a divorce lawyer.

I'd be happy to give you more information on ~~poisons that are unlikely to be detected on autopsy~~ local legal options if you'd like to contact me through my email address on the website.

Debbie

CHAPTER 15

DEBBIE

It's a few minutes before two o'clock when I pull into the parking lot for the *Hingham Household* newspaper.

The office is in a small strip mall next to a Chinese restaurant and below a massage parlor. I didn't eat that much at Rochelle's house, because I was avoiding the sandwiches, and I have to admit that Chinese food and a massage sounds pretty good right about now. Maybe I'll make a stop after Garrett and I talk about whatever was *so* important that it couldn't be done over the phone.

The words HINGHAM HOUSEHOLD are etched in black lettering on the glass door, although a few of the letters have rubbed off so that it reads HIN HAM HOUSEHO. I turn the knob and enter the small space, walking past the few scattered desks leading to the lone office occupied by Garrett Meers. I had always imagined that the offices of a newspaper would be big and bustling, but this place is the opposite of that. It's small and carpeted and usually so silent, you can hear a pin drop. It smells vaguely of cigarettes, which is strange since I don't think anyone who works here smokes.

The only one who is here today is Garrett's secretary, Sierra. She's so gorgeous that it's not surprising that I've seen Garrett checking her out when he thinks nobody is looking. Sierra looks up briefly when I enter the office, but she doesn't say a word and even avoids eye contact. I find that odd, because usually that girl can't shut up.

And something else about the office sets off an alarm bell in the back of my head:

Bernice isn't here.

Bernice is a senior editor at the paper, and even though Garrett is the editor in chief, Bernice makes all the important decisions. I generally submit my column directly to her, and I'm not convinced Garrett even reads it.

It wouldn't be strange for Bernice not to be in the office, because I'm sure the last thing she wants is to sit at that creaky wooden desk all day. However, the emptiness of her desk is what strikes me as a red flag. There are usually stacks of paper on her desk, a nameplate, and a photo of her daughter grinning at a state fair. All that has vanished.

"Hi, Sierra," I say. "I'm here to see—"

"Go on in," Sierra tells me, since she has obviously been expecting me. It's yet another slightly disturbing red flag.

I knock on the door to Garrett's office, even though it's slightly ajar. He calls for me to come in, and I slip into his broom closet of an office. Garrett is in his early forties, maybe a year or two younger than I am, and he's always clean-shaven and well dressed. He likes to project the image of the paper being more important than it is. After all, who is he dressing for when we are the only ones here?

"Hi, Debbie." He tries to smile, but only the left side of his lips turns up. "Have a seat. Please."

I oblige, taking the seat in front of his desk, smoothing my dress so that the hem stretches over my knees. I can't push away the sinking feeling in my chest. "Is everything okay? Where is Bernice?"

Garrett opens his mouth, but instead of answering that question, he just shakes his head. "I need to talk to you about a column you did a little while ago."

"Okay..."

"There was a woman who wrote to you, talking about a problem with her husband," he reminds me. "And this is the advice you gave her..." He picks up a printed copy of the *Hingham Household* off his desk, which is already dog-eared to the offending page. "You said, 'Your husband is using money as a way to control you. You don't need his permission to get a job. You don't need his permission for anything! My advice is that you should speak to a divorce lawyer.'"

I remember the column well. I don't often tell women to leave their husbands, believe me. I'm not a licensed therapist, and I certainly can't offer that kind of advice based on the tiny snippet presented to me in letters from readers. At least half of the women write in with complaints about their husbands, and I can never tell them what I *really* think, although I'm always itching to do so. But what that woman was describing was so egregious, I couldn't help myself.

"Yes," I say. "The financial abuse guy."

"Well, she left him."

75

I nod, pleased. "Good."

"Not good." Garrett looks at me like I've lost my mind. "Debbie, what were you thinking? You can't tell complete strangers to leave their husbands."

"Isn't *my job* to give advice?"

"Right, about gardening or getting stains out of shirts." His voice is completely exasperated. "You can't tell a woman you've never even met to get a divorce!"

"I can if he's so clearly abusive!"

"You don't know that…"

"He wouldn't let her have her own credit card." I tick off the man's sins on my hands. "He put her on an allowance even though she's a grown woman. He wouldn't let her get a job of her own. What sort of decent husband treats his wife that way? Would you treat your wife that way?"

"It's none of your business, Debbie."

"None of my business!" I burst out. "Garrett, I write an *advice column*. That's what I do. People ask me for advice, and I give it to them. It's up to them if they follow that advice."

"Not anymore you don't."

I stare at him. "What?"

Garrett lets out a long sigh and massages his temples. "The husband is threatening to sue us. This guy means business. The only way he would retract the lawsuit is if I fired you. And Bernice."

Well, that explains Bernice's empty desk.

"Why did you have to fire Bernice?" I feel terrible about that most of all. She's a single mother with a daughter in college. At least I have Cooper's income to lean on. "I'm the one who wrote the column."

"It was Bernice's decision to print the letter," he says. "She knew what she was doing."

"It was good advice." I clutch the hem of my skirt in my fists, which have suddenly grown sweaty. "That woman needed help, and I told her the truth. You're really going to fire me for helping a woman who was being abused?"

"This is a family-oriented paper," Garrett reminds me. "That's what our advertisers expect. You can't tell people to get a divorce. You just can't, Debbie."

"So you're just going to give this asshole everything he wants so he doesn't sue you?"

"Actually, I agree with him. You should not have gotten involved. If Bernice had shown me the column, I would've told her not to print it."

I'm sure Bernice did show him the column, but as usual, my lazy boss didn't bother to look at it. Now that Bernice is gone, he's screwed. Who will put the paper together? I doubt he even knows how. But I'm sure he'll find some other sap to do all the work while he sits there pretending he's important.

Garrett rises from his seat, his spine abnormally straight. "I'm going to have to ask you to leave now. Sierra will escort you to the door."

"Escort me?" That buzzing in my head starts up again. I take a deep breath, trying to calm myself. "What do you think I'm going to do?"

He doesn't answer that question. What I really want to say is that if I did want to stir up some shit, I doubt scrawny little Sierra could stop me. Luckily for him, I plan to go quietly.

I have a desk in the office, although I've barely got

anything in it. Sierra babysits me while I grab a legal pad out of the desk and a few pens. I also have a color photograph of Cooper with the girls in my desk drawer. Nobody offers me a box, so I just carry everything in my arms.

"I'm sorry, Debbie," Sierra says, looking uncomfortable, "but I have to ask you for your key."

I had forgotten I even have a set of keys, but I check my key ring, and sure enough, there is a mystery key that I suspect opens the door to the office. The buzzing in my head grows louder as I work it free and hand it over to Sierra's waiting hand. She goes through the rigamarole of testing it to make sure it's the correct key and that I'm not giving them a fake one. As if it wouldn't have been super easy to make a copy if I wanted to.

It's funny that they're so worried about the key. That isn't the thing they should be worried about me having. At the thought of this, the buzzing suddenly stops.

"Sorry about this," Sierra says. "I always liked your column. You gave really good advice."

I hug the legal pad to my chest. "Garrett doesn't think so."

"Well, it's just so important that the paper is family oriented," she says. "The sanctity of marriage, you know?"

"Uh-huh."

"There's nothing more important than the bonds of marriage," Sierra says sagely. "So you can't violate that by telling a woman to leave her husband. And our advertisers feel the same way. Without them, the paper would be done. You know that."

"Yes," I say. "I do know that."

Sierra walks me all the way to the door and makes sure that I leave without a fuss. As I trudge back to my car with my meager belongings, I can't suppress a jolt of sadness. Even though it was just a silly little local paper, I enjoyed my job. I liked giving advice. My own life has felt like a mess, but when it came to other people, I always seemed to know exactly what they should do.

It's time to start taking my own advice.

CHAPTER 16

The brownies are still in the oven when the front door slams shut.

It's too early for Cooper to be home. And Lexi is likely frolicking around God knows where with her boyfriend. I checked her location with Findly ten minutes ago, and she was at the Hingham Shipyard. So unless it's a burglar, which I suppose is possible but unlikely in the middle of the day, it must be Izzy.

"Izzy?" I call out.

No answer. But the footsteps coming from the foyer sound like hers. I pride myself on being able to distinguish the members of my family just based on their footsteps. Izzy's are quiet but surefooted. That's what makes her so good at soccer.

Sure enough, a few moments later, my younger daughter's face appears at the entrance to the kitchen. I turn to acknowledge her, even though she has not yet said one word.

"Hi," I say.

"Hey."

I open the door to the oven to check on the brownies, and the scent of chocolate quickly fills the kitchen. I inhale deeply and sigh. It's one of my favorite smells.

"Why are you always making brownies?" Izzy complains.

I look at her in surprise. First of all, I am not "always" making brownies. In fact, the last time I made them was nearly a year ago, for a holiday bake sale at her school. And second of all, what child complains about *fresh baked brownies*? Even *Lexi* doesn't find fault in my baking.

"Sorry," I say. "I guess that means you don't want any."

"Ew, no."

Ew? I can only shake my head, but that's fine. Even if she wanted to try one, I wouldn't give it to her.

Izzy is still standing at the door to the kitchen like she wants to tell me something, but she's completely silent, her backpack lying at her sneakers. It's unusual because between my two girls, Izzy is the chatterbox. She never stops talking, whereas Lexi always chooses her words more carefully. (Especially in the morning, when talking is verboten.)

"So what happened with soccer?" I ask her.

"Nothing." She lifts a shoulder halfway as if she's too tired to actually shrug. "I got sick of it."

I find that really hard to believe. Izzy has been playing soccer since she was in kindergarten. Every Saturday morning, bright and early, I would drive her to the local middle school where they had soccer practice for the grade school kids. Finding parking during soccer practice was a stressful and sometimes terrifying experience, but as soon as I found a spot, Izzy would burst out of the car in her pigtails and cleats and soccer socks. (I still don't understand what soccer socks are, but I obligingly bought them every single year.) Practice was her favorite part of the whole week.

So no, I don't believe she quit.

"Lexi says you got kicked off the team," I remind her.

"She doesn't know what she's talking about. I quit."

It was so easy to tell when Izzy was lying when she was little. When she was about three years old, she stole some chocolate chip cookies from the kitchen, and she swore her innocence, but the whole time, her lips were stained with chocolate and cookie crumbs. Little kids are so clueless.

She's a much better liar now, but I have no doubt that she didn't quit soccer. She would *never* quit soccer.

"You're not going to call Coach Pike, are you?" she asks in a worried voice.

"Of course not."

"Because that won't change anything."

"I told you, I'm not going to call him."

"You swear?"

"I swear." I let the oven door bang closed. "Do you think I don't have anything better to do than call your coach? He probably wouldn't even answer the phone anyway."

Her shoulders relax after my reassurance. "I'm going to do my homework. I've got a ton of homework this year." The fog in her eyes clears slightly. "So it's actually *better* I don't have soccer."

Bullshit. But okay, I'll pretend to believe it if it makes her feel better. "Izzy?"

She avoids my gaze. "Yeah?"

I consider asking if Coach Pike ever peeked in on the girls in the locker room the way Lexi's friend said he did. But I have a feeling that even if it's true, she'll never tell me the truth.

"Do you need any help with your homework?" I finally ask.

"Nope."

She never does.

Izzy doesn't ask me about my own day, but that's not surprising. She couldn't care less about my day. She's a good kid, but it doesn't matter to her that my magazine photo shoot got co-opted. She might care that I lost my job at the newspaper if it means less money for the family, but we've got Cooper's job to rely on, so it probably won't even register.

It's not worth mentioning, honestly. My kids have more important things to think about than their mother's drama. Besides, I can handle it.

Izzy gives me one last suspicious look, because she knows that I'm not good at leaving things alone when I'm upset over them. But she doesn't question me further. After a minute, she picks up her backpack and heads in the direction of the stairwell.

I always keep my promises to my children. I promised Izzy I wouldn't call her soccer coach. And I won't.

I'm going to drive down there.

CHAPTER 17

COOPER

After five miles on the treadmill, I don't feel any better. I used to run track in high school and the beginning of college. I was pretty good for a while, although I had some issues during my last two years of college and I dropped off the team. And later, I graduated and then got married, and especially after I had kids, I didn't have time for exercise.

When you're in your twenties and even thirties, you can stay in pretty good shape without hitting the gym. But at forty? Forget it. So when Jesse suggested the two of us join Titan Fitness, I decided it was time to get back in shape.

Jesse and I have been holding each other accountable. We both wanted to get back in shape, so we made sure to hit the gym at least three times per week. Jesse is better about it than I am. He often stays later than me, and today, he practically had to drag me here. *Come on. It will make you feel better.*

He's usually right. Working out at the gym has been great for me in more ways than one. Jesse does a mix of weights and cardio, but I usually stick with the treadmill with just a little bit of weightlifting. Still, the difference is noticeable. Not only in my strength and endurance but also in my appearance.

After I cool down on the machine, I towel off the sweat on my face. Even though I've got a sweat stain on my collar, I notice a woman on the elliptical giving me an appreciative look. I look back for just a little too long, and she winks at me. That's when I quickly avert my eyes and hurry over to where Jesse is lifting weights.

"I'm going to head out," I tell him.

Jesse puts down the weights and takes a long chug from his water bottle. He wipes his mouth and looks up at me. "Are you okay, Cooper? Do you want to go out for a drink or something?"

Definitely not. "I just want to go home and get this over with."

"You're going to tell Debbie?"

Christ, the last thing I want is to tell Debbie. What I'd really like is to start searching for another job and not let her know until I've secured something. But God knows how long that will take. And it's not like I'm not keeping secrets from her already. Something has to give.

"I'll figure it out," I say.

He frowns at me. Like my wife, Jesse is a problem solver. When something is wrong, his instinct is to figure out a way to fix it. "You know, this could be the best thing that ever happened to you."

"Uh-huh."

"Really," he insists. "I mean, you said yourself that

it was turning into a dead-end job. Now you can find something better."

"I'm sure you're right," I say, not feeling at all sure that he's right.

"We should do something this weekend," he says. "So you don't sit around the house moping all day."

"Yeah, maybe."

"What do you want to do?"

I can't think of anything I want to do. It will take all my effort not to lie on the sofa wallowing in despair. What I *should* be doing is posting my profile on all the job-hunting websites and contacting recruiters. All stuff I hate, but I have to do it.

Still, I can think of one thing that might cheer me up.

"Let's go to the firing range," I say.

Jesse grins at me. "Yeah?"

"Sure, why not?"

"You're on."

Yes, I do own a gun. One of the major sources of discord in my marriage is the fact that I purchased one a few years ago after there were a few burglaries in our neighborhood. Debbie was adamantly against it, citing admittedly accurate statistics about how people who own a gun are more likely to shoot a family member than an intruder. But in the end, I won out and bought it. The compromise is that I keep it in the garage, locked up, and I only use it at the firing range. The kids don't even know it's there.

And I enjoy firing the gun. After everything that happened this week, it will feel good to quite literally blow off a little steam.

I take a quick shower at the gym and throw on a

change of clothes. I'll be home before dinner but not early enough for a long conversation before we eat. I still don't quite know what I'm going to say to Debbie. Lately, she has seemed different. More…fragile. More distracted.

That's why I can't be entirely honest with her. Not now.

I return to the front desk to sign out with my card. That woman from the elliptical who had been smiling at me earlier passes by, somehow even more alluring in her jeans and sweater than she was in her skintight workout outfit. My gaze is drawn to her like a magnet, and it's only when she winks at me that I manage to rip my eyes away.

Not a good idea, Coop.

"Have a good workout today?" Cindy, the woman who works the front desk, interrupts my thoughts.

Am I imagining it, or is there a bit of an edge to her voice? "Uh, yeah. Thanks."

"You know," she says, "your *wife* was here earlier, working out."

Yes, that was definitely an edge to her voice. But she wouldn't tell Debbie I was ogling some other woman, would she? I barely looked! "Oh. Okay."

"Well," Cindy says, her tone back to neutral, "have a great evening!"

I nod wordlessly and head straight home before I can do anything else stupid.

CHAPTER 18

DEBBIE

So I'm not going to the high school *only* to see Coach Pike. I also have to drop off the cans for the food drive.

I realize that doesn't make it better, but somehow in my head, it does.

Even though it's after hours, the administrator who works at the front desk, Elena, is still around. She buzzes me into the school, and her eyes light up at the brown box filled with cans that I've got in my arms.

"Debbie!" Elena grins at me. "I knew you'd come through."

"Yes, and I can skip the gym after carrying this over here," I joke, even though I already had my workout for today.

I set the cans down on the counter while Elena taps at some keys on her computer. I linger there for a moment, trying to figure out the best way to handle this.

"Hey," I say, trying to make my voice as casual as possible, "would it be okay if I popped over to speak to Coach

Pike for a minute? I need to talk about the soccer schedule with him. There are a few days that Izzy can't make it in."

"Sure, go right ahead," Elena tells me without looking up from the computer screen.

She trusts me. She doesn't think that there's any chance that I'm going to do anything I shouldn't. But in my defense, I'm not going to do anything terrible. I would just like to have a conversation with the soccer coach about why he felt the need to cut his best player. If that's not an honorable intention, I don't know what is.

After all, what is more honorable than protecting your child? If my parents had protected me better...

Well, no point in thinking about that right now.

I already know that Coach Pike has his office on the first floor, not far from the soccer field. While I walk down the high school's familiar hallways, I reach into my purse to pull out the brownies wrapped in tinfoil. I am certainly not beyond throwing chocolate at a situation to make it better.

I get lucky. Soccer practice has already ended, and the coach is sitting at his desk, shuffling through some papers in front of him. He is in his fifties, and I'm pretty sure he's bald or at least bald*ing*, but I can't know for certain since I've never seen him without a baseball cap on his head. He's got a Hingham Prep T-shirt on, which stretches over the folds of his belly. He actually seems to be in poor shape for somebody who coaches sports, but who am I to judge?

I rap on his open door, plastering a smile on my face as I hold out the tinfoil-wrapped brownies as a peace offering. "Coach Pike?"

He raises his eyes. I'm still wearing the yellow dress

89

that I had on during my meeting at the newspaper, and I can feel Pike's gaze crawling up my body. I squirm and clutch my purse to my chest with my free hand.

"Can I help you?" he asks me with a lecherous smile. I never liked this man, but I like him even a little less right now.

"Yes," I say. "I'm Isabel Mullen's mother."

"Oh." The smile instantly drops off his lips. "I see."

"I brought you these brownies." I bring them over to him, glad to have an excuse for entering the office. "I was hoping we could chat."

Coach Pike accepts the brownies, peeking under the foil wrapping with a look of approval. He doesn't suggest that I sit down, but I do it anyway.

"I wanted to talk to you about Izzy," I say. "I found out today that she was cut from the soccer team."

"Yep" is all he has to say on the matter.

"Well, that confused me," I continue, "because, as you know, she's a great player. I watched her play all year last year, and I think she's one of your strongest players. So I just don't understand…"

Pike peels back the tinfoil to discover that I wrapped the brownies in several layers of plastic wrap. He looks like he's considering unwrapping them, but he decides against the effort. "They look good."

"They taste good too."

He stares at the chocolaty treats thoughtfully, considering his next words. "Actually, the brownies are part of the problem."

"Ex…excuse me?"

"At the end of last season," Pike tells me, "I told Izzy that she was too slow, and she needed to lose some weight before the next season. Fifteen pounds at least. But twenty would be better."

My jaw drops. "You...you told my fifteen-year-old daughter that she needs to drop twenty pounds?"

"I told her she needs to be faster," he corrects me. "I suggested that losing weight might be a way to be faster. But she's not any faster, and on top of that, she's five pounds more than she was last year at this time. We've got two extra girls on the team, and someone had to go. So I had to cut her."

"Izzy is plenty fast!" I protest.

"With all due respect, Mrs. Mullen, you're not the soccer coach, are you?" He taps on the tinfoil of the brownie tray. "I'm a soccer coach, and I'm the one who can tell you who is fast enough. Not you."

It suddenly makes perfect sense that Izzy was mad at me for making brownies. She was mad because my fit, perfect daughter somehow felt like she needed to be smaller.

"Look," he says, "I agree that Izzy has potential. If she can lose the weight and get faster, maybe I'll consider taking her back."

"So it's about speed." I shift in my chair. "How fast does she need to be? Like, if we do some running, how fast does she need to—"

"Faster than she is now," he says without further explanation. "And like I said, the best way to get faster is to lose weight. The treadmill won't cut it." He pauses to fold his arms across his chest. "And anyway, nobody wants to watch a bunch of chubby girls running around the soccer field. That eyeful isn't going to make the crowd happy. Hell, *I* don't want to see it."

My head is spinning. I can't *believe* he just said that about a bunch of teenage girls. I want to repeat this conversation to the principal, but he'll just deny it. If I ever doubted Lexi's story about the coach "accidentally" walking into the locker room, that doubt is gone. If he hadn't kicked Izzy off the team, I'd have insisted she withdraw to avoid any further interactions with Pike.

Izzy can't play the sport she loves because of this man. And worse, he's making her feel bad about herself. He's making her feel like she needs to change.

And he's ogling teenage girls while they're changing in the locker room.

"I'm sorry I can't just give in to everything you want." Pike shrugs, not looking the least bit sorry. "But that's not the way the world works, and it's better she learns that sooner rather than later."

"She deserves to be on the team," I say through my teeth, although I no longer want her on *his* team.

"If you want to help your daughter, help her lose that weight," he says to me. "Stop making brownies all the time. And while you're at it, it wouldn't hurt for you to lose a few pounds yourself."

My teeth are clenched so tightly, I can't believe one of them doesn't crack in half. I take a breath, trying to calm myself. I count to ten in my head, then get to my feet.

"Thank you for your time, Coach Pike," I say.

He nods at me. "Anytime."

I turn around and exit the coach's office. All I can think of is that I need to get out of this school before I scream.

But I can't leave now. I have one more stop to make before I go.

CHAPTER 19

COOPER

The house is dark when I get home.

I had thought Debbie would be in the kitchen, working on dinner, and I'm relieved that she isn't. I didn't want to be bombarded with questions the second I walked through the door. Although there likely won't be *that* many questions. Only one.

What happened with your boss?

The thought of it makes a cold sweat break out along my hairline. It's a familiar feeling, one that I have grown to hate. All I can think is that there's only one thing that will make me feel better. There's only one place I can go right now.

I've got to get out of here.

Before I can bolt, I hear the garage door crank open. Damn, I waited too long. I brace myself, knowing that Debbie will be here in another minute. My whole body tenses up.

"Cooper?" Debbie's voice fills the living room

before I even see her. "Why are you standing there in the dark?"

"I, uh…" I don't have a good answer for her question. Debbie flicks on the light, and I blink a few times as my eyes adjust. "I just got home."

"Sorry I'm late," she says. "I was at the grocery store, and it was a lot more crowded than I expected."

Except she's not carrying any groceries. That's weird.

She looks good though. She's changed out of the clingy dress she was wearing this morning, but she looks great in everything. I still remember the first day I met her, over twenty years ago now, and it was like a bolt of lightning hit me. I hadn't been thinking about marriage before that, but I knew right away I wanted to marry Debbie. This was a woman I'd never be able to get out of my head.

"How was your day?" I ask her before she can ask me. "Oh, hey, how was the photo shoot?"

She was so excited about it. I'm sure we can kill at least fifteen minutes going over the details.

"It went great," she says in a chipper voice. "I can't wait for you to see the pictures."

I can't wait either. I'm not into gardening like Debbie is—the truth is, I find plants boring in the same way that other people find tax codes boring—but I'm excited because she's excited. Maybe I can get one of the photos professionally framed so we can hang it in the hallway. I can do it as a surprise when the article comes out.

I wait for the rush of details about the photo shoot. Debbie loves to tell me all about her day, and I'm usually happy to listen, but right now, she's strangely quiet. I guess she's worn out from all the excitement.

"So, uh," I say. "Anything else happen today?"

She taps her chin as if thinking about it. "Not really. Just an ordinary day."

"Oh."

"So…" She grins at me. "How did the conversation with Ken go?"

Well, that didn't take long.

"It didn't go…great."

The smile fades from her lips. "What do you mean?"

I can't bring myself to tell Debbie that I didn't get the promotion and then decided to quit. Christ, what will she think of me? So instead, I tell her a version of the truth. "The partnership isn't going to happen. It's off the table."

Eventually, I'll have to admit to her that I quit. Even worse, I'm going to have to find another job without the benefit of a reference, although my last boss from a decade ago might still vouch for me. If I don't find something quickly, we'll have to move. Hingham is expensive, and it's barely in our price range as it is. We are pretty screwed right now. The thought of it makes me feel like there's a noose tightening around my neck.

At least we've got Debbie's newspaper job to tide us over. It's not much, but it's something. Worse comes to worst, I can beg for my job back—probably with a pay cut.

"Did he say why?" Debbie presses me.

"Not really." I avoid Debbie's eyes and instead look at our clock mounted on the wall. "Hey, are we going to have dinner soon?"

The question throws her off. She obviously doesn't have a meal prepared, because she just got home. From wherever she was, which definitely wasn't the supermarket.

Where could she have gone? And how is it possible that she doesn't have dinner ready? Debbie has dinner ready at six thirty on the dot every night. You could set a clock by it.

"It will be a little while before dinner," Debbie admits. "An hour? Sorry about that—busy day."

"You know what?" I rest a hand on my belly and pretend to wince. "I'm starving. Do you mind if I just run out and grab some fast food? Is that okay?"

Debbie is a stickler for family dinners, so I expect her to protest. But instead, she smiles at me. "Of course. I'll probably just throw together some sandwiches for me and Izzy. Lexi is having dinner out with Zane tonight."

Debbie makes a sour face the way she always does when she mentions our daughter's boyfriend. I have to admit, I don't think much of the kid either. But I realize my opinion won't mean much to Lexi.

"So anyway," she says, "go out and get something greasy. I'll hold down the fort."

My shoulders sag. It's becoming harder and harder to come up with excuses to slip out in the evening. "Do you want me to bring you back anything?"

She tilts her head thoughtfully, and she looks so sweet at that moment, I can't help but feel a jab of ice-cold guilt. "I would never say no to french fries."

"You got it."

As if fries would make up for lying to her face.

Before I leave, I tap out a quick text message on my phone. Then I snatch my car keys from where I left them on the mantel in the living room and head out the front door. Last year, Debbie—who I might have mentioned is a genius—installed an app on our phones called Findly. It's sort of like Find My Friends, but with much more impressive accuracy.

Jesse was shocked when I told him there was a tracking app on my phone that allowed my wife to know where I was at all times. He announced that I must be pretty whipped to allow her to install something like that. At the time, I couldn't imagine anything I would be doing that I wouldn't want Debbie to know about.

And now, as I walk out the front door, I toggle off Findly. If she asks, I'll tell her I must have been in a dead zone, but I'm sure as hell not sharing my location with her for the next couple of hours. She can't know where I'm going.

CHAPTER 20

HARLEY

I always shower after I get home from Titan Fitness.

Yes, there are showers at the gym. But seriously, they're gross. If the members knew how seldom they were cleaned, they wouldn't shower there either. Showers are *not* self-cleaning, believe me.

Besides, I love long, luxurious, hot showers. I love standing under the burning hot water until my skin turns beet red. I keep turning the heat higher and higher until I'm certain that I'm going to be boiled alive like a lobster in a pot. I stand there until all the hot water is gone, and only then do I come out and wrap myself in a warm, fluffy towel.

Like I said, I love showers.

I have a little basement apartment on a dead-end street, where there's only one other house that appears to be abandoned, possibly condemned from the looks of it. The couple that lives in the main part of the house are super old and deaf, and they keep to themselves, so it feels a bit like I'm living here by myself. One of these days, I'm probably going to come upstairs to give them my rent check and find one or both unresponsive in the living room. But until then, it's a nice quiet place to live.

Just as I'm wrapping a towel around myself, my phone pings with a text message. I find it lying on the nightstand in the bedroom and smile when I see the message waiting for me.

Can I come over?

I type out my response:

Absolutely. ETA?
Fifteen minutes.

Oh, yay. That will give me just enough time to blow-dry my hair and apply some makeup for the perfect no-makeup look. I'll get dressed, but there's no need to bother with too many clothes, considering they'll be coming off again shortly, if you know what I mean.

When I'm done dolling myself up, I look myself over in the full-length mirror in my bedroom. Just enough makeup? Check. Hair sexily tousled? Check. Tank top showing just a little too much cleavage? Check.

I look hot. Much hotter than *her*. I mean, it isn't even close.

While I'm in the middle of practicing smoldering looks in the mirror, there's a knock on my door. My heart speeds up in my chest the way it always does when he knocks, and I race across my apartment, practically tripping over an ottoman.

That's how you know you really like somebody. When you nearly suffer bodily harm in your eagerness to answer the door for them.

I throw it open, and he's standing there, looking a bit guilty like he always does, but at the same time really sexy. Maybe it's sexy that he's guilty. He says he's never done anything like this before, and I believe it. But there's no doubt he wants to be here—badly. His gaze is flooded with desire.

"Hey, Harley," he says.

I smile at him, that flutter in my chest that I always get when he shows up at my door. God, he's sexy.

"Hey, Cooper," I say.

He pauses one more beat, and then he steps inside the apartment. He doesn't waste another second before kissing me. His wife will be expecting him home soon, so there isn't a ton of time for foreplay. I might be his first affair, but he's not my first married man. Not even close. I know the score.

"When is Debbie expecting you back?" I ask him as he kisses my neck. I hate to talk about her when we're having sexy time, but I need to be practical. I want to know how long we've got.

"I've got about an hour."

Long enough.

Cooper doesn't waste any time. He picks me up easily, because he's been working out. Good thing he has, because that's where we met. At the gym. When I saw him doing laps on that treadmill, I couldn't help myself.

As he carries me to the bedroom, I can't help but think to myself that one of these days, at the end of the hour, he's going to decide that this time, he's not going back to her.

CHAPTER 21

I know what you're thinking. I'm a terrible person. A home-wrecker.

And you wouldn't be *wrong*.

But the truth of the matter is that humans are not meant to be monogamous. Especially men. Biologically, they have a compulsion to spread their seed to as many women as possible. And also biologically, Debbie is past her childbearing years, whereas Cooper, at forty-six years old, has many reproductive years ahead of him.

Biologically, Cooper is designed to want me.

Cooper and I are lying together in bed. He has his arm around me, and we're plastered together with sweat. He plants a kiss on my forehead, and it's so sweet, it almost kills me that he's going to have to run out of here in another few minutes.

"What if you stayed?" I suggest.

He lets out a pained sigh. "I wish I could. Believe me. Debbie and I are like strangers who are forced to live together."

"That sounds terrible."

"It is." He swallows. "I was losing my mind until you came along, Harley. I wish I didn't have to pretend anymore."

"Then don't. She doesn't own you."

"Uh, she sort of does." Cooper holds up his left hand with the wedding ring on his fourth finger. "A divorce would be rough. She'd take everything."

"Just half of everything."

But Cooper shakes his head. I've dated a lot of married men, and I know they'll tell me what they think I want to hear, but I truly believe he doesn't love Debbie anymore. He hasn't in a long time. He's been sleeping in the guest room for years, but he still can't leave. She's not stable, and a divorce would send her off the deep end.

And now that I've gotten to know Debbie, I know what he means. The woman poisoned her neighbors after all.

It was not my intention to befriend the wife of the man I'm hooking up with. I mean, I'm not a complete psychopath. But then one morning, I was talking to Cindy at the front desk of the gym, and a fortyish woman with a pleasant but somewhat angular face and hair pulled back into a neat ponytail swiped her card, and the name Debra Mullen popped up on the computer.

So of course, I was curious. I'm only human. It's not like I went to her house and stalked her.

I'm not a stalker in general. But to be fair, Cooper is impossible to stalk. The man has no social media presence, which isn't uncommon among men his age. When I couldn't stalk him online, the only way to learn more about him was to do some real-life reconnaissance.

Even so, I just meant to have a *conversation* with her. But every time she mentioned Cooper's name, I found myself hanging on her every word. She seemed to have no idea how much trouble her marriage was in. Or else she was trying to hide it from me. After all, you don't go around telling strangers that you haven't had sex with your husband in two years.

So I figured if we were better friends, she might be willing to confide in me about Cooper. That was when I invited her to get coffee with me.

One thing led to another, and suddenly we were getting coffee regularly, and then she was inviting me to her book club, and now suddenly we are best friends. I get the feeling she doesn't have a lot of friends, and the truth is, neither do I. Cooper would be furious if he knew I was spending time with his wife, so I have been careful not to mention it.

At some point, this is going to blow up in my face. I can't maintain my friendship with Debbie while sleeping with her husband. One day over dinner, Debbie is going to mention her new friend Harley to Cooper, and he'll probably choke to death on a carrot or something.

Although maybe that's what I *want* to happen. Well, not the choking on a carrot part. But I *want* Debbie to know that her husband is messing around behind her back. I want her to boot him out the door. Because when she does, he'll come straight here.

My relationships with married men rarely end well. In fact, the last one, with a man named Edgar, blew up in my face quite spectacularly. But I've got a good feeling about Cooper Mullen.

Cooper extracts himself from my embrace and rolls

out of bed. In the dim light of the bedroom, I watch him get dressed. He's over a decade older than I am, but he's in fantastic shape, and it's all I can do to keep from pulling him back into bed. He could do better than Debbie. He must know that.

"Will you be back tomorrow?" I ask him.

I wait for the flash of annoyance on his face, but it never comes. "I'll try to get away if I can." Then he adds, "No promises."

It's not easy being the other woman. I know, I know, cry me a river, but it's a hard life. We can't be seen in public, and when all the major holidays roll around, I'm alone. Forget about double dates.

But very soon, I won't be the other woman anymore.

Cooper is the one. The more time I spend with him, the more certain I am that it's true. And very soon, Debbie will know it too.

CHAPTER 22

DEBBIE

When the porch lights go on, I assume it's Cooper, back from his fast-food run. Until the lock on the front door fails to turn.

I come out to the foyer and peek through one of the windows overlooking the front porch to see who is out there. I shouldn't be entirely surprised to find Lexi and Zane standing on the porch together. My instinct is to back away slowly before I have to watch my daughter make out with her boyfriend. It's the last thing I want to see.

Except they're not kissing. They're talking to each other, and even though I can't hear what they're saying, Lexi has her hand on her hip, and her lips are turned down. All the while, Zane has a self-satisfied smirk on his face.

Zane pulls his phone out of his pocket, and he's pointing at the screen. Lexi makes a grab for the phone, and he holds it just out of her reach. The expression on her face makes it look like she wants to scratch his eyes out.

What's going on out there?

If I quietly crack open the window, I might be able to hear what they're saying. Not that I want to eavesdrop on my daughter, but… Okay, fine, *yes*, I want to eavesdrop on my daughter. She'll never tell me on her own what they've been discussing. This is my only option.

But before I can attempt to wrench open the window, Zane reaches out and grabs Lexi's arm. Even though I'm sure he's done a lot more than that when they're alone together, the discomfort on her face is palpable. She tries to pull her arm away, but he won't let her go. And all the while, he's got that smirk on his face.

I forget all about the window and go straight for the front door. I pretend like I was on my way out, even though I don't have my purse, and now that I think about it, I also don't have shoes on. So it's not much of a ruse, but it's enough to startle both of them.

Instantly, Zane releases Lexi's arm.

"Oh, hello!" My attempt to pretend to be surprised is somewhat short of an Oscar-winning performance but good enough. "I didn't realize you two were out here."

"Zane is leaving," Lexi says tightly.

Zane's hair is hanging in his eyes, and it makes me want to grab a pair of scissors from the kitchen and snip it off. Actually, I would rather snip something else off, but I'd settle for a haircut, I suppose. Or anything that would wipe that smirk off his lips.

"I'll talk to you later, Lexi," he says.

She doesn't say anything, but after a few beats, she nods.

I step back to let Lexi enter the house and shut the door behind her, having abandoned any pretext of going outside. I'm just glad Lexi is inside and safe. I only wish Cooper would come home too, especially since his location sharing seems to be off. Maybe he's in a dead zone.

I expect Lexi to run upstairs to her room without another word like she often does these days, but instead, she just stands in the middle of the living room as if she's not sure what to do next. I am desperate to ask her what happened between her and her boyfriend on the porch, but I know from experience that it won't go well.

"What are you doing?" she finally asks me.

She doesn't say it like she usually does. Her typical way of asking me what I'm doing is to say "What are you *doing?*" Basically, she's trying to indicate that whatever I'm doing is weird and unacceptable. But now she asks like she's genuinely curious. And I have to come up with an answer.

"I'm tidying up the living room." *And definitely not spying on you and your boyfriend.*

She looks at me with interest. When Lexi was little, she and I used to have a weekly cleaning session. When Izzy was a toddler, the house used to get cluttered, so every Sunday, Lexi and I would clean together. She loved it. I used to let her run the vacuum, and she looked so hilariously adorable trying to push around a vacuum that was almost as big as she was. I've probably got hundreds of photos of her with that vacuum cleaner, but it makes me too sad to look at them.

I brace myself for some critical comment from Lexi about my housekeeping skills, but instead, she says, "Do you need any help?"

The living room is already spotless. I vacuum and dust every single morning after I make the beds and do the dishes from breakfast. But if Lexi is offering to help me, I'm not going to turn her down.

"Could you vacuum the floor for me?" I ask her, even though there probably isn't even one speck of dust on the living room floor.

Lexi's eyes light up. "Sure."

She follows me to the closet where I keep the vacuum cleaner and other cleaning supplies. As I am pulling it out, unwinding the cord from where it always seems to get tangled, I decide to take a chance. I know I'm tempting fate, but I'm dying to know what was happening on the porch. More importantly, I need to know if my daughter is in some kind of danger.

So I say as casually as I can, "By the way, how are things going with Zane?"

Naturally, it was the absolute wrong thing to say. I have been a mother of at least one teenager for four years, and I should have known better.

Her eyes immediately narrow. "Why?"

The cord is caught on something, and I give it a yank, trying to work it free. "No reason."

"Were you *spying* on me?" she snaps at me. "Is that why you came out on the porch and were being so weird?"

To be fair, I am *always* being weird in Lexi's assessment. "I wasn't spying on you. I swear."

But only because the window was closed and I couldn't hear anything.

"So why did you open the front door?" she demands to know.

"I was looking for your father," I say weakly.

Lexi doesn't believe me, which is probably fair. She regards the vacuum with sudden disdain. "I don't really feel like doing chores right now. I'm going to go upstairs."

"But..." The cord finally pops free from the closet. I brandish the vacuum in my right hand. "Just do a quick lap around the living room. It will be fun."

"Fun?" Her voice is dripping with sarcasm. "I don't think being your maid is *fun*. And anyway, I've got homework to do."

And I've lost her.

She stomps up the stairs to her room without another word. I should have been more careful. I should never have brought up Zane. When she's ready, she'll tell me. Or maybe she won't tell me, and I'll just notice he's not around anymore.

And if he does anything to hurt her, he'll be very sorry.

CHAPTER 23

An hour later, Cooper comes home.

He's been gone for two hours total, which is quite a long time for a fast-food run. Fast food is *fast*—it's in the name. He walks through the front door, clutching a bag of french fries that have stained the brown paper with their grease. The smell is intoxicating, but I don't have much of an appetite.

Cooper has been gone most of the evening, and I don't know where he's been. Not only that, but it's not the first time he's disappeared like that. Always with an excuse.

And he always turns off his location sharing.

I rise from the sofa to confront him. "Where have you been?"

"I told you, I grabbed some dinner." His eyes avoid mine. "Then I was just…you know, driving around a bit. I had to clear my head."

"I see…"

"Sorry." He holds out the bag of fries, and I obligingly

take it from him. "If I thought you needed me home sooner, I wouldn't have stayed out."

Except that's another lie.

"I was worried," I say. "I tried to see where you were, but Findly didn't show your location."

"Sorry... I was on some back roads. Probably going in and out of dead zones."

And another.

I bring the bag of french fries to the kitchen, and Cooper follows behind. I pour each of us a cup of diet cola and pass his across the kitchen table, where he drops into one of the seats. He stares down at the drink, eventually taking a sip, but he doesn't reach for the fries. Neither do I.

"Cooper," I say.

"There's something I need to tell you, Debbie." He takes a shaky breath. "I..."

I brace myself for whatever is coming. Whatever he has to say isn't going to be something I want to hear. He's not going to tell me, *Hey, Debbie, I just won the lottery. Let's go buy a mansion.* He drops his eyes, staring down at his hands.

"I quit," he says.

"*What?*"

"When Ken told me I didn't get the promotion." He's still looking down at his hands, unable to meet my eyes. "I threatened to quit, and he didn't budge. So...I did it. I quit."

That was the last thing I expected him to say. I knew that speaking to Ken Bryant could put Cooper's future with the company in danger, but this is not the outcome I anticipated. Cooper isn't the sort of impulsive man who quits when he doesn't get his way. That buzzing in the back of my head starts up again, and I feel my hands clench into fists.

"It sucks," Cooper acknowledges. "But…I'm sure I'll find something else."

"Did he say why he wouldn't promote you?" My voice is louder than it should be for this hour of the night. "He must have given you a reason!"

He flashes me a wry smile. "He said I'm not management material. And that he doesn't need me."

"Is he out of his mind?" I know what Cooper does at that company, and they'll be lost without him. "Why would he say that?"

"I don't know, but he made it clear I would never be a partner."

This time, I snatch up a few of the fries from the bag. They've been sitting in the bag too long and have gone cold. I wonder how long Cooper was driving around with them.

"This is absolutely ridiculous!" I say. "You can't let him get away with this!"

"I just want to move past it," he says, "and find something else. This… It could be a blessing. I was never going to become a partner there, so maybe I can find something better."

He could be right. Cooper deserves better than that job, but all I can think about is how we're going to pay the mortgage.

"Anyway," he adds, "we've got your salary from Dear Debbie to tide us over until I find something new."

Oh right, I never told Cooper that I got fired. Today was not a great day for the Mullen family.

I open my mouth to share this little revelation, but I

can't make myself do it. Cooper looks miserable enough, and I can't bring myself to drop one more thing on him right now.

He'll look for a job, and I'll look for a job. Between the two of us, we'll find something. We'll be okay.

"Ken made a huge mistake." I reach to take both of his hands in mine. "You're his best employee."

Cooper just shrugs sadly. "Maybe."

"You are," I insist. "Trust me, Ken Bryant is going to regret letting you go. *Deeply.*"

Cooper seems a bit skeptical, but I know what I'm talking about. Sooner than he thinks, Ken is going to be sorry for what he's done.

CHAPTER 24

FROM *DEAR DEBBIE* DRAFTS FILE

Dear Debbie,

Debbie, I am exhausted! My husband snores like a
dang chainsaw! I swear, I haven't had one full night of
sleep since the day we said, "I do"! Every night, it's the
same deal. He falls asleep in two seconds flat, and that's
when the gosh darned racket starts. I have to lie awake
and listen to what sounds like a grizzly bear giving birth
right next to me!

I've tried it all! Earplugs, giving him a little nudge
(or not so little shove), and nothing works! If I don't
figure out what to do soon, I'm going to have to pack
up and sleep in the bathtub! Do you have any advice to
save my sanity?

Sleepless in Hingham

Dear Sleepless,

Snoring is a very common problem in adults, especially men. It's been estimated that one-quarter of all people snore on a regular basis! And of course, it's a big problem for the partners they sleep with.

There are several things your husband could do to reduce his snoring. Regular exercise and reduced alcohol intake can help with snoring. Weight loss can also be helpful. Also, side sleeping is less likely to result in snoring, so if your husband sleeps on his back, tell him to roll over!

If none of that works or your husband doesn't want to do anything to reduce his snoring, there's a little trick that's 100 percent effective:

The next time your husband wakes you up from his snoring, take your pillow off the bed, and hold it over his face. Then with your hands, apply medium to firm pressure over the center of the pillow. The noise level may briefly intensify, but I guarantee that within five minutes, the snoring will have stopped. Permanently.

Happy sleeping!
Debbie

CHAPTER 25

DEBBIE

I wake up at two in the morning, my heart pounding.

I had considered setting an alarm, but I didn't want to risk waking Cooper. Thankfully, he is still asleep, snoring softly beside me in bed. In the light of the moon, he looks much younger. He looks just like he did when we first met all those years ago. I still remember how happy he seemed when I agreed to go out with him, like he couldn't believe his luck.

Cooper doesn't stir as I climb out of bed. He is generally a sound sleeper, but it helps that I put some opium in the diet soda that I poured him when we were eating the french fries. The colorful flowers in my garden look a lot like windflowers, but that's not what they are.

Yes, I grow opium poppies in my garden.

Technically, it's not illegal to grow them in your own backyard. It's only when the quantity reaches the level of acres and you're manufacturing opium to sell to others that it becomes problematic. I suspect the neighbors would frown on it, and God knows what Zane would do if he knew. So I tell everyone that they're windflowers.

Of course, I don't *just* grow opium poppies. Really, they're only a small part of my garden. I'm also partial to lantana with their bright, tropical colors as well as hibiscus flowers with the bright bold red pop. I also have a small patch of dark red *Carapichea ipecacuanha* berries, which is what they make syrup of ipecac from. It's quite a powerful emetic.

I started harvesting the opium out of curiosity. What can I say? I get bored easily, especially now that the kids are teenagers and don't need me every moment of the day. I watched a video about it online, which taught me what to do. You make vertical cuts in the poppy pod in order to "bleed" out the opium. I've been doing it for years now, and I've accumulated quite the little stash.

I suppose this is what happens when somebody has an IQ of 178 and no job except for writing a weekly advice column. I do write those apps for our phones, but I've become so quick at it, they don't take much work anymore. My brain is screaming for stimulation.

Cooper continues to snore as I get dressed in a pair of jeans and a black sweater. I tie my hair back in a bun to keep it out of my face and creep downstairs to the first floor. I have quite a lot to do tonight and no time to waste.

The first thing I do is grab the three refill packs for the Japanese beetle traps. And then I enter our garage, which is where we keep the shovel that Cooper uses to dig us out during the winter when it snows. Armed with both, I leave the house.

The weather is a bit cool for the sweater I have on. Really, it's more like jacket weather, but I expect after digging a bit, I'll have worked up more of a sweat. Anyway, this won't take long.

I walk down the block to the bottom of the hill where Jo Dolan lives. I pass Rochelle's house on the way, which is silent and dark like everyone else's house. I took a stroll by her property at around eight o'clock this evening, and there was no sign of a party. I suspect Rochelle was still vomiting by then.

After a few minutes, I reach Jo's garden. Under the cloak of darkness, the roses look almost ominous. They look like they might come to life and kill me at any moment. Especially if they knew what I'm about to do to them.

But I'm not too worried about killer plants. What I *am* worried about is cameras, but I don't see any of those. I'm fairly sure that Jo isn't the sort of person who mounts cameras on her property. She really ought to though. It took me less than five minutes to install our door cameras—one in front and one in back—and install the software on my phone to monitor them at all times. It's a good source of security, and it's also a great way to spy on my older daughter when she's on the porch with her boyfriend.

When I'm satisfied that there is nothing recording me, I find a good spot at the periphery of her front yard and start digging in the mulch. It takes me about five minutes to dig a shallow grave in which to bury the first refill pack, and then I bury the others at two more locations in the garden. When I straighten up, I brush off my hands on my jeans and inspect my handiwork.

This will do nicely.

Next, I return to my home. It's only two thirty, and I should be exhausted, but the adrenaline is pumping through my veins, and I feel like I could run a marathon. Actually, maybe running a marathon would be a better outlet for my frustration. Oh well, too late.

When I get inside, I drop the shovel back in the garage and climb into my Subaru. I recognize there is some risk in programming the address of my next destination into my GPS, but I have to take that chance. Massachusetts is impossible to navigate without a GPS, and it would be far worse to wander the streets in the middle of the night. Besides, my final destination is only a fifteen-minute drive away in Weymouth.

I follow the GPS directions, turning onto dark streets lit only by dim streetlights. After about fifteen minutes, the British accented voice on my phone announces, "You have reached your destination."

I pull over down the road, recognizing that it could be problematic to park directly in front of Coach Robert Pike's house. Back when I was sitting in his office, I had an uncomfortable buzzing in the back of my head. I'm still buzzing now, but it's different. This time, I'm buzzing with *excitement.*

I took a detour to check out Pike's house earlier on my way home from the school, just to make sure that he didn't have any cameras on his property. But like Jo Dolan, Pike is not a camera sort of guy. Guard dogs maybe. But I didn't hear any of those earlier either. This isn't a swanky neighborhood where burglars are likely to break in.

Also, he's not married and has no children. He lives completely alone.

My heart is still thrumming as I climb out of the car and step onto the street. I walk quickly and purposefully in the direction of Pike's home. I'm not adept at picking locks, but I did notice one other thing when I was standing in front of his home earlier—something that made me feel confident that I would be able to get inside when I needed to.

When I reach Pike's front lawn, I notice that he has two sprinkler heads separated by only a little over a foot. The one on the left has a brass-like cap, and it seems to be jutting out of the soil slightly more than the other one. I look around, checking one more time to make sure everybody in the neighborhood is sound asleep, and then I crouch down next to the brass sprinkler head. I reach down, and it lifts out easily.

It's fake.

As quickly as I can, I unscrew the bottom of the fake sprinkler head. Sure enough, a key falls into my hand, as do a few twenty-dollar bills. I don't want the money, and I'll be putting the key back when I'm done. Nobody can know I was here, and if Coach Pike ate at least one of those brownies, which I am almost certain he must have done based on how he was eyeing them, he's going to sleep through the entire night. Long enough for me to do what I need to do.

I take a deep breath and walk in the direction of his front door.

CHAPTER 26

COOPER

I wake up at three in the morning, feeling sick to my stomach.

I don't know if it was something I ate. Maybe it was those french fries that Debbie and I shared, because I haven't felt quite right since then. Then again, I only ate, like, six or seven fries. That doesn't seem like enough to unsettle my stomach.

I sit up in bed, rubbing my abdomen with one hand and my eyes with the other. I sit there for a moment, debating if I want to attempt to throw up, and then decide against it. And that's when I notice Debbie isn't in bed beside me.

That's weird.

Maybe she got sick from the french fries too. But that doesn't explain where she went. I can see from here that she isn't in the master bathroom. If she was feeling sick, where would she have gone?

By now, I'm too keyed up to sleep, so I stumble out

of bed. All at once, a wave of dizziness hits me. The urge to vomit suddenly becomes overwhelming, and I make a mad dash for the toilet, where I empty the contents of my stomach in one impressive expulsion. I cling to the side of the toilet for a moment, waiting for the dizziness to pass.

"Debbie?" I croak.

I don't know why I'm calling her name. She's clearly not here. But my instinct when I'm sick is to call out for my wife.

I finally manage to get back to my feet, although I'm not as steady as I'd like. Debbie definitely is not in the bedroom. Presumably, she's downstairs. Maybe she decided to make herself a cup of tea to settle her stomach. Actually, that sounds pretty good.

Maybe I'll go downstairs and join her.

I don't bother to change out of my undershirt and boxers as I make my way out into the hallway. Over the last several months, Debbie has been acting strangely. I can't quite put my finger on what it is, but it's *something*. Every single day since we first started living together, Debbie has made the bed after we got up for the day. Then six months ago, she suddenly stopped making the bed.

It's not that I care if she makes the bed. Frankly, I prefer not having to wrench the blankets out from under the mattress every night. But I can't figure out why she stopped. And when I mentioned it, she just shrugged and changed the subject.

And now she forgot my lunch this morning. And tied my tie like a kindergartner might do it.

It feels like she's keeping something from me—like there's some sort of unspoken distance between us that is growing wider every day. I could blame it on the secrets

I've kept from her, but everything I've done recently is *because* of the distance.

As I walk down the stairs, clinging to the banister, I make up my mind. I'm going to come clean.

This could be a big mistake. She's going to be *pissed*. She might even decide to leave me. I wouldn't blame her, but the right thing to do is to be honest. Get everything out in the open, and then we'll figure out how to deal with it.

I know how it looks. But I swear, I'm not a bad guy. And I want to be a good husband. That's *all* I want. I just…I screwed up. I love Debbie. Isn't that what matters?

But when I get to the bottom of the stairs, the first floor is completely dark. I click on the light switch at the base of the stairs and look around, but there's nobody here. Debbie isn't in the kitchen having a cup of tea. She's not here at all.

"Debbie?" I call out, just to be sure.

Nope. Nothing.

Even so, I wander the first floor of my house for several minutes, just confirming she's not asleep on the sofa or something. But there's no sign of my wife anywhere.

Where the hell did she go?

My next stop is the garage. It doesn't seem possible that Debbie would have left the house at three in the morning, but when I push open the door to the garage, her car is gone.

I get an uneasy feeling in the pit of my stomach that replaces the nausea. For some reason, my wife left the house in the middle of the night, and she went far enough that she took her car. Where could she possibly have gone?

A wave of dizziness washes over me, but I do my best

to push it away. I don't know why I feel so sick. Yes, it's the middle of the night, but I don't feel like I'm tired. I feel...

I feel drugged.

But how could I be? I didn't take anything that would alter my consciousness in any way. I didn't have anything to drink tonight. I haven't taken so much as a baby aspirin.

Again, I have to cling to the banister as I make my way back upstairs to where I left my phone. Once at the top of the stairs, I hold on to the wall as I go down the hallway in the direction of the master bedroom. I make it back into my bed, and then I grab my phone from where it's charging on the nightstand.

I bring up the Findly app. There are flashing dots on the map indicating where each member of my family is. Both of the kids are home, thank God. I don't know what I would think if both of them were missing as well. But Debbie's dot is not positioned over our home, and as far as I can see, she is still sharing her location.

I squint down at the screen. It looks like she's at an address in Weymouth. It doesn't sound familiar to me. In fact, as far as I can remember, I don't know anyone who lives in Weymouth, although it's just the next town over.

When I click on her dot, a street name pops up. There's no guarantee it's 100 percent accurate, but just in case it is, I scribble it down on the notepad that I keep on the nightstand. It's barely legible but good enough.

I stare at the address, trying to figure out where Debbie would be at this hour. An affair with another man? Christ, that would be...awful.

Maybe I should call her. Instead of lying here, wondering what the hell she's doing, I could call her right now and demand to know where she is. It would certainly be a reasonable thing to do.

But before I can call her, the dot on the screen starts moving. Wherever she went, she's leaving right now.

I drop my phone and rest my head on the pillow. Debbie is only fifteen minutes away, which means she'll be home soon. As soon as she gets home, I'm going to ask her where she was. We're going to sit down and have a long discussion about…well, about everything.

Like I said, it's time to come clean. Her dirty laundry and my dirty laundry.

Except about two minutes after I vow to talk to my wife as soon as she gets back home, I pass out and don't wake up till the next morning.

CHAPTER 27

DEBBIE

I wake up early the next morning feeling oddly refreshed, even though I took a little middle-of-the-night excursion.

Cooper is passed out next to me in bed, snoring more loudly than he usually does, drool pooling in the right corner of his mouth. Unsurprisingly, he's still out cold.

I slide out of bed as quietly as I can and hit the shower. There's nothing like a nice, hot shower to start the day, and I turn up the temperature as high as it will go. Cooper always takes lukewarm showers, but in my opinion, a shower can never be hot enough. You could drop me in a pot of boiling water, and I'd turn up the heat a few degrees.

I dress quietly, putting on another dark blouse with a pair of wide leg jeans that have recently become all the rage. Lexi seethed when I first wore them, because she felt wide leg jeans belonged to *her* generation, and I was "too old" to pull it off. But I actually think they're very flattering.

The hallway of the second floor of my house is silent—both girls have another hour until their alarms go off for the day. I should be back before that happens.

I get in my Subaru, and twenty minutes later, I am pulling up in front of Kenneth Bryant's house. Unlike last night, the street is well lit, and there are people leaving their houses to start their day. Still, I'm pretty sure nobody will notice my unassuming vehicle. And it's not like a middle-aged housewife attracts any unwanted attention around here.

The lights are on in Ken's house as I approach the front door, my purse slung on my shoulder. Cooper told me Ken's always the first one at the office in the morning and the last to leave, so I was certain he'd be awake when I arrived. He's probably enjoying a nice cup of coffee while reading the morning news.

I press the doorbell.

A minute later, the locks turn on the other side of the door. The door cracks open to reveal a tall man with thin hair and even thinner lips. I've never met him, because Ken Bryant never had any interest in socializing, but I recognize him from photos. He narrows his eyes at me.

"I don't speak to solicitors," he barks at me.

My, what a lovely greeting. How about *hello*?

"Actually," I say, "I'm Debbie Mullen." He looks at me blankly, so I add, "Cooper's wife." He still looks confused, so I further clarify, "Cooper Mullen. Your employee."

"Oh." He allows the door to swing open another inch. "Right. Cooper's wife. Dottie."

"Debbie." I clear my throat. "May I please come in?"

Ken looks like he's considering slamming the door in my face, but after a moment of deliberation, he steps aside to allow me to enter. It's a start.

I've never been inside my husband's boss's home, and it's about what I expected. It's a large living space but spartan and without personality. I've seen homes staged for viewings that had more personality than this house. He has a leather sofa, but he doesn't offer me a seat.

"You probably want to talk to me about Cooper getting a promotion," he grumbles.

"Well," I say, "yes. My husband has been with your company for a long time, and he's a hard worker."

"He's also extremely replaceable." He cinches his tie a little tighter around his neck, and I imagine grabbing it and cinching it as tight as it can go. "He does his job and nothing more. He brings nothing special to the table. He's the most ordinary employee I've ever had, and when he goes, there will be five more candidates just like him who will work for less money."

"I think you're wrong."

He shrugs. "With all due respect, your husband quit, and I think I'm better off without him."

I reach into my purse, sifting through what feels like an endless supply of bunched-up napkins. I pull out a pair of leather gloves, and Ken frowns as I slide them onto my hands.

"What are you doing?" he asks me. "Are you cold?"

I don't answer his question. The gun I pull from my purse answers it for me.

"Wh-what..." he stammers, his face turning pale. "What are you doing?"

I gesture at the sofa with the barrel of the gun. "Please have a seat, Mr. Bryant."

He clutches his chest, and for a moment, I wonder if nature will do the job for me. But then he collapses onto the sofa, and he's still conscious. I need him to stay with me long enough to bind his wrists, then march him upstairs and into the bedroom.

"What are you doing?" he asks me again. "This isn't about Cooper's job, is it? Because I—"

"Stop talking," I say in a sharp voice that silences him instantly.

I stare down at the older man, who is trembling on the living room sofa. Then I look down at the gun gripped in my right hand. Am I really going to do this? It's one thing to cut some wires in a fuse box or poison sandwiches, but it's an entirely different thing to...

I am about to cross a line. And once I do, I won't be able to go back. Then again, this has been a long time coming.

I'm glad I wore black to hide the bloodstains.

CHAPTER 28

COOPER

The phone is ringing.

It feels like it's been ringing for a while. I'm lying in bed, my head throbbing slightly, willing it to stop. And it finally does stop when the phone goes to voicemail, but whoever it is just calls back again. It's an endless cycle.

"All right, damn it!"

Through my haze, I recall that there could be a name on the screen that I don't want Debbie to see. Frantically, I feel around on my nightstand, but when I grab my phone, the screen is black. My phone isn't the one that was ringing. It's *Debbie's* phone that's ringing. Over and over and over. My relief is replaced by curiosity.

That's when I become aware of another sound. It's the sound of the shower running in the master bathroom. I had told myself I was going to stay awake until Debbie got home, but I clearly failed at that task. I passed out almost immediately after lying down, and right now, I feel like I got hit by a truck. My mouth feels like the Sahara Desert.

Why do I feel hungover?

Debbie's phone stops ringing, and I say a silent thank you. But then thirty seconds later, it starts again. I throw Debbie's pillow on top of my face, trying to stifle the sound of the ringing phone. But it's no use. Whoever is calling my wife wants to talk to her *really* badly.

"Debbie?" I call out. "You coming out soon?"

There's no answer, but she's definitely in there. I can hear her singing, which is weird because Debbie doesn't usually sing in the shower.

Finally, I give in. I grab the phone off the nightstand next to Debbie's side of the bed. The name on the screen is Garrett Meers. Debbie's boss.

What the hell is he calling about over and over again? They can't possibly have a news emergency that involves Debbie. First of all, my wife writes an *advice column*. What's an advice column emergency? Somebody has a party in fifteen minutes and doesn't know how to get grass stains out of her dress?

But clearly, Garrett is freaking out. Which is also weird, because I met the guy once, and he seemed pretty laid-back to me.

I swipe to take the call, and before I can even say hello, Garrett's voice booms in my ear, "Debbie! Debbie, what the hell did you do?"

"Uh, hello?" I say.

Garrett is momentarily thrown off by the sound of my voice. "Who is this?"

"It's Cooper." Because he doesn't respond, I add, "Debbie's husband."

"Where's Debbie?" he demands to know. "I need to talk to her right away!"

I struggle into a sitting position, and the pounding in my head intensifies. "Sorry, she's in the shower."

"Then get her out of the shower! I need to talk to her *right now!*"

"Uh, no?" I rub my eyes. "Whatever is wrong—"

"Whatever is wrong!" he bursts out. "There's *pornography* on the newspaper's website. That's what's wrong! And it's not just pornography, it's... Look, I know Debbie has the password for our website. Just because I fired her—"

"You fired Debbie?" I repeat, unable to keep the astonishment out of my voice.

That throws Garrett for a loop. "Oh. I thought she would've... Well, anyway, yes. There was an issue with a lawsuit, and... Sorry, but I didn't have a choice. But what the hell? She needs to get it down this minute!" His voice is getting louder with each word. "Do you understand what I'm saying? She's going to *ruin* me!"

"Why can't you take it down yourself?" I ask impatiently.

"She changed the password! I'm locked out!"

As Garrett is talking, I navigate to the website for the newspaper on my own phone. No offense to Debbie, but the *Hingham Household* is the most boring newspaper I've ever seen. The website generally contains their logo and the top news story in Hingham, which is probably, I don't know, a PTA meeting where they're trying to decide what to watch on the middle school movie night. But instead of that, the only thing on the screen is a video that seems to be playing on a repeat loop.

It's a video of two people having sex. And one of those people is Garrett Meers.

I don't know who the other person is, but I met his

wife, and it's not her. The whole thing looks like it's taking place in an office, on top of a desk. I'm guessing it's the office at the newspaper.

Wow. He's right. He really is screwed.

"We've already had half a dozen advertisers call to cancel their contracts with us." His panicked voice has turned pleading. "And my wife… If she sees this…"

Even though it's rude, I bark out a laugh. "You really think there's any chance your wife isn't going to see this?"

"Go to hell!" Garrett snaps back at me. "Debbie has gone too far this time!"

I frown at the phone, suddenly overtaken by a feeling of déjà vu. This is the exact same conversation I had with Brett yesterday morning, when he accused Debbie of messing with his fuse box.

She certainly has the technical skills to do this. And if she got fired yesterday, that's a motive right there. She would have needed to obtain the footage of Garrett with that other woman, but she's the one who installed the cameras outside our front door. She certainly knows how to plant a hidden camera.

And yet I still don't believe it. I always tell Debbie to advocate for herself more, because she's constantly letting herself get pushed around. She's great at giving advice, but she never takes mine. I can't envision her doing something this diabolical. It's not her style.

"Look," I say, "Debbie didn't do this…"

"She did it!" he insists. "And I swear to God, she is going to pay for this. I'm going to make sure she pays."

Okay, that's enough. I understand he's upset, but *nobody* threatens Debbie. "Watch what you say about my wife," I say.

"Oh yeah?" Garrett seems unimpressed. "Or else what?"

"If you so much as breathe on her," I growl into the phone in a voice that actually sounds fairly scary, "I'm going to drive over to your house and break your face."

I can hear the sharp inhale of breath on the other line, and with that, Garrett finally goes quiet. I take the opportunity to end the call. A second later, the phone starts ringing again, but I put it on silent.

Could I actually break Garrett Meers's face? I don't know. I have been going to the gym a lot lately. I've never thrown a punch in my entire life, but if he did anything to hurt Debbie, I would definitely make him pay.

"Who was on the phone?"

I didn't even notice that the shower had turned off, and Debbie has come out of the bathroom, wrapped in a terry-cloth bathrobe. Her hair is still wet and slicked back from her face with water. She looks so small and vulnerable. Innocent. Except...

Did you break into our neighbor's house and wreck his fuse box?

Did you post a video of your former boss banging his secretary?

Where were you last night?

What are you hiding from me?

"That was Garrett," I finally say. "He's upset about something with the website. It looks like he..."

Instead of saying it, I show her my phone, where the video is still playing on repeat. If a picture is worth a thousand words, a video pretty much says it all. Debbie's eyebrows shoot up.

"Oh!" she says. "I guess Garrett really is sleeping with Sierra. So much for being a family man, huh?"

I keep my gaze trained on her face, watching for her reaction. "He thinks you're the one who posted the video."

"Does he?" She laughs. "What does he think? That I hid a camera in his office months ago to get something I could someday use to embarrass him?"

"Uh, not in so many words…"

"Well, that's a little ridiculous." She cocks her head at me. "Don't you think?"

I don't know what to say to that. "He wants you to take it down. He says they already lost a bunch of advertisers. And he's worried his wife will see it."

Debbie gives the video one last look, then hands my phone back to me. "I'm sure somebody already sent his wife an email letting her know about the video."

"You…you think so?"

"Oh yes." She bobs her head. "And as for getting it down, I'm sure that somebody from tech support can reset the password for him. That man spirals into a panic far too easily."

"Debbie." I swallow a hard lump that has formed in my throat. "You weren't the one who… I mean, did you…"

For a moment, she just stares at me. My head is still pounding, but all I can do is stare back into my wife's brown eyes. I've known her for nearly half my life, but I'm starting to wonder if I know her at all.

What have you done, Debbie?

Just when I can't stand it another second, she pipes up, "Of course not! Where would I even get a video like that?" Then she smiles at me. "I'm starving. Do you feel like pancakes?"

"Uh, sure."

She's still humming to herself as she gets dressed and heads down to the kitchen to make us breakfast.

After Debbie is gone, my gaze drops to the small pad of paper by the bed. If I had any delusion that what happened last night was some sort of wild dream, the address scribbled in my handwriting indicates otherwise. I stare at my writing for a moment, not sure what to do. I was so tired when I wrote it, the street name is nearly impossible to make out. It seems to say "Main" but just as easily could say "Maple" or something completely different.

I rip the paper from the pad and stare at it for a moment. And then, for reasons I can't entirely explain, I stuff the piece of paper into the top drawer of the nightstand before heading for the shower.

CHAPTER 29

DEBBIE

I'm making pancakes for breakfast.

When I got out of the shower, I had over one hundred unread text messages from Garrett Meers as well as quite a few voice messages. I deleted all of them, then I blocked his number. He can deal with this on his own. After all, I'm not his tech person. I was just the advice columnist, and I was fired, so the way I see it, none of this is my problem.

Also, right now, I need to focus all my attention on making pancakes.

I don't make them from scratch. I'm not freaking Betty Crocker. I have a box of powdered pancake mix, although I do have some tweaks to make them taste better. I use milk to mix the batter rather than water, and I also add a dash of cinnamon. And once you put it in the pan, you have to cook it *just* the right amount of time, flipping the pancakes halfway through. It's not foolproof, but it's considerably easier than programming a phone app to track your family members.

Izzy comes into the living room first this morning. She hears the sizzling pancakes in the frying pan, and her eyes widen in that same excited expression that Cooper gets when I make him a dinner he particularly enjoys.

"Want some pancakes?" I ask her.

She does. I can see it all over her face. She is torn apart by the inner turmoil of wanting to eat pancakes but also feeling like she needs to lose twenty pounds to get back on the soccer team. The urge to wrap my arms around her in a hug is almost overwhelming. I miss the days when a hug could fix everything and a well-placed kiss could heal any ouchie instantly. These days, I have to be a bit more creative.

"I'm not hungry," she finally says.

Great. Coach Pike has given my daughter an eating disorder.

Fortunately, that won't be a problem very soon.

Lexi is the next to enter the kitchen, clomping on the hardwood floor in her Doc Martens that she's been breaking in for the last two years. She's wearing a pair of oversize cargo pants, which I suppose are slightly better than pajamas. She's also not wearing her giant headphones. She walks right up to me at the stove, and I stiffen, waiting for her critique of whatever I'm doing. Last week, she informed me that I was *breathing* too loudly.

"Mom?" she says.

"Yes?"

She chews on her right thumbnail. "Can I have a ride to school?"

My first instinct is to ask why Zane isn't driving her like usual, but I'm pretty sure that won't go well. So this time, I keep my fool mouth shut. "Of course. Would you like some pancakes, sweetheart?"

She hesitates for only a split second. "Okay."

"I'll maybe have one pancake too," Izzy speaks up, and I'm so happy, I could cry.

I portion the pancakes out onto two plates, and I'm placing them on the kitchen table in front of my girls when a loud horn sounds from outside. I cringe. I assumed because Lexi asked for a ride, that punk wouldn't be spreading his noise pollution through our neighborhood this morning.

"Is that Zane?" I ask cautiously.

Lexi drops her eyes to the plate in front of her. "Mom, can you tell him that I'm getting a ride with you today?"

"Sure, honey. Of course."

I wipe my hands on my blue jeans and head over to the front door. Sure enough, Zane's Kia is parked in my driveway at a strange angle. I slip on my flats and step onto the front porch, not bothering with a jacket. This won't take long.

Even with the windows closed, I can hear his music blasting. I don't know what he's listening to. It's definitely not anything I've heard on the radio. I know it's hard for "old people" like me to enjoy new music, but this song genuinely sounds like a man hacking up phlegm repeatedly. He leans on his horn one more time, and I clench my teeth.

I walk down the steps of the front porch right up to Zane's car. He is absently bobbing his head to the music, his shaggy hair in disarray. Once again, I fantasize about what I'd do to him with a pair of barber scissors. Then I tap on the car window.

I have to tap a second time, because he doesn't notice me the first time. He's probably half deaf from the music.

(If one could call it music. I can only imagine that whoever recorded this did it as some sort of psychological experiment to see if anyone would listen to the sounds of bodily functions.) Finally, he swivels his head to look at me and rolls down the window.

"Hey, Mrs. Mullen." As he looks up at me, I can't help but notice how hollow his cheeks are, like he's much older than he really is. "Where's Lexi?"

"I'm bringing her to school today."

"But I'm *here*."

"Right. And now you can leave."

Zane rolls his eyes. "Fine. *Whatever*."

Without any warning, he backs the car out of my driveway, practically running over my foot. I watch him speed off, keeping my fingers crossed that this will be the last time Zane ever comes here to eat all the food in our kitchen and drink our alcohol.

But somehow, I have a bad feeling that it's not.

CHAPTER 30

FROM *DEAR DEBBIE* DRAFTS FILE

Dear Debbie,

I can't stand my daughter's so-called boyfriend. She thinks the sun rises and sets on that boy, but I see right through him. He drives much too fast, he is barely passing his classes in school, and he's as lazy as the day is long. And don't even get me started on his attitude problem. The mouth on that boy!

Every time I try to talk some sense into that little girl, she acts like I'm overstepping my bounds! She gets all huffy, like I'm just supposed to sit there twiddling my thumbs while she throws her life away on an asshole.

Please tell me how to open my daughter's eyes before it's too late! Do you know of any reverse love potion recipes? I'll pay anything!

Sincerely,
Hates the Boyfriend

Dear Hates the Boyfriend,

Unfortunately, I don't know any recipes for reverse love potions. Wish I did!

I'm sure you know that when it comes to teenagers, the more you try to convince your daughter to dump her boyfriend, the more she'll stubbornly want to stay with him. You might do better by trying the opposite approach and getting to know him better. Perhaps you can invite him over to your house for a nice home-cooked dinner. After an hour of bonding over a pot roast, I bet you'll find that he isn't as bad as you thought he was!

And if after your family dinner is over, you still feel the same way, I would suggest that you sneak out to his car while he's busy with your daughter after dinner. It's a simple process to snip the brake line. You say he drives fast, but with no brakes in his car, I bet he'll go even faster!

Debbie

CHAPTER 31

DEBBIE

After leaving a plate of pancakes for Cooper on the kitchen counter, I drive the kids to school.

It's about a ten-minute drive. There's a brief fight over which of the girls gets to sit in the front, which reminds me of all the fights they used to have in the car when they were little. When I picked them up from school, they would argue over who got to tell me about their day first. We tried to divide it evenly, but since there were five days in the week, I told the girls that if the date was an even number, Lexi could talk first, and on odd days, it would be Izzy's turn. It was an excellent opportunity to teach them about odd and even numbers.

Lexi wins out and climbs into the passenger seat beside me. She has brushed her dark brown hair back off her face into a ponytail, and she looks so much like me, it feels like I'm looking into a time machine taking me back to when I was seventeen years old.

I wish I had a time machine. I wish I could talk to

seventeen-year-old Debbie and warn her about everything that was going to happen to her. The first thing I would have told her would be to stay home that night during the second semester of her sophomore year.

If I had, everything would've been different.

The drive to school is blessedly free of conflict, and Lexi only criticizes my driving twice. But when we pull up to the drop-off line for students, a police car with flashing lights is parked in front of the school.

"What's going on?" Izzy pipes up from the back seat, craning her neck to get a better look.

"Maybe some kid got arrested!" Lexi says a bit too eagerly.

"I'm sure it's fine," I murmur, waiting patiently for the drop-off line to creep forward. "It's just one car."

"But the lights are flashing, Mom!" Izzy points out.

Very true.

We finally pull up in front of the school, and both girls climb out of the car. Like all the other kids, they are ogling the police car, trying to figure out what's going on. I remember how it used to be when I was a kid and there was something out of the ordinary going on at school. A burst of excitement in the otherwise monotonous day.

Oh, who am I kidding? I loved school. But it was still fun when there was *drama*.

After the girls are out of the car, I would ordinarily drive back home, but I too am curious about the parked police car. So I pull around the side of the school and park in the guest lot. There aren't a lot of spaces, and I have to circle a few times to find a spot that would really be better suited to a compact car rather than my SUV. But I work my parking magic and squeeze into the spot.

After parking, I walk around to the front of the school again. The police car is still parked with the flashing lights, but there's no other indication of what's going on. It could be anything from a bomb threat to some drugs found in a locker. But I'm fairly sure I know why the police are here.

This is going to be interesting.

CHAPTER 32

A group of parents are milling about close to the school. I recognize one of them—Tabitha, who still looks a little green after our book club meeting yesterday. I approach her, plastering a disarming smile on my face.

Tabitha looks less than thrilled to see me, but she manages a halfhearted smile. "Hello, Debbie."

I touch her arm in a gesture of sympathy. "How are you feeling today? Still throwing up?"

At the question, several of the other women flash us an alarmed look.

Tabitha frowns at me. "I'm totally fine, thanks."

"Are you sure? You look a bit peaked."

"I'm not *peaked*," Tabitha says through her teeth. "I'm *fine*."

Several of the women are now staring at us, so I decide to let her off the hook. I nod at the police car. "Do you know what's going on?"

Tabitha is not excited to talk to me, probably because

she's embarrassed that she vomited in my presence yesterday, but she's also an incorrigible gossip. She battles her emotional turmoil for a moment, then finally says, "Somebody called the school and said they saw a camera in the showers of the girls' locker room."

"A *camera*?"

"A nanny cam—like for *recording*." She clutches her chest, her eyes wide. "Can you *imagine*? Some sicko was recording high school girls taking a shower!"

Now the question of the day: "Do they know who?" I ask.

She shakes her head. "There are no security cameras that record outside the locker room and obviously none *in* the locker room. So I'm not sure if they have any suspects."

Oh, come on. I'm pretty sure the anonymous tipster mentioned a name.

I endure another twenty minutes of speculation among the group of women, and I'm tempted to turn around and go home. I'm sure I'll hear how it plays out on social media. But just as I'm about to give up and go back to my car, the doors of the school burst open. The police are leading a man out of the building in handcuffs.

"Oh my God!" Tabitha grabs my arm tightly enough that her nails bite into me. "It's Coach Pike!"

It is indeed Coach Pike. His hands are cuffed in front of him as the police escort him out of the school. He makes the mistake of turning in our direction, and every single woman whips out her phone practically in unison and snaps a photo of the coach being arrested.

"I didn't do it!" Coach Pike is yelling. "That camera wasn't mine! I don't know how that stuff got on my phone!"

"Yeah, right," Tabitha mutters to me. "Does he really think anyone believes that? What a creep."

"*Such* a creep," I agree. And then, just to add more fuel to the fire, I add, "I used to see him staring at the girls' butts during soccer practice. I'm not at all surprised."

"Oh my gosh!" another mother exclaims. "I always knew there was something off about him!"

The dam has burst, and now all the women are excitedly exchanging stories about what a jerk Coach Pike was. We're still sharing anecdotes when the police car drives away with the coach in the back seat.

CHAPTER 33

COOPER

D ebbie burned the pancakes this morning.
   She's never burned pancakes in the entire time I've been married to her. She's not a gourmet cook, but she never *burns* things. And the pancakes weren't just a little on the brown side—they were *black* on the bottom with an acrid odor. The entire kitchen reeked.

   It seemed like a particularly ominous sign.

   When I get to the office, Mrs. McCauley is sitting primly at her desk. She gets to her feet when she sees me. "Mr. Mullen, can I have a word?"

   I don't really feel like having a conversation with Mrs. McCauley, but I obediently approach her desk. "What's going on?"

   "Mr. Bryant has decided to take a spur-of-the-moment fishing trip," she says. "He informed me via email this morning that he would be absent for the rest of the week."

   Fantastic. That means I don't have to see him.

"Of course," she adds, "that doesn't give you a license to spend the next two days having a vacation of your own. I promised him that I would keep an eye on you and the rest of the staff."

I don't doubt that she will. However, Mrs. McCauley always leaves at four thirty on the dot, which means that I'll be cutting out at four thirty five. I'll head to the gym and blow off some of my nervous energy.

After disentangling myself from Mrs. McCauley, I head to the small break room to get a cup of coffee. Jesse is already there, sipping from his own mug. "Hey, Coop," he says.

"Hey, man."

We have one of those coffee pod machines in the break room, but Ken refuses to provide the pods, so Jesse and I split a box of them. We keep them in the cabinet over the sink, so I grab one to make my own coffee.

"Must be nice to be the boss and get to take a spur-of-the-moment fishing trip in the middle of the damn week," Jesse muses.

"I'm glad he's gone."

Jesse is silent for a moment, sipping his coffee. Despite the fact that Mrs. McCauley is watching us, he doesn't seem particularly eager to get to work. He's good at his job, but he has a more relaxed attitude, which is something I envy about him.

"Don't take this the wrong way," he says to me, "but you look like shit, Cooper."

I squeeze my eyes shut as I wait for the coffee to fill my cup. I need some caffeine like nobody's business. "Yeah, I feel like shit."

"Everything okay, buddy?"

I shoot him a look. "Is that a serious question?"

He flinches. "I'm sorry. I'm being an ass."

"No," I grunt. "*I'm* sorry. It's just been a weird couple of days. And Debbie... I don't think she's taking the whole thing well."

"That Debbie." He shakes his head. "She's kind of... intense, isn't she?"

I know what he means. I've always known Debbie was different from everyone else, but now it's gotten to the point where friends seem to be noticing. "What gives you that idea?"

"Well..." He takes a thoughtful sip from his coffee mug. It has a cartoon dog on it. "Remember when the four of us went to dinner together at that little Italian place?"

"Yeah..."

"Do you remember how the waitress was flirting with you?" When I look at him blankly, he elaborates. "She was giggling at everything you said, and then at one point, she put her hand on your shoulder."

"I don't think I noticed."

"Well, Debbie sure did." He lowers his mug onto the counter. "She was super cold after that. I swear, she deliberately spilled her drink so the waitress would have to clean it up. And she didn't leave any tip on your half when we split the bill. I actually kicked in extra so the waitress wouldn't get stiffed."

I remember that part now. I remember Debbie tossing in her own credit card when we were splitting the bill, which surprised me because I am the one who usually pays for meals. Technically it was the same joint credit card, but we fall into the typical gender roles, and I'm the one who pays. This time, it was Debbie who used her credit card though.

And apparently, she had a good reason.

"Debbie has serious jealousy issues," Jesse observes.

"You really think so?"

"For sure." He slugs my shoulder playfully. "I get the feeling Debbie has a fiery side."

"Not that I've ever seen."

Jesse grins. "You giving her something to worry about, Coop?"

A cold sensation runs down my spine. The coffee finishes pouring into the cup, and I snatch it from the machine. "I better get to work. Mrs. McCauley is probably writing down everything we do."

"I'll bet." He snickers. "She's probably going to provide Ken with minute-by-minute updates. Although I get to leave for an hour to water Ken's plants. He texted me to assign me that dubious honor."

That makes me feel even worse. The last time Ken took a fishing trip, I was the one he asked to water his plants. I can understand after our conversation yesterday, though, why he wouldn't want me wandering around his empty home. Not that I'd take a piss in his plants or anything like that, but, well, I'd be tempted.

As I trudge back to my office with my cup of coffee, I can't seem to shake a sensation in the back of my head that something isn't entirely right here. Ken goes fishing all the time, but he usually gives us a few weeks' notice. And there's something strange about the fact that the people he told were contacted electronically rather than with a phone call.

Impulsively, I grab my phone and find Ken's number

under my favorite contacts. The last thing I want to do is chitchat with my boss after our conversation yesterday, but my Spidey sense won't stop tingling. Something is wrong.

I grip the phone as it rings in my ear. Again and again until it goes to his terse voicemail:

This is Ken Bryant. Leave a message.

If he went on a fishing trip, it makes sense he wouldn't have phone service. Or else he left his phone behind while he's sitting in the middle of a lake, just him and his fishing rod. That's the most logical explanation.

So why can't I turn off this buzzing in the back of my head? Maybe it's because in all the years I've known Ken, he has never once taken a spontaneous vacation. Every time he's taken so much as an afternoon off, he's given us several weeks' notice. This is very strange behavior.

Maybe I should go check on him.

But that might not be a great idea. If he *is* home, Ken wouldn't appreciate it if I showed up at his front door. And if he's not home, that sort of thing might be looked at as trespassing by a disgruntled employee.

I'm sure he's fine. I'm sure he'll be back on Monday.

CHAPTER 34

DEBBIE

Without my advice column to work on, I spend the morning in my garden.

I love gardening. I find the repetitive motions of planting, watering, and pruning to be very relaxing. Almost meditative. I feel so much satisfaction after spending the day outside when I look out on my yard at the fruits of my labor. Multiple studies have shown that gardening reduces stress, anxiety, and depression. After working for a morning in my backyard, I feel so relaxed and zen.

Screw that *Home Gardening* magazine. They can go straight to hell.

Opium poppies are actually surprisingly easy to grow. They are my favorite of all the flowers in my garden. I've been doing it for years, so I've got it down to a science. Unlike my children, who change every single year, leaving me fumbling to keep up, poppies follow a natural and predictable cycle. My little poppy flowers are nearly at the end of their annual cycle.

In a month or so, I will shake the seeds all over the garden to begin the cycle anew. I'm careful to strategically plan the distribution of seeds, and by spring, the flowers will bloom in bright bursts of color. The color is so vivid that it almost seems to glow with a mystical intensity. At the height of the season, my garden looks ethereal.

By the late fall, the petals will have fallen off the flowers, and the pods will start to bloom. I will then harvest them for seeds. And, of course, opium.

Today, I walk out into my yard barefoot. I don't do it all the time, but I love gardening in my bare feet. I love the feel of the dirt between my toes, and it almost makes me feel like I'm *part* of the garden. My task for the morning is to get rid of all the stray leaves that have fallen into the yard, and there are enough of them that it keeps me busy for nearly two hours. By the end, there's soil caked into my fingernails and in the creases of my palms, and of course, my feet are caked with it.

As I'm washing the dirt off my hands in the kitchen sink, I think about what I want to make for lunch. I pull out my phone and idly check the website for the *Hingham Household*. It's the only local paper, so they might have a news update on Coach Robert Pike. But nope, it's still that video of Garrett and Sierra having sex on his desk. Apparently, he hasn't managed to get it down yet.

Oh, Garrett.

While I've got my phone out, another idea hits me. It might be nice to have some company. So I reach for my phone and shoot off a message to Harley:

Sorry for the late notice, but any chance you'd like to grab lunch?

Immediately, three bubbles appear on the screen. Harley doesn't usually work on Thursday mornings, so she must be home.

Sure! But I don't have a lot of time. I'm teaching a spin class at one.
No problem. What if I bring some food to your house? I can make sandwiches.

Before she can respond, I quickly add:

No avocados. I promise.

The response takes longer this time. She's clearly thinking hard about what she wants to say. It probably doesn't help that the last time I made sandwiches, three people got seriously ill with food poisoning. But I'm not going to give Harley food poisoning. I'm sure she realizes that.

Sure thing! See you soon!

She texts me her address, and I enter it in my GPS. She lives outside Hingham, over in Rockland, but it won't take me too long to get there.

As for our lunch, I decide to go the healthy route and make the two of us a salad using the tomatoes, cucumbers, and lettuce in my fridge. No avocados, although I love avocados in a salad. I grab a bottle of miso ranch dressing and load everything into my car.

I pull out of my driveway, and as I'm rolling down the block, I notice there's a bit of a commotion in front of Jo Dolan's house. A man is standing next to a tripod, holding an expensive-looking camera in his hand, and Jo is standing in front of him, yelling and waving her hands wildly. The argument seems to be attracting some attention from our neighbors. Even Bev who lives across from me has made the trek down the street and is standing on the sidelines and gawking.

Curious, I pull over on the side of the road and climb out of the car, leaving my salad and dressing in the passenger seat. I don't want the salad to wilt, but I'm sure this won't take long.

"Bev," I whisper to my neighbor, "what's going on?"

Bev giggles. "Looks like Jo has a little insect problem."

I turn my attention to Jo and the man with the camera. Now that I'm closer, I can see the veins standing out in Jo's scrawny neck. Her housedress is swaying in the wind.

"I have the best rose garden in all of Hingham!" Jo is ranting at him. "You won't find better roses than mine. I guarantee it!"

The man flashes her an exasperated look. "I don't care how nice your roses are. I'm not photographing a garden infested with *bugs*."

"There are hardly any bugs!" Jo shouts.

The man gives her an "are you kidding me?" look. That's when I swivel my head to take a look at Jo's rose garden.

Wow, there are Japanese beetles everywhere.

Japanese beetles are shiny, metallic green with bronze wings. The tiny insects are clinging to the blades of grass and the leaves and petals of Jo's precious roses. It almost looks like every Japanese beetle in the Hingham area—hell, maybe every beetle in Massachusetts—has congregated in

Jo's rose garden. It's practically a swarm. Soon, they will have devoured all the flowers and leaves, leaving behind a patchwork of holes and lacy remnants.

Those trap refills worked even better than I hoped.

"*You!*" she cries. "Did *you* do this to my garden?"

"Me?" I feign astonishment. "You really think I have the ability to bring a swarm of Japanese beetles to your garden? I'm not a beetle whisperer, Jo."

"You were jealous yesterday!" she reminds me. "You were mad that I stole your photo shoot."

"Yes." I nod. "And I did mention something about *karma*, didn't I? I guess I was right about that."

Jo narrows her eyes at me, but there's nothing she can do. She doesn't know anything about the three traps buried in the mulch of her yard that are attracting every Japanese beetle in the area. And until she finds them, she'll never get rid of the pests.

I hope she never finds them.

CHAPTER 35

It's a similar length ride to Harley's as it was to get to Coach Pike's place. Thankfully, even though it's close to lunchtime, there isn't much traffic. Her house is on a dead-end street, which contains one other house that looks like it's empty, possibly abandoned. She wrote in her text message that I should go around back to find the door to her basement apartment.

I arrive at Harley's door, balancing the salad dressing in one hand and the Tupperware in the other. When she opens the door, she's wearing her workout uniform, her pink-streaked blond hair tied back into a neat ponytail. Her stomach is peeking out, and the outline of her abs is visible.

"Debbie!" Her face lights up at the sight of me. "Come on in! I'll show you around Casa Harley."

I laugh as I step inside and Harley relieves me of my salad and dressing. "It's so quiet here. There isn't even one other car on the street."

"I barely see my landlords who live upstairs," she says. "They mostly stay inside, but right now, they're in Michigan visiting their grandchildren, so I really am completely alone. They won't be back till Monday."

"You should throw a wild party."

Now it's her turn to laugh. "Oh, don't worry. I've got plans."

We take a little tour of the apartment. It's small, but she makes the most of the space. She has a comfy-looking blue sofa with a TV tray set up in front of it, and Japanese doors separate the kitchenette from the living area. She has managed to stuff a queen-size bed, a bookcase, and a dresser into her bedroom, with just enough room to walk between them.

"Nice place," I say appreciatively as I look around the bedroom. It reminds me a bit of an apartment I rented back in my pre-Cooper days.

Then my gaze drops to her dresser. There's a T-shirt crumpled up on top of the dresser, and it looks several sizes too big for Harley to wear. Before I can stop myself, I pick it up and realize that it's a man's T-shirt.

And there's something achingly familiar about it. Not just about the way it looks but the way it *smells*.

"I sleep in that," Harley says quickly, tugging it out of my hands. "I love sleeping in oversize T-shirts. Don't you?"

Except the T-shirt doesn't smell like Harley. The entire apartment is heavy with the distinctive scent of her perfume or laundry detergent or whatever it is. But that T-shirt smells different. Like men's cologne and something else.

Sweat.

"Well," I say brightly, "why don't we have some lunch?"

"Sounds great!"

I follow Harley back to the living room, but I realize that I have suddenly lost my appetite.

CHAPTER 36

HARLEY

I can't decide if I should tell Cooper that his wife discovered his shirt in my bedroom.

I couldn't believe it when she zeroed in on it. She couldn't quite recognize it—she wasn't certain—but she was suspicious. And then she brought it to her nose and sniffed it. I thought for sure I was busted when she did that. After all, a woman knows what her husband smells like.

Yet she didn't say a word. So maybe we're safe.

The funny thing is that when she went back into the living room to eat the salad with me, I was almost disappointed that she didn't call me out on it. Maybe I wanted to get busted. I didn't have to invite her to my house—we could have met somewhere else closer to the gym. And even if we did meet here, I had plenty of time to stuff that T-shirt in a drawer, but instead, I left it right where she could find it. It was almost exhilarating when Debbie picked up her husband's T-shirt, trying desperately to place it.

Right now, we're in my living room, eating the salad she made. It's nothing special but it tastes pretty good, thanks to that miso ranch dressing. I'll have to ask her where she got it. It's been a long time since I had a friend I could share recipes with.

It makes me sad to think that I don't have any close friends anymore. My last one was my college roommate, Mariah. But Mariah got married and had a baby, and after that, every text message exchange we had included a photo of her baby doing something she thought was "so adorable." I couldn't even talk about the weather without her sending me a photo of her baby holding a thermometer or something. I finally snapped and told Mariah that I had absolutely no interest in the constant photos of her ugly daughter. After that, our friendship sort of fizzled.

Debbie is talking about her garden now, which is obviously her favorite topic, but I don't care about her stupid flowers. There's only one reason why I've become friends with Debbie Mullen, and that's to pump her for information about Cooper, although, as always, I try to be casual about it, like I barely even remember who he is.

"So…" I take another bite of salad, crunching the lettuce between my teeth. "How is your husband doing? What did you say his name was? Carter? Connor?"

She gives me a funny look that I can't quite interpret. "Cooper."

"Right. So how is Cooper?"

Her tone is disinterested. "He's fine."

"What did you say he does for a living?" I prompt her. "Something in an office?"

"He's an accountant."

"Right." I snap my fingers as if I didn't already know all this. "That's sort of boring. He's a bit of a nerd then?"

"A bit," she concedes, although I disagree. Cooper might be an accountant, but he's definitely not a nerd. Nobody who saw him with his shirt off would think so. "Not as much as me. And he's hopeless with any technology. He needs my help to turn on the computer."

I already know that's true. It has made stalking Cooper online an exercise in frustration. I prefer men who post everything they do and everywhere they go on social media so I can gauge exactly what they're thinking. But Cooper is older than me—old enough that posting minute-to-minute updates online is not a priority for him, like it is for a lot of men my age or younger.

"He sounds nice," I say before she can start talking about her garden again. "You're lucky to be married to a nice guy."

She doesn't answer me right away. She seems to be considering her response carefully as she stabs a piece of tomato with her fork. "He's nice" is all she says.

"Good father?" I press her. I like the idea of Cooper being a good father. Mine was shit. I don't want to blame everything bad I've done on daddy issues, but it would have been nice if he ever said two words to me, that's all I'm saying.

"Great father," she confirms.

She doesn't seem eager to discuss this, but I can't help myself. I'm desperate for any little morsel she can tell me about Cooper Mullen, even if it means giving myself away.

"It must be hard to be married for so long," I say. "I would think that after five or ten years, a lot of the romance gets sucked out of it."

Debbie's eyebrows shoot up to her hairline. Uh-oh, maybe that was too far. I got greedy. But I am desperate for a tearful confession that she and Cooper don't love each other anymore and that he hasn't touched her in years. I don't want everything he told me to be a lie.

"Marriage can be hard," she says quietly.

I wait for her to elaborate, but she doesn't. I grudgingly respect that she isn't trashing her husband, but maybe that says it all. If she and Cooper were stupidly in love, she would say so. She's embarrassed to admit that her marriage has fallen apart.

Cooper is the one. Every time I meet with him, I'm more sure of it. And now that I know Debbie, I understand why he's desperate to get away from her.

I just have to handle this exactly right.

CHAPTER 37

DEBBIE

My head is spinning as I drive back home from Harley's apartment.

That T-shirt. That T-shirt in her bedroom. I can't get it out of my head. The smell is still lingering in my nasal passages. Tugging at me.

I know that smell.

This changes everything.

There's a car behind me, riding my ass. I'm going the speed limit. Actually, I'm going five miles *above* the speed limit on a street littered with stop signs, but that is not fast enough for the man behind me. Every time I slow to a halt at a stop sign, he instantly leans on his horn until I start moving again.

Why is everyone in such a *hurry*? Is he a surgeon rushing in for an emergency appendectomy, and the appendix will literally *explode* if he spends more than one second at each stop sign?

I am not in the mood for this.

If this were any other week, I would have pulled over and let the guy go around me. I hate being tailgated—it stresses me out.

But this time, I don't pull over. In fact, I stay a bit on the left to make it hard for him to get around me if he did choose to illegally cross the double yellow lines. And each time I stop at a stop sign, I spend a little more time there. He leans on his horn the whole time.

Finally, after playing this game for several more minutes, I hit the brakes at yet another stop sign. I count to ten in my head while the man behind me leans on his horn.

One one thousand. Two one thousand. Three one thousand...

I only make it to seven before the man gets completely fed up with me. He swerves around me, blowing through the stop sign at a good thirty miles per hour.

A split second later, the cop car I saw lying in wait turns the corner, its lights flashing.

I go through the stop sign, and I swerve around the man, who is waiting in his car for the cop to come out and give him a ticket. I flash him my middle finger, and he pays me back the same courtesy. I just barely catch the look on the police officer's face, who thinks that the man's hand gesture was meant for him.

Well, that was fun.

A few minutes later, I am back in my own neighborhood. When I turn onto my block, I pass Jo Dolan's garden. I've only been gone for an hour and a half, but the Japanese beetle situation has clearly worsened to a critical level. If they weren't a swarm before, they definitely are now. Jo is standing in the middle of her yard, looking miserable. It's safe to say that the photo shoot is off. Although perhaps some entomological publication would be interested.

As soon as I pull into my driveway, I dig my phone out of my purse. Despite a few distractions on the way home, I still can't stop thinking about that T-shirt. Studies have shown that smells trigger greater brain activity than visual stimuli due to the direct connection of the olfactory bulb to the amygdala (which is responsible for emotions) and the hippocampus (which is responsible for memories).

Before I can stop myself, I call Cooper. He picks up quickly, which I take as a good sign.

"Hey, Debbie," he says. "Everything okay?"

I want to ask him if he can explain that shirt to me, but I can't seem to push the words out. Things are bad enough without forcing Cooper to lie to me.

That is, lie to me *again*. Because he's already been lying to me. I knew it the second I realized he turned off the location sharing on his phone.

"I'm fine," I say. "Just wanted to check in."

"Okay..." He sounds confused, which is reasonable considering I don't usually call him in the middle of the day to check in. "Are you sure you're okay?"

"I'm fine. Really."

Under other circumstances, I would think he was being sweet and concerned. Ever since we met, Cooper has worshipped the ground I walk on. He never judged me for the things other people have judged me for.

Although, like him, I have my secrets. There are things I never told him, because I never told anyone. And maybe that's part of the problem. I never gave myself to him one hundred percent.

I start to mention the news of Coach Pike's arrest, but

then I think better of it. He'll find out about it sooner or later. Better he doesn't hear about it from me.

"When will you be home?" I ask him.

"Maybe six? I was planning to hit the gym again today."

Of course he is. "Okay. Just…be home in time for dinner, all right?"

"I always am."

"Have you talked to Ken again?" I blurt out, even though I recognize it's the last thing he wants to talk about. "I mean, maybe you should ask him about…"

"Getting my job back?"

He's right. That was exactly what I was going to say.

Cooper is quiet for a moment as he absorbs the reality of our situation. Neither of us have jobs, and we've got a huge mortgage and a college tuition looming next year. "He's out of town. Until Monday."

"Oh. Well, maybe Monday then."

"Maybe."

It doesn't matter. Cooper won't be talking to Ken Bryant on Monday. Nobody will be talking to Ken on Monday or ever again.

CHAPTER 38

HARLEY

I'm glad to see Cooper show up at the gym today.

I wasn't sure if he'd be here, because he usually only comes three days a week. But when I emerge from my Zumba class, there he is, grunting as he lifts weights in a seated position. I stand in the corner of the room, about ten feet away from him, waiting for him to acknowledge me. When he doesn't even glance my way, I walk right over to him.

"Harley…" He looks startled to see me. "What are you doing here?"

"I *work* here."

His gaze darts around the room anxiously. His friend that he often comes with is on another machine, working out, but he's not looking at us. "I told you, we can't talk here. It's too dangerous."

Too dangerous. This is a man who is scared shitless of getting caught by his wife. Scared because she's completely out of her mind? Or scared because he still loves her and doesn't want to lose her?

"Well, sorry." I plant one hand on either hip, pushing my breasts forward. Cooper *definitely* notices. "I've just been missing you today."

Cooper opens his mouth, and at that moment, I am absolutely certain he is about to tell me that we need to cool it. I've seen that look before, and that's always what's coming. I brace myself, waiting for him to say the words.

But he doesn't say it. He just reaches out, gives my hand a quick squeeze, then pulls away.

"Not here, okay?" he says. "We have to be careful here."

My shoulders sag in relief. "Right. I'm sorry."

"But I'll see you later, okay?"

"Tonight?" I ask hopefully.

He shakes his head. "I can't get away tonight. Tomorrow?"

"Tomorrow," I agree, smiling at the delicious thrill that runs through every molecule of my body at the thought of an hour of pleasure with Cooper. "What if you come for dinner?"

He hesitates so long, I'm almost positive he's going to tell me no. Getting to have dinner with your boyfriend when you're the other woman is one of those pie-in-the-sky things.

"*Please*," I say softly.

"Okay," he finally agrees, and I almost jump up and down like a little kid. "I'll come at six-ish. I'll tell Debbie I'm staying late at the office."

I'm floating on a cloud as I make my way to the front desk to pick up my schedule for tomorrow. I barely even notice the disapproving look on Cindy's face when she hands me my schedule—until she won't let go of the piece of paper.

"Harley," she says in a low, firm voice.

I try to tug the paper out of her hands, but she still won't let it go. "What? What's wrong?"

"He's *married*," she says.

Ugh. This is not what I need right now. I tug harder on the paper, and finally, Cindy releases it from her grasp.

"I know he's married," I hiss at her.

"Then why are you messing around with him?"

Cindy doesn't get it. She is single and seems to have no interest whatsoever in dating or sex. She's old—even older than Debbie—but she's actually pretty attractive. She could have a partner if she wanted, but she doesn't want one. She must be one of those women who hates sex. You can't expect somebody like that to understand.

"This is actually none of your business," I tell her quietly.

Cindy blinks at me. "You're right," she says. "It's none of my business."

I celebrate a little moment of triumph, but then I realize that if she wants, Cindy could tell Debbie what's been going on. If she tells Debbie that her husband's been cheating on her with me… Well, I do want Debbie to find out, but not like that. I want her to find out in a way that I can control.

That means that I have to be the one to tell Debbie that her husband is cheating on her. I just have to figure out how to break the news.

CHAPTER 39

When I get home from the gym, there's a car I don't recognize parked on my deserted, dead-end street.

I squint at the windows of the car to see if there's anyone inside, but it's too dark. My first instinct is to make a U-turn and hightail it out of here. I'm not sure where I'd go—a bar? Back to the gym? All I know is that the mystery car doesn't signify anything good.

Then again, I'm exhausted. All I want is to get into my apartment and take a nice, long shower, slip into a pair of comfy pajamas, and binge reality TV. I don't want to let some stranger in a silver SUV scare me away from my own home.

So I pull into the driveway, my fingers crossed that my upstairs landlords have a relative visiting and the owner of this vehicle has nothing to do with me.

No such luck though. The second I grab my purse and climb out of my car, the door to the SUV cracks open. Whoever is in that car has been waiting for me. Waiting for God knows how long, which means I won't be able to get rid of them quickly.

The driver of the SUV is a middle-aged woman who reminds me a bit of Debbie. She has graying brown hair pulled into a neat bun, and she's wrapped in a trench coat. My first thought is that it's Edgar's wife, even though I remember what she looks like, and this woman doesn't really resemble her. There's something familiar about her though.

My stomach sinks as the woman takes purposeful strides in my direction. I thrust my right hand into my purse, feeling around for the small can of pepper spray I keep inside. I've never used it before—never even tested it—but there's a first time for everything.

"Harley Sibbern!" Her voice is brimming with fury. "That's you, isn't it?"

I freeze, wondering if I should make a run for it. I imagine the woman chasing me down, grabbing me by my ponytail, and tackling me to the ground. "Yes…"

"I'm Lisette Inghram," she says. When I look at her blankly, she adds, "Edgar's sister."

"Oh." Shit. "How…uh, how is he doing?"

"You mean after you wrecked his family?" Lisette raises her eyebrows, which are in dire need of grooming. "After you got him to leave his wife, then decided you didn't want him?"

That's not an entirely fair assessment of the situation. Edgar and I had an affair about a year ago, and yes, I did convince him to leave his wife of thirty years. But unlike Cooper, who has a lot of compelling *physical* attributes, Edgar was three decades older than me, seriously balding, with a weak chin and beady eyes. His most attractive feature was the fact that he was quite wealthy.

He failed to mention that the wealth belonged entirely to his wife. He also failed to mention that he had signed an ironclad prenuptial agreement and would be left penniless in the divorce. So really, he completely misrepresented himself to me. *I* was the victim here. I mean, did he think I was going to still live in a basement apartment, working for a second-rate gym as a trainer when I'm *forty*? He was delusional if he thought that.

And it's certainly not my fault that his wife didn't want to take him back. Or that his three children didn't want to have anything to do with him.

"He hung himself," Lisette blurts out.

"*What?*"

"You heard me." Her furious eyes fill with tears. "He lost everything because of you, and he couldn't take it anymore."

Again, this is not fair. His wife is at least 50 percent at fault. "Is he...dead?"

I calculate in my head how much flowers sent to a funeral home will set me back.

"He's still alive," she croaks. "But he has an anoxic brain injury. He can't walk...can't speak...can't feed himself. He's in a nursing home now and needs twenty-four-seven care."

"Well, I'm sorry to hear that."

Lisette looks like she wants to slap me, and I take a step back. "*Sorry?* That's all you have to say for yourself?"

My fingers finally locate the bottle of pepper spray, and my shoulders relax slightly. "What do you want me to say? Edgar was an adult, and he made his own bed. I didn't force him to leave his wife. And I didn't force him to hang himself."

"Wow." She shakes her head as if she's never met anyone quite as horrible as me. What a drama queen— just like Edgar. "You're heartless."

"What do you want from me?" I retort. "What am I supposed to do? Take him back?"

She wipes her eyes with the back of her hand. She's probably the only person in the entire world who's sad about what happened to Edgar. I didn't get the sense he had many friends.

"You could visit him," she says.

"Visit him?"

She nods. "The nursing home is only an hour away from here. He doesn't talk much, but he smiles when he's happy. You could sit with him and hold his hand. It…" She takes a breath. "I think it would mean a lot to him."

I stare at her, waiting to hear the punch line to what has got to be a joke. She wants me to drive an hour out to some nursing home to hold hands with a *vegetable* who— full disclosure here—I didn't even like very much when he was healthy. Physically, Edgar wasn't my type, but his wealth made him sexy. Once that was gone, my feelings for him deflated.

"You've got to be kidding me," I snort. "I'm not doing that!"

Lisette flinches. "You don't have to go every week…"

"I'm not going *ever*." I readjust my purse on my shoulder, keeping my hand on the spray bottle. "I'm sorry Edgar couldn't even manage to kill himself properly, but that's not my problem. There's no way I'm wasting even one more minute of my time on him."

Circles of pink appear on the older woman's cheeks. "You bitch," she breathes.

She raises her hand, and now I'm fairly sure she means to slap me. But I'm ready for her. I yank the bottle of pepper spray from my bag, and it turns out that it's actually quite easy to dispense. I press the button at the top of the can, and a cloud of toxic mist releases into Lisette's face. She halts with a screech, followed by a lot of coughing and rubbing her eyes.

"Stay away from me, lady." My voice is firm and devoid of emotion. "If I see your car around here ever again, I'm calling the police."

She's still rubbing her eyes, which probably need to be washed out with water. But that's not my problem, any more than her brother is my problem. What's done is done. I turn around, go into my apartment, and lock the door behind me.

CHAPTER 40

FROM *DEAR DEBBIE* DRAFTS FILE

Dear Debbie,

Oh, I don't know what to do, Debbie! My husband doesn't like my cooking, and it just about breaks my heart. He jokes that I should win an award for the worst cook in the whole country, and while I try to laugh it off, I can't help but feel like I've let him down.

I have tried everything to make myself into the wonderful chef my husband deserves. I've followed new recipes, watched online tutorials to improve my skills, and most of all, I put a large dollop of love into every meal. The funny thing is, my kids and I think they taste just fine, but my husband has a much more refined and sophisticated palate. I hate disappointing him every night.

Do you have any advice on how to become a better cook and bring a little more joy to the dinner table?

Sincerely,
Hopeless in the Kitchen

Dear Hopeless in the Kitchen,

Cooking a delicious and nutritious meal is important in any family. Have you tried taking a cooking class? Getting instructions from a real person can be extremely helpful! Also, encourage your husband to cook something for the family so he can show you the sorts of dishes he enjoys (and understand how difficult it can be).

If none of that works, I would encourage you to try some new and interesting way to flavor his food. For instance, ethylene glycol, also known as antifreeze, has a lovely, sweet taste. If you put a healthy dollop into his food, it will enhance the flavor, and I promise you, he will have no complaints once he finishes!

Debbie

CHAPTER 41

COOPER

When I get home from the gym, Debbie is cooking dinner in the kitchen.

She doesn't need to do that every night. I could bring home food, or I could try to cook. My cooking isn't anything to get excited about, but I'm a smart enough guy. I can figure out how to put together a meal. Especially now that I'm not going to have a job.

"Is dinner almost ready?" I ask her.

Debbie looks up from the saucepan and smiles at me. But there's something off about her smile. I can't quite put my finger on it.

"Almost," she confirms.

"Can I help?"

She pauses for a beat, then nods. "Can you set the table? And fill up the water glasses."

I take four glasses from the cabinet over the sink and set them down on the counter. I grab the jug of spring water in the refrigerator, but there's only enough in it to fill two glasses.

"Do we have any more?" I ask her.

"Just fill it up from the tap," Debbie says.

I raise my eyebrows. "I thought Lexi won't drink water from the tap. She says it tastes metallic to her. Isn't that why we have this?"

Debbie laughs. "Cooper, I've been refilling that jug from the tap for the last two years. Lexi doesn't know the difference."

I had no idea she was doing this. I agree that Lexi's teenage obsession with not drinking our perfectly fine tap water was weird, and it's sort of funny that she can't tell the difference, but I don't know how I feel about the fact that Debbie has been lying to our daughter for two years. And even worse, I had no idea about any of it. Aren't we partners in this whole parenting thing?

I finish setting the table, and then I do one better and let the girls know to come down to eat. Izzy bounds down the stairs almost immediately, but Lexi is slower on the descent. She's also uncharacteristically silent. Lexi has been so moody ever since she turned fourteen. Is that typical for girls? Thank God Izzy isn't moody like that—I don't think I could deal with *two* kids telling me that I need to find a new barber because my haircut makes me look like a dork.

"The police were at school all day today," Izzy babbles as Debbie brings out a large plate of food. We always get served family style, especially since lately you never can predict how much the girls want to eat. They will consume anything between a full plate of food and five noodles. "They were even still there when I left the building!"

"The police?" I repeat.

Izzy stares at me in amazement. "You didn't hear? Mom didn't tell you?"

I look at Debbie questioningly, but she is busy scooping pasta and white sauce on her plate. It seems like an issue involving the police would be something that Debbie would have thought to mention to me. Apparently not.

"No," I admit. "What happened?"

"Coach Pike was *arrested*," Izzy says. "He had a camera in the girls' locker room in the shower."

I let out a gasp. "He was recording teenage girls taking showers?"

"I heard the camera was just put in and hadn't started recording yet," Izzy says.

Thank God. The thought of what could have been on that footage is traumatizing.

"My friend Ayan told me he's saying he didn't do it, but, like, I heard they found a program on his phone that connected to the camera. So he definitely did it."

A program on his phone that connected to the camera. Just like what we have at our front door.

"I'm sure he did it," Lexi mutters. "Coach Pike is a total creep, and everyone knows it. I'm just surprised he was stupid enough to get caught. I mean, did he really think he could put a *camera* in the girls' locker room and nobody would notice?"

She's right. Anyone who did that is just begging to get caught.

"So, Izzy," Debbie says, "now that Coach Pike is gone, do they know who will be coaching the girls' soccer team?"

"Mrs. Laslo is going to take over," Izzy says. "And she says even though Coach Pike told me I was off the team, I can join up again. She's not strict like he was."

"You were off the soccer team?" I ask in surprise.

"Jesus, Dad," Lexi says. "Get with the program."

She's right. I clearly have no idea what's going on in my family right now. But in my defense, I did just quit my job yesterday.

Izzy lowers her eyes to her plate of food. "The coach said I wasn't fast enough."

"And that was ridiculous," Debbie chimes in, her eyes suddenly animated. "You were the best player on the team. I don't know what he was thinking. Not only was he a despicable pervert, he was also a terrible coach."

Izzy shrugs.

"Well," Debbie says, "thankfully, that's a mistake on his part that will now be corrected. I suppose at least *some* good came out of the terrible thing he did."

I look over at Debbie again, sitting across from me at the dinner table. She has already made a dent in her food, but the lump of pasta on my plate is just sitting there. Izzy and Lexi have also piled pasta on their plates, although Lexi seems to be eating only one noodle every several minutes. I'm the only one who isn't eating at all.

"Aren't you hungry, Dad?" Izzy asks me.

Actually, I'm not. I don't think I've ever been less hungry in my life.

I wipe my hands on my napkin and push my chair back from the dinner table. It makes a loud scraping sound on the floor. "I'll be right back," I announce.

All three faces look up at me questioningly.

"I just need to run upstairs and…" I clear my throat. "I need to check something for work. It'll just be a minute."

Debbie gives me a funny look. My excuse sounded weak, because it *is* weak. I don't need to check something for work. But there is something I need to take a look at, and my thoughts won't stop racing until I do.

I hurry up the stairs to our bedroom. I shut the door behind me, although it's not like anyone will be following me. I perch on the edge of the bed, on the side where I usually sleep, and wrench open the drawer of the nightstand.

The crumpled paper that I stuffed inside this morning is still there. The one where I wrote down the address that popped up when I did the search for Debbie in her Findly app. And now I dig my own phone out of my pocket.

I don't know the full name of Izzy's soccer coach who kicked her off the team. However, typing a few keywords into Google quickly brings up the news article about a high school sports coach named Robert Pike who was arrested for filming minors in the girls' locker room at the high school.

He's saying he didn't do it, but, like Izzy said, they found a program on his phone that connected to the camera.

I scroll away from the news article, and the next thing I search for in my phone is "Robert Pike home address." Instantly, the address of the home he owns in Weymouth pops up on the screen.

My scribble from last night is hard to read, but there's no doubt the street name is the same.

Debbie was at Coach Pike's house in the middle of the night. Then the next morning, he was arrested for having incriminating software on his phone.

There's no way that could be a coincidence.

But it also seems impossible. Could my sweet, unassuming wife really have broken into the coach's house while he was sleeping and installed something on his phone? Mild-mannered housewives don't do things like that.

Just like they don't break into the neighbor's basement to destroy their fuse box. Or post pornographic videos of their bosses online.

I stare at the piece of paper with Pike's address on it, trying to figure out what to do with this information. If my wife did all those things, she is an incredibly disturbed individual. She would be somebody in need of serious psychiatric help. Because if she could do all that, who knows what else she could be capable of?

She could be dangerous.

CHAPTER 42

DEBBIE

It seems like Lexi has broken up with Zane.

Ordinarily, this would be cause for great celebration. I do not like that boy, and I'm grateful that he won't be in my house again or blasting his horn in our driveway. Lexi could do way better. *Nobody* would be way better.

But it's hard to celebrate when Lexi is clearly upset. She's barely said five words during dinner, and she took only a few bites of the pasta I made. It wasn't exactly a gourmet meal, but she usually eats what I put in front of her. Tonight, she's completely uninterested.

Cooper also seems distracted. He went upstairs with an excuse about checking something for work, but his laptop is sitting on our coffee table. So what was he checking? All I know is that when he came back downstairs, he looked pale.

Only Izzy is happily scarfing down her food. One out of three isn't bad, but it could be better.

"I have to do homework," Lexi mumbles as she pushes her chair back.

"You barely ate anything," I point out. "Didn't you like the dinner?"

She lifts a shoulder. "I'm not hungry."

"Do you want me to make you something else?"

"Oh my God, Mom." Lexi glares at me. "I told you, *I'm not hungry*. Stop asking me a million times if I want to eat something else."

I bite my lip to keep from pointing out that I only, in fact, asked once. "Fine. Go do your homework."

Izzy announces she has homework too, although at least her plate has been practically licked clean. I'm thrilled she's eating normally again, but it's hard to celebrate when Cooper is at the table, pushing a clump of noodles around his plate.

"Not hungry either?" I ask him as the girls climb the stairs to go to their respective rooms.

Cooper lifts his eyes, blinking as if surprised to see me still sitting at the table with him. "Oh," he says. "I, uh, I guess not."

"Are you okay?"

Of course he's not okay. Instead of getting a promotion, he just lost his job. He's got to be worried sick about how we're going to pay the mortgage and afford Lexi's college tuition. But there's a look in his eyes that makes me think there's something more going on. Something that he hasn't shared with me.

He opens his mouth as if to reply, but before he can, his phone's familiar generic ringtone fills the room. It's the same chimes the phone came with, because he doesn't know how to change it. He digs it out of his pocket, angling the screen so I can't see it. He sucks in a breath.

Who is calling him? What is he hiding from me?

"I, uh…" He jumps from his seat, an uncomfortable smile on his face. "I better take this."

He rushes away from the table, his phone pressed to his ear. As he's leaving the room, I can just barely make out the sound of a voice on the other end of the line. A *female* voice. A few seconds later, the door to our bedroom slams shut.

Hmm.

I rise from my own chair to clear the table. Not one person in my family thought to take their dishes to the sink. Cooper will occasionally load or unload the dishwasher, but the kids *never* do. Do they think there's poison fumes trapped inside and if they open it to put a dish inside, the fumes will be released, killing us all? Based on their behavior, I have to assume that yes, they *do* think this.

I scrape the uneaten pasta off the plates and into the garbage disposal, wondering what's going on with Lexi. She's never in a good mood, but she seemed even more upset than usual tonight. Should I try to talk to her? Unfortunately, it never goes well when I initiate conversations with my daughter about her love life. Yesterday, she practically bit my head off when I mentioned Zane.

Also, I have enough problems of my own. I was fired from my job, although that wasn't much of a loss. Cooper also just quit his longtime job, and even before that, he was acting incredibly strange. And that mysterious phone call that made him dash off to our bedroom has made me uneasy. Really, I should be sitting *him* down for a talk. (Although I also think it would be better to keep my mouth shut when it comes to my husband. At least until I'm ready to share my own secrets.)

Something about Lexi keeps tugging at me. There are times when the best thing to do is leave her alone, but my gut is telling me something more is going on right now.

I'm going to try to talk to her.

I load the dishes into the dishwasher, then walk through the kitchen to the stairwell. I climb the stairs to the second floor, and when I get to the door of Lexi's room, my fist poised to knock on the door, I hesitate. The door to the master bedroom is at the other end of the hallway. Cooper is likely still on the phone, and if I press my ear against the door, I'll be able to hear his end of the conversation.

Maybe I should do it. There's something going on with Cooper that he is reluctant to talk to me about, and a little spy work is the only way to find out the truth. And it's not like Lexi is going to spill her guts to me if I try to talk to her. She'll likely be mad at me, because she'll have decided I'm not allowed to talk to her when the moon is in waning gibbous or something along those lines.

I'll try this weekend. I'll offer to take her shopping, and I can gently probe about what happened with Zane. Not that we have a lot of money to drop on a shopping trip, but maybe we can go to that thrift store she likes. We can probably get her a whole wardrobe there for two dollars.

I drop my arm, ready to walk away. And I almost do, but at that moment, something stops me. Something makes me freeze in my tracks.

It's the sound of sobs coming from Lexi's room.

I turn around, and this time, I knock on Lexi's door

without hesitation. The crying immediately ceases, and she calls out. "What is it?"

"Lexi, honey?" I say. "Can I come in?"

There's a long silence on the other side of the door. I suspect she's debating whether she should tell me to get lost. But then she calls out in a voice laced with resignation, "*Fine.*"

Lexi is curled up in her bed, her knees tucked close to her chest, her lanky arms wrapped around them. Her face is streaked with tears, her eyes bloodshot. It looks like she's been crying for a while and was just managing to keep it quiet until now.

If Zane hurt her, I'll kill him.

Actually, I won't have to. Cooper would do it first. He may not know every detail of our children's lives the way I do, but if anyone posed a threat to them, he'd risk his life to save them just like I would.

I close the door behind me. I approach her cautiously, like she's a scared animal that might scurry off at any moment. I finally settle down at the edge of her bed, my right butt cheek half hovering in the air.

"Sweetheart," I say as gently as I can, "what happened?"

She shakes her head, and a tidal wave of fresh tears falls from her eyes. Her shoulders shake with sobs, and I scoot down the length of the bed to wrap my arms around her. I rock her the way I did when she was small, and after a moment, she is clinging to me.

"Mom," she sobs. "Mom…"

"It's okay," I tell her in my most soothing voice. "I promise, it's okay."

"It's not okay!" she gasps. "He…he has pictures!"

What?

I pull away from her, inspecting her red and swollen face. "Pictures?" I say in a voice I hope belies the sick sensation in the pit of my stomach.

She covers her eyes with both hands and bobs her head.

"What pictures?" I ask in that same gentle tone, even though what I really want to do is grab her shoulders and shake her until she tells me what the hell is going on.

"Zane…he…he has…" She gulps, struggling to catch her breath. "He has pictures of me. Pictures where I'm…"

I'm trying really hard not to react with horror. "Where you're *what*?"

"You know," she mumbles.

"Like…" I cringe. "*Sex* pictures?"

"No." She shakes her head vigorously. Thank *God*. "But…you know…you can see my…my boobs."

Oh no. Well, it could be worse. It could definitely be better, but it could be worse too.

"He said he'll show everyone!" She buries her face in her hands. "He's going to share it with all his friends unless I…"

"Unless you what?"

"Unless I…" She doesn't lift her face. "Unless I…you know…"

If she says "you know" one more time, I might scream. "Unless you *what*?"

"Mom." She finally raises her face, her eyes pleading. "We haven't…and he wants to…"

That buzzing starts up again in the back of my head. I want to *kill* that bastard. "Are you saying," I begin as I try to keep my voice from trembling, "if you don't have sex with him, he's going to send the naked photos of you to all his friends?"

She doesn't answer, but another wave of tears spills over. Her shoulders start to shake. "My life is ruined!"

I grit my teeth. I don't know if I've ever been this angry in my entire life, and I've been *really* angry. How *dare* he? This is my little girl! What sort of person would do something like that?

"What will I do?" she wails. "If he sends it to his friends, they'll send it to their friends, and then the whole school will get it! How will I even get into college?"

"Maybe he's lying," I say, although I agree that Zane seems like the sort of person who would do something like that. "Maybe he won't really send it to anyone."

"He did it before!" she cries.

What?

"He transferred to our school between sophomore and junior year," she explains. "His family moved here from Florida. And apparently, this girl he was dating during sophomore year sent him a naked picture, and he circulated it everywhere. He *showed* it to me."

"Seriously? And he didn't get turned in for doing that?"

"His friends all covered for him. Nobody would say where the photo came from. Eventually though, everyone was passing it around."

Wow. I never liked Zane, but this is next level.

"My life is ruined!" Lexi reaches for me, and I wrap my arms around her, holding her tightly. "I can't believe I was so stupid. How could I have let him take those pictures?"

"It's *not* your fault," I say.

I'm annoyed that it happened, but I mean what I'm saying. I can imagine the way Zane must have pressured her. She's only a kid—seventeen is such a baby!—and she desperately wanted her cool boyfriend to like her. I understand exactly how it happened.

"Listen to me, Lexi," I say. "I promise you, we will figure this out. We are not going to let Zane win."

Her bloodshot eyes widen. "You're not going to tell the principal, are you?"

"Lexi..."

"You can't!" She grabs my arm. "Mom, if you tell them, everyone will find out! And he'll circulate the photos anyway!"

"Lexi..."

"Promise me!"

I don't know if she's right, but the way Lexi is grabbing my arm, she certainly thinks so. And she has a point. If I go to the school, these things do have a way of getting around. Even if he doesn't do anything with the photos, the mere existence of them will be a rumor that spreads like wildfire.

No, I've got to deal with this in a different way.

"I promise," I say. "I won't tell anyone at the school. But I need you to promise me something."

She blinks at me, her eyes wet.

"I want you to promise me that you will trust me," I say. "I want you to trust me when I say that I will make absolutely sure those photos of you never get out."

"But how can you—"

"*Trust* me, Lexi."

She hesitates for only a moment, but then she says, "I trust you."

I see that trust in her eyes. Even though she's not a little kid anymore, she still believes that I can fix things for her.

I am seized by the sudden almost irrepressible urge to tell her everything. I've never told anyone what happened to me. Not my parents, not Cooper, not anyone. I wish I could tell her, even though I know I can't.

I just wish she knew that I used to be just like her. I was carefree and intelligent, and yes, beautiful, even though I didn't know it at the time. And then something happened that ruined my life. That's why I refuse to let anything like that happen to her. Because I love her more than anything, and I want her life to be as good as mine promised to be before I was raped during my second year of college.

CHAPTER 43

This is a story I have never told before.

Don't worry, there won't be any graphic details. The truth is, I don't remember much, which is part of why I never went to the police, although there were a lot of reasons I kept it to myself. All I really remember is what happened before and how it all ended. So if it sounds confused or if I can't account for big blocks of time, that's why.

It doesn't mean I'm lying.

I was in the second semester of my second year at MIT and loving it. The first year is pass/fail, so my last semester was the first time I had received any letter grades, and they were good. Okay, I'm being modest—they were great. I got all A's. And I wasn't taking, like, intro to bullshit. I was taking challenging computer science classes in which several of my classmates were just barely scraping by.

Like I said, I can't help but wonder what could have been.

It was my roommate, Selena, who talked me into going

to a frat party, although I don't blame Selena for what happened. I had been to a few fairly tame parties over the last year and a half, but a large percentage of the guys at MIT were in fraternities, so those parties were supposed to be a lot more interesting. To be clear, they weren't interesting to *me*, just more interesting in an objective sort of way.

I had big plans to do some coding that night and had even purchased a large bottle of Mountain Dew in anticipation. But then Selena went on this whole rant about how I was never any fun and how I was going to graduate from college a virgin, which would be bad for some reason. I finally agreed to go to the party just to get her to stop talking and also because my wrists were sort of hurting from coding twelve hours straight the day before.

She lent me a dress from her own closet and spent about fifteen minutes going through my hair with a curling iron. She also managed to do my makeup for about ten minutes before I told her to stop. When she had done all that I was allowing her to do, I looked at myself in the full-length mirror in the communal restroom in the hallway and actually thought I looked pretty good. I cleaned up nice.

When I came back into our dorm room, Selena let out a low whistle. "Hey, sexy," she joked.

"Don't make me change my mind."

She frowned at me. "Can you lose the glasses?"

I could not. I was half-blind without them. That was before I discovered the miracle of contact lenses. When I was in college, the idea of sticking my fingers in my eyes was too horrible for words.

We walked over to the Zeta Pi fraternity, which was nearly a thirty-minute hike in the nippy March night. Actually, it wasn't too bad for me, because I was wearing a pair of flats, a coat, and a hat. Selena, on the other hand, was wearing heels and no coat, which meant she complained bitterly during the entire walk.

It's funny what I remember about that night. I can still hear Selena's gripes about the cold echoing in my ears. *I think my underwire has frozen to my skin, Debbie.*

We finally got to the party at about ten o'clock, and it was well underway. In stark contrast to the frigid night air, the frat house was way, *way* too hot. It was also strangely humid, and all the work Selena did to make my hair smooth and shiny was immediately undone. I shrugged off my coat and stuffed it in a bedroom referred to as "the coat room" without any confidence that I would ever get it back. There was music playing, and the bass was so loud that it made my head throb.

An hour later, I wanted to leave. Badly. Selena and I had managed to stay together for the first twenty minutes, but then some guy started chatting her up, and she disappeared. Nobody was chatting me up. I was just sitting in a corner, sipping from a cup of Coke, wishing I knew the way home. Too bad neither GPS nor Uber had been invented yet.

That was when he found me.

I'm glad I was wearing my glasses, because I got a good look at his face. He looked like an upperclassman. A junior or a senior. Not that he looked a lot older, but he just had that confidence about him, like he'd been here a while, and he knew what was what.

"You look miserable," he observed.

I looked up at him. He wasn't remarkable looking, but he had dark brown hair that curled endearingly at the ends and fell in his eyes. He was cute.

"It's loud down here," I admitted. "I'm getting a headache."

"I know." He took a swig from the paper cup in his hand. "By the time I graduate, I'll be lucky if I have any hearing left."

I smiled.

"I'm Hutch." He stuck a thumb at his own chest. "I don't think I've ever seen you here before."

"I'm Debbie."

"Nice to meet you, Debbie." He grinned at me, and I was sort of proud that this cute upperclassman frat boy was flirting with me. "Looks like you're almost done with your drink. Can I get you another one of whatever you're having?"

"It's just a Coke " I said.

"Well, no wonder you're not having a good time," he said, and at the time, I had to admit it was a good point. "How about if I get you another Coke, but you let me put a little bit of rum in it." He positioned his thumb and forefinger about half an inch apart. "*This* much."

And because he was cute and older and was flirting with me, I said, "Okay."

He got me a rum and Coke, which was only the second time I had had alcohol during college and only the third time in my whole life. At the time, I assumed everything that happened after that was because I had zero alcohol tolerance, but later, when I really thought about it, I was pretty sure that one drink could not have done that to me.

Hutch dropped something in my drink. Maybe not a roofie, but he put *something* in there to make sure I wouldn't be able to fight him off.

198

We sat and talked on the couch for a bit. He asked me what dorm I was in, and I told him Baker. He asked me what I was majoring in, and I told him course 6 (computer science). He was majoring in course 14 (economics). He asked me another question that I couldn't hear because the music was so loud, and that was when he suggested going upstairs, because it would be quieter up there. I told him yes, and I was grateful because it was too loud downstairs, and all I'd been wanting since I got here was some peace and quiet.

That's when the memories start to get a little fuzzy.

I remember walking up the stairs to his room. I sort of remember his room. There were two twin beds... No, wait, it was a bunk bed. There was a desk. It must have had a desktop computer on it, because we all had desktops back then. I think I told him I was tired, and he suggested that I lie down on his bed.

The next thing I remember was feeling like somebody was trying to shake me awake. But when I cracked my eyes open, I realized that wasn't what was happening at all. Hutch was on top of me, his cute hair falling in his eyes. He had pulled up my dress and pulled down my underwear, and he was...

My first thought was that I was confused. Was I so drunk that I had told him this was okay? That didn't seem possible. It definitely *wasn't* okay. I was still a virgin, and what he was doing... It hurt.

I opened my mouth, and my throat felt painfully dry. Somehow, I managed to crack out, "No. Stop."

I expected him to roll off me, full of apologies. But he didn't do that. He just kept thrusting, oblivious to my plea.

"*Stop*," I said, louder this time. I tried to push him

away, but—I clearly remember this part—my arms felt like I was moving through molasses. "Please stop!"

This time, he replied with a twinge of annoyance, "Don't worry. This will be over in a minute."

It was actually *two* minutes. I know because I counted every second.

And suddenly, it was over. He rolled off me and zipped up his pants like nothing had happened. And then…he left.

I was really out of it. I lay there in that bottom bunk for anywhere from ten minutes to an hour, trying to figure out if it had really happened or just been a nightmare. The only thing that convinced me it was real was the soreness I felt and the blood on my underwear when I got home.

My head was swimming, but I managed to pull myself out of bed. I stumbled through the crowd downstairs without talking to anyone. I didn't bother to find Selena or even my coat. I walked out the front door, and even though it was freezing outside, I barely felt it. To this day, I have no idea how I made it home. But I must have, because I woke up the next day in my own bed in my dorm room.

I tried to tell myself that it wasn't a big deal. In my head, I didn't even use the R word. I went to a party, had a little too much to drink, and had sex with a guy I barely knew. It was a one-night stand. Selena had had them, and it wasn't a big deal. It would only become a big deal if I let it be a big deal.

I had always been a strong person. Smart, capable. I had gotten into MIT after all—the only person in my graduating class in high school. I was the next Bill Gates. This wasn't a big deal. I would get past it.

Except I didn't get past it. I had nightmares every night, and I would wake up covered in sweat. I was sleeping in two-hour chunks and walking around with permanent bags under my eyes. Everywhere I went on campus, I kept thinking I saw Hutch. It was never him though. It was always some other boy with a similar haircut, but it didn't matter. My grades started slipping. Then they started plummeting.

After getting straight A's the first semester, I failed every single class my second semester. I didn't even show up for two of the final exams.

A counselor at the school talked to me about my decline. She tried to ask what happened to me, but I refused to tell her. I just said that I was feeling unmotivated, and I needed a break from school. I went home for the summer, hoping some time away would heal me.

I never went back.

I almost told Cooper what happened to me a thousand times. He was the first guy I dated after I left college. He was so sweet and patient with me, although he had no idea why I was so anxious when it came to sex. Even without telling him anything, he was understanding. In the end, I was scared to tell him the truth because I thought he would respect me less. And then after we were married, I was scared to tell him because I thought he'd be mad at me for not telling him sooner.

And now, after twenty years of marriage, it's far too late.

Besides, he's got secrets too. Plenty of them.

The idea that Zane might be trying to do to my daughter what Hutch did to me fills me with a rage so burning hot, I feel like I could tear that punk kid limb from limb. But of course, I can't do that. I don't want to go to jail. And physically, I'm not sure I could do it. I'm not some sort of superhero (supervillain?) capable of ripping a person apart with my bare hands.

Anyway, what I will do to him will be much, much worse.

CHAPTER 44

I wait until everyone is asleep.

I have to be very careful tonight. Even after drugging Cooper last night, I'm fairly sure he woke up while I was gone. And since I didn't know I'd be sneaking out after dinner was over, it would have been a challenge to slip him something again. I'll just have to be very quiet.

I slide out of bed at midnight. Cooper appears to be asleep, but I am extra quiet as I extract myself from our shared blanket. Before going to bed, I stored a change of clothes in the living room so I wouldn't wake him while I dressed.

But my first stop is Lexi's room.

I don't have to be that quiet this time. My eldest daughter sleeps like the dead. Last year, a fire alarm went off in the house in the middle of the night, and I had to shake her awake to make sure she didn't burn alive.

I tiptoe into her room and snatch her phone off the nightstand where it's charging. Then I quietly leave.

I don't make a habit of spying on Lexi's phone, but I do require her to give me the passcode so that I can get in if I need to. This is not information that I have taken advantage of in the past, and the truth is, it would not have surprised me if she changed the passcode. But when I punch in the six digits, the phone unlocks.

I'm in.

For a moment, I'm tempted to look through her photos to try to find the pictures she was telling me about, but then I decide not to. I'm not here to snoop. I'm here to take care of a situation for my child.

Zane is one of the top contacts on her phone. She hasn't blocked him, possibly because she's monitoring the situation. I don't want to read all the text messages between the two of them, but the last message from him makes me see red:

If you don't want the whole school to see those photos, you should stop being such a little cocktease.

Oh my God, I want to kill him.

I have to take a few deep breaths to calm myself down. My hands are shaking as I tap out a message to Zane:

Can we see each other now? I'll sneak out and take my parents' car.

There's a chance he could be asleep, but I remember overhearing him say that he never goes to bed before two in the morning. Sure enough, three bubbles appear on the screen. He's typing.

Have you reconsidered?

Kill him with my bare hands. Rip him limb from limb.

Yes. I want to see you. I'll do anything you want.
You're so smart. I knew you'd come around.

Yes, Lexi is smart. That's why she told her mother what was happening.

Can we meet at the playground in the shipyard? We'll be the only ones there.

The Hingham Shipyard used to be an actual shipyard many years ago but is now an area on the marina with homes, shopping, and recreation activities. I used to take the kids to the playground there when they were little, followed by lunch at Wahlburgers. During the day, it was always busy, but it will be completely deserted at this time of night. And I happened to notice on a recent excursion there that there were no cameras around the playground.

I'll be there in 20 minutes.

CHAPTER 45

I arrive fifteen minutes later.

Zane is chronically late, so I didn't need to rush, but on the other hand, he also drives like chaos incarnate, so it seemed possible that he might show up on time or even early. I need to beat him to the playground.

As expected, the playground is completely empty. It's officially "closed after dusk," as if any children would come here to play at one in the morning. It's a medium-size play area with tire swings, a play structure with a green plastic slide, and wood chips covering the ground that threaten to enter my shoes with each step.

Last night before bed, I went out and bought a six-pack of beer. It's not the sort of thing we ever keep in the house, because Cooper and I don't care for beer, but I need it tonight. As soon as I get to the playground, I crack open a can.

Then I add the opium. Enough to knock him out.

I certainly would never drink from a mystery can left

on a playground, but I'm not Zane, who is eighteen years old with a penchant for getting in trouble. I place the beer in a prominent location on one of the benches lining the playground. Then I position myself behind a set of bushes. And I wait.

Zane is ten minutes late. When he arrives at the playground, he looks around, expecting to see Lexi waiting for him there. From my hiding place, I can see a flash of annoyance over his gaunt features. He might not wait for her.

Thankfully, I brought along Lexi's phone for just this reason. I type out another message to Zane:

My mom got up to use the bathroom, so I got out a little late. I'll be there in 15 minutes.

He reads the message, frowning. Is he going to wait for her? I have to do something to seal the deal. So even though it kills me, I type:

I want to do it right on the bench in the playground.

The message serves a dual purpose. First, it will ensure that he waits for Lexi, even though she's not actually coming. And second, it gets him thinking about the park bench.

Sure enough, he walks over to the bench and sits down. I squint at him in the moonlight as he messes with his phone. I imagine he's looking at the photos of Lexi, and I want to wring his neck.

Most of the time, I am able to push what happened that night with Hutch out of my head. But right now, it's like he's whispering in my ear: *Don't worry. This will be over in a minute.*

I will not let that happen to my daughter.

It takes Zane a few minutes to notice the beer can. He glances at it a few times, then finally picks it up. He seems surprised that it's nearly full. Then he sniffs it.

Opium does have an odor. It smells sort of sweet, with an earthy overtone to it. It reminds me a little of the smell of maple syrup. I'm hoping that the yeasty odor of the beer will mask the opium. I watch Zane contemplating the can. Hopefully, I've taught my own children better than to drink from a random container left in the park, but I have a strong feeling Zane will have no qualms about it if he thinks it's alcohol.

Drink it. Come on, drink it, you piece of shit!

And then he does. He's drinking it. He downs the entire can of opium-laced beer in what looks like five gulps.

I stay poised with my phone in case he looks like he's going to take off, but after about five minutes, he doesn't seem as fidgety as he was before. Fifteen minutes later, he is yawning and rubbing his eyes.

Half an hour later, he is out cold.

I wait another ten minutes, just in case. In the meantime, I make sure to delete the entire conversation between Zane and my daughter's phone so she'll never find out we met tonight. While I'm at it, I also block his number. I shove Lexi's phone into my purse and walk over to where he is lying strewn across the bench. He had been messing with his phone, and it fell out of his hand and is lying on the grass below the bench. I pick it up.

Unlike Coach Pike's phone, which I opened using his

fingerprint, this is the type of phone that unlocks by facial recognition. This generally means that your eyes must be open to unlock it. However, during the summer, I walked in on Lexi and Zane in my kitchen, and he was complaining about how his phone wouldn't unlock if he had his sunglasses on. I overheard the conversation and told him that you could turn off the "Attention" function on the phone so that it does not require you to be looking at it in order to unlock. When he seemed confused, I offered to do it for him. He handed me his phone, and I changed the settings personally.

That's how I know that when I hold the phone up to his face, it will unlock, even though his eyes are closed.

I step back into the shadows in case Zane wakes up, although it doesn't look like that's going to happen anytime soon. After deleting the conversation between his phone and Lexi's that led him to the playground, the next thing I do is scroll through the photos on his phone and find the ones that Lexi sent him. I delete them all. It's entirely possible he has them saved somewhere else, but deleting those photos is not my primary purpose.

I'm here to do something else.

Lexi told me that he had done this before. During his sophomore year, he dated a girl whose picture he sent around the school. Considering he was a sophomore, that girl was likely around fifteen years old. Which means that legally, he was distributing child pornography.

Now I must find the digital fingerprint of what he did.

It's not fun searching Zane's phone. I have to scroll through a lot of conversations with his friends involving my daughter, none of which are flattering. I find one from yesterday that particularly raises my blood pressure.

You still dating that Lexi chick?
Ya but she sucks at going down on me. Will probably
dump her soon.
She needs lessons from Yvonne.
I think she's too stupid to learn.

At some point, I put down the phone and just stare at
Zane, who is still lying unconscious on the park bench.
I'm going through all this trouble to find incriminating
photos, but it doesn't have to be this difficult. I've got a
Swiss Army knife in the glove compartment of my car. I
can walk over, get it, and chop off his dick. That would be
justice, and it would certainly solve the problem!

I suppose it would create other problems though.

It takes me nearly half an hour of searching before I
find what I'm looking for. The photo of that poor girl is
still in his camera feed, because of course he'd be too naive
to ever delete it. She looks only fourteen or fifteen. She's
completely naked, and she appears so deeply uncomfortable, I almost really do get that Swiss Army knife. He has
shared this photo multiple times, and the evidence is all
there. Right on his phone. He never deleted any of it.

And he called *my daughter* stupid.

I screenshot everything, then I create an anonymous
email account. I send everything to both the high school
administration and the local police department, noting the
approximate age of the girl.

I allow myself a smile. Tomorrow will be interesting.

CHAPTER 46

When I get home from my little errand, I find Cooper waiting for me in the living room.

He's in his undershirt and boxers, and only the small light is on next to him, giving his face an eerie glow. I should have guessed he would be up. He hasn't been sleeping well, and the absence of my body next to his in bed might have been enough to jolt him awake.

He stares at me, his frame rigid. He must've heard my car enter the garage, so he knows I've been driving. I can't pretend I was taking a stroll around the neighborhood. Plus, I failed to turn off the Findly app, which was a terrible oversight. Although maybe on some level, I wanted him to know where I had gone.

"Debbie," he says.

When he speaks, I smell it. He must've discovered the rest of the beers that I left in the back of the refrigerator. Cooper isn't much of a drinker, but I guess I can't blame him right now.

"Hi," I say weakly.

"Where were you?"

I try to smile, although it feels like plastic on my face. "I was just driving around."

He frowns. "Were you at the shipyard?"

Just as I suspected—the tracker on my phone gave me away. I will definitely have to shut it off next time. The same way he does when he disappears somewhere he doesn't want me to know. He's much better at keeping secrets than I am.

"I couldn't sleep," I say. "I was just driving around. I thought it would make me tired."

He struggles to his feet. His brown hair is tousled from sleep, and he has a day's growth of a beard on his face. When I first met him, I had not been on a date in a very long time, but he seemed so sweet and earnest when he asked me. I was afraid of men for a long time because of Hutch, but for some reason, I wasn't afraid of Cooper. He was, in fact, the first man who didn't give me that sick feeling of fear in the pit of my stomach. He didn't seem like he would ever hurt me.

When did that change?

"Debbie," he croaks, his voice pleading.

I know what he wants. He wants me to tell him the truth about everything. But there's no way I can do that. It's far too late.

"Where did you go last night?" I counter. "When you told me you were getting dinner and you were gone for two hours?"

His eyes widen in alarm. "I…I told you. I just went for a drive."

"A drive?"

"Yes, of course." His voice takes on a defensive edge. "What do you *think* I've been doing?"

Why should I tell the truth when he's been lying to my face?

When it's all over, he'll know everything. And maybe there will be a way he can understand.

"I'm tired," I say. "I'm going to bed."

I push past him, through the living room into the stairwell. I expect him to follow me up to the bedroom, but he doesn't. He stays in the living room, and that's where he spends the rest of the night.

CHAPTER 47

FROM *DEAR DEBBIE* DRAFTS FILE

Dear Debbie,

I think my husband might be cheating on me.

I can't be entirely sure, but all the red flags are there. He is completely uninterested in having sex with me and has been for several months now, even when I try to initiate. Sometimes I'll call him during the day and can't reach him at times when he should be available. On another occasion, he told me he was going out with friends, but when I texted the wife of one of these friends, she said her husband was home with her. And worst of all, I have smelled perfume on him that definitely was not mine!

When I ask him about it, he becomes very defensive. He says he feels hurt that I think he would do something like that.

What do you think? Do you think my husband is cheating on me, or am I being a "jealous wife"?

Sincerely,
Worried Wife

Dear Worried Wife,

I agree that a lot of your husband's behavior is concerning for infidelity. Unfortunately, when a man is cheating, it is common for him to become overly defensive when confronted.

If you are highly suspicious that your husband is cheating on you, one thing you can do is search to see if he has an alternate phone that he's using. Along those lines, he may have an alternate email address. If you can't find anything on your own but you're still suspicious, you may want to consider hiring a private investigator. If your private investigator turns up signs of infidelity, you may then want to consider hiring a lawyer. Or a hit man.

So as you see, you have many options.

Debbie

CHAPTER 48

DEBBIE

The next morning, I make sure to wake Cooper up before the girls come downstairs. It won't help matters if they discover their father sleeping on the couch. He looks at me with bleary eyes, then stumbles upstairs to take a shower or catch up on the sleep he missed during the night. He's holding his back—the sofa is not the most comfortable place to sleep.

Lexi seems to be in slightly better spirits than last night. She isn't crying at least. But like Cooper, she looks tired. She probably tossed and turned a lot during the night, but thankfully, she never discovered that her phone was missing. I managed to return it to her nightstand without waking her.

Izzy, on the other hand, is in a *great* mood. She's back on the soccer team, and she doesn't have to deal with a coach who is always putting her down. I should have gotten rid of Coach Pike ages ago.

I scramble up some eggs and put them on toasted English muffins. I have been making myself fiber cereal every morning, but I throw caution to the wind and make myself an English muffin with eggs as well.

"Would you like a ride to school again?" I ask the girls as I lay the plates of food down on the kitchen table.

"Yes," Izzy says eagerly. She'll never turn down a ride.

Lexi, who isn't even wearing her headphones this morning, nods as well. "Sure. But I've got a physics test first thing in the morning, so I can't be late."

"Do I ever get you there late?" I challenge her.

She flashes me a grudging smile. "Not too often."

"Try *never*." I return her smile as I join them at the table. I am, in fact, habitually prompt. "Anyway, finish your food, and then we'll go."

Lexi looks down at the three plates in front of us, then over her shoulder at the stove. "Aren't you going to make a plate for Dad?"

Well, that's quite the loaded question. I open my mouth, not entirely sure how I'm going to respond, and that's when the doorbell rings.

The sound sets off my nerves. There's nobody who could be waiting at the front door that would have anything good to say. Is it Jo Dolan, wanting me to pay for her extermination bill? Brett Carlson, looking for me to pay for his broken fuse box? Garrett Meers, who hilariously *still* can't seem to get the porn video down from the newspaper website?

"I'll get it," I say.

I abandon my eggs and hurry to the front door, where our visitor seems to be in the process of putting all their weight on our doorbell. And when I get there, my heart sinks. It's somebody far worse than Jo or Brett or Garrett. It's Zane.

217

And he looks *pissed*.

I guess that's not a surprise. I dragged him out in the middle of the night, then he got stood up by his girlfriend who he thought was going to do God knows what with him in a public playground. I wonder what time he woke up on that bench. He's lucky it's a safe area, even in the middle of the night.

Honestly, he has some nerve coming over here after the way he threatened her, but I have to pretend like I don't know about any of this. Lexi would kill me if she had the slightest idea what I did.

"Where's Lexi?" Zane demands to know.

I fold my arms across my chest. "She's eating breakfast at the moment. Can I help you?"

He looks like he's not quite sure what to say. He can't exactly tell me that my daughter stood him up in the middle of the night. So he says the one thing that he can say: "She blocked me on her phone!"

To be fair, *I* blocked him. Because he deserved to be blocked, and also, if I didn't block him, he was going to blow up Lexi's phone with messages asking where she was last night. In the interest of her never finding out what I did, I couldn't let him send her any text messages.

"That's her business," I say tightly. "Do you have any messages you want me to pass on?"

"Yeah." His lower jaw juts out. "Tell her she's a bitch."

I have to admit, that one surprises me. I didn't think he had the gall to say that to my face. But it makes the next thing I have to say so much easier.

"I'll be sure to let her know," I say sarcastically. "Also, I have a little message for you as well, Zane."

He rolls his eyes. "Yeah?"

218

"That's right." I smile brightly. "I just wanted to make sure that you are aware of what happens to a sex offender in prison."

That wipes the smug look right off his face. "What?"

"A sex offender," I repeat. "Like, for instance, somebody who passed around naked photos of a fifteen-year-old girl, which would legally be considered child pornography."

For a moment, there is a flicker of fear in his eyes. "I don't know what you're talking about."

"Oh, I think you do." I raise my eyebrows. "Anyway, if that person were eighteen or older and were to be caught—and these days, digital footprints make it *so* easy to get caught—prison would be a rough time for him. Prison is especially difficult for sex offenders. They often get attacked by other inmates to punish them and elevate their own social status."

Zane takes a step back, nearly stumbling on his own feet. "What?"

"And then when you finally get out," I continue, "you have to put yourself on the sex offender registry everywhere you live for the rest of your life. You have to let your employers know. Any woman you date can look you up and…well, cancel. And good luck finding a place to live when you have to tell landlords you're a sex offender."

"Okay…" Zane is shaking his head, all the anger vanished from his face. He looks decidedly freaked out. "Look, just tell Lexi that I can't drive her to school anymore."

"Will do!" I say cheerfully.

I close the door in his face and return to the kitchen, where my sandwich is still waiting for me. I slide back into my chair and pick up my egg muffin.

"Who was that, Mom?" Lexi wants to know.

"Nobody important."

I take a bite out of the muffin. It's delicious.

CHAPTER 49

COOPER

I've been in a fog all morning.

I don't know where Debbie went last night. I mean, geographically, I know where she went. But I don't know why she would go to the shipyard in the middle of the night or what she was doing there.

I don't think she was out there for a tryst with her lover. Debbie wouldn't do that. She just…she wouldn't. But if that's not what she was doing, then what the hell *was* she doing?

Part of me wanted to confront her in the morning, but instead, I end up avoiding her. I'm dead tired and not in any condition to have a serious discussion right now, and I'm pretty sure this is going to be a *very* serious discussion.

We do have to talk though. I'll lay it all on the table— everything I've been keeping from her. And if she hates me? Well, I hope she doesn't hate me. I hope we can find a way to work through it. I'll do counseling, whatever she wants.

But this needs to come to an end. The lying and sneaking around need to stop.

It's a miracle that I manage to get to work on time. Ken might still be on his fishing trip, but Mrs. McCauley is keeping track of the exact millisecond when each of us arrive and will be reporting back to Ken when he returns. Not that it matters, considering I've already handed in my two weeks' notice. But I don't want to give him an excuse to kick me out even sooner. I desperately need that last paycheck.

(Who am I kidding? I'll probably be on my knees, begging for my job back the second Ken returns to the office.)

When I get to the office, Jesse is standing behind Mrs. McCauley at her desk. The two of them are both staring at her computer screen with identical furrowed brows.

"What's going on?" I ask.

Jesse raises his eyes from the screen. "It looks like there's money missing from the company account."

What?

"Money missing?" I repeat numbly.

Mrs. McCauley peers up at me through her spectacles. "I noticed the discrepancy this morning. Quite a bit has gone missing, and it looks like it's been going on for several months now."

"Are…are you sure?" I stammer.

"Of course I'm sure!" Mrs. McCauley seems offended at the suggestion that she could get anything wrong. She *is* very rarely wrong. "I suppose it's possible that Mr. Bryant moved the money himself. I've been trying to reach him on his phone since I got in, but he's not picking up."

"Well, he's fishing," I point out.

"He usually picks up his phone when he's fishing," she says. "You know how he is about not missing calls."

That's true.

"It was probably him who moved the money," Mrs. McCauley says thoughtfully. "Hopefully at least. It does look like it was done internally."

"Internally?" I repeat. "You mean by someone who works here?"

Jesse looks up at me and grins. "Did you take the money, Coop? Fess up!"

He is joking around, but I have a terrible sinking feeling in my stomach. It doesn't feel like any of this is a coincidence. Ken Bryant randomly disappears on some fishing trip in the middle of the week, and nobody can locate him. And then a bunch of money disappears from the company account, and it looks like an "inside job."

And where does Debbie keep going in the middle of the night?

"I guess you should just keep trying to reach him," I mumble. "He'll want to know about all this right away."

Maybe I'm suspicious over nothing. But I can't seem to push away the feeling that a noose is closing around my neck.

CHAPTER 50

DEBBIE

I've come up with a new idea for a phone app.

It hit me while I was driving back from the shipyard last night. It's called Punish Your Husband.

I spend the whole morning working on it, although it's a little more involved than I initially intended. I've coded half a dozen apps in the last decade, but this one seems like the sort of app that could really take off. And now that I'm no longer working, I've got plenty of time to develop Punish Your Husband. I can't spend every moment of my day working in my garden, tending to my opium poppies.

If I build the app and sell it, I bet I can make a good chunk of change. We could certainly use the money right now.

I wonder what Cooper will think of it.

I've just finished jotting down more ideas when my phone starts ringing. When I see Izzy's name on the screen, I nearly drop the phone trying to answer it. She never calls me during the day. "Izzy?"

"Mom!" Her voice is breathless. "You've got to come pick us up right now!"

"What?" Is it some sort of half day that I'm not aware of? Random half days seem to occur with alarming frequency. "Why?"

"Because," she says, "a kid smashed his car into the school!"

"*What?*" That was the last thing I expected her to say. "How did that happen?"

"I have no idea," Izzy says. "It was some senior guy, and I heard he was really drunk. I don't know what happened, but they're sending everyone home. There's, like, an ambulance and a fire truck and everything."

"Is he okay?"

"I don't think so. I heard he's pretty badly hurt."

"Where's Lexi?"

"She's in her classroom," Izzy says. "We all are. They won't let us leave the classrooms that we're in until someone comes to get us. So you have to come get us."

"I'm on my way. Don't move."

"I can't, Mom! They won't let us!"

I go into emergency mode. I send Lexi a text message to let her know that I'm on my way, because I'm sure she'll be calling next. Then I grab my keys and head for my car. All the while, I try to convince myself that this isn't what I think it is, even though the evidence is concerning.

A boy smashed his car into the school, drunk at nine in the morning. A kid who obviously wasn't thinking straight. He was a senior.

Is it possible that the senior who crashed his car is...

No, it couldn't be.

Although…

I hop in my car and drive as quickly as I can in the direction of the high school.

CHAPTER 51

I make great time driving to the school, but as soon as I get there, it's a mess. There are cars backed up several blocks away, and it only seems to be getting worse. I could have walked to the school ten times over in the time it takes me to drive there.

It looks like they have evacuated the kids from the building, but now they're standing in clusters outside the school with their teachers. When I finally get to the pickup area, a teacher comes to my car window and asks me the names of my children and their grades.

"Isabel Mullen, tenth grade, and Alexa Mullen, twelfth grade," I tell her.

The woman has a clipboard in her hand, and the process happens faster and more efficiently than I anticipated. I thought I'd receive a few wrong kids before my own showed up, but only a minute later, Lexi and Izzy are being herded in the direction of my car. I expect the usual fight for the passenger seat in front, but Lexi goes right for the back seat without a word. Izzy slides into the seat next to me.

I peer in the rearview mirror at my older daughter. Like last night, her eyes are swollen.

"It was Zane!" Izzy announces, her eyes wide. "Zane was the kid who crashed his car!"

"He…he was?"

Despite everything, I'm stunned. After my conversation with Zane, he must have found something to drink and got toasted.

"I heard he got an email calling him to the principal's office," Izzy continues her story without missing a beat. "I guess he was in trouble for something—I don't know what. But we all heard the crash when his car hit. The whole school *shook*."

Wow, I must have really freaked him out with my story about being a sex offender.

"Is he dead?" I ask.

Izzy just shakes her head, and I can hear Lexi sniffling quietly in the back seat. I guess nobody knows. But the fact that an ambulance came seems to indicate that he's probably still alive. For the moment.

"Lexi honey?" I say. "Are you all right?"

She doesn't answer me. Instead, she just sobs, tucked in on herself. I don't understand why she's crying. That asshole was *blackmailing* her. He was threatening to ruin her whole life.

We drive in silence the rest of the way home, broken only by the sound of Lexi's sobs. I don't know what to say, and my experience as the mother of teenage girls is that everything I say is always wrong, so it's better to keep my mouth shut. As they say, it's better to remain quiet and have your teenagers think you're an idiot than open your mouth and say something they can text their friends about.

When we get back into the house, Izzy does that thing where she walks through the door and scrolls through her phone at the same time. After a moment, she looks up.

"He's alive," she says as she perches herself on the edge of the sofa. "They took him to the hospital."

"That's good," I say, and I mean it. Well, kind of.

"But he's badly hurt," she reports. "Jana says he broke his neck."

At this new revelation, Lexi bursts into hysterical tears. Shockingly, she's even more upset than she was last night. Her face is buried in her hands, and her whole body is shaking with sobs.

I don't understand it. Zane was *horrible*. He tricked her into giving him naked pictures of her, and he threatened to show them to the whole school. He was blackmailing her into having sex with him. What part of this makes her *sad* that he's hurt?

"Lexi honey." I put my arm around her shoulders to attempt to comfort her. "Why are you crying?"

"Why am I crying?" she repeats incredulously. "My boyfriend has a broken neck!"

"But last night, you had a problem," I point out, "and now it's fixed."

Lexi looks up at me with her tearstained face, which is frozen in an expression of horror. "Not like *this*," she chokes out.

With those words, she squirms out of my half embrace and runs up the stairs two at a time. The last thing I hear is the door to her room slamming shut so hard that the windows rattle.

Well, I don't get it. She had a problem, and I *fixed* it. I wish somebody had done that for me when I was in trouble. Maybe my whole life would have been different.

In any case, I don't regret what I did. I never told Zane to get drunk and smash his car into the school, for God's sake. Yes, I did indicate how bad it would be to be labeled a sex offender, and I'm sure when he got that email from the principal, it spooked him. But *he* was the one who crashed his car. I didn't have my foot on the gas. Everything that happened was simply…karma.

CHAPTER 52

Lexi doesn't leave her room for the rest of the morning and the early afternoon.

I check on her a few times. I knock on the door, and when she snaps at me to go away, I feel better. If she is angry at me, that's a healthier emotion than feeling sad over that loser who she never should've been dating in the first place. He was never good enough for her. She's an honor student taking four AP classes! As far as I can tell, he barely even bothered to go to class at all, and I overheard him mocking her for wanting to stay in to study.

Good riddance.

I intermittently check the news for updates on Zane. The website for the *Hingham Household* is still just porn, but there are plenty of other news articles about the accident. All the articles I find confirm the story I heard from Izzy. They don't mention that Zane had been called to the principal's office for a disciplinary issue, but I imagine that's something they're trying to keep quiet.

The articles also confirm that he is very much alive, although his injuries do sound serious. One of them mentions a broken neck and says that he has been rushed to emergency surgery.

At about two o'clock, I head upstairs to check on my girls.

I find Izzy studying in her bedroom. She is sitting cross-legged on her bed with a pencil in her mouth. It's actually something that Cooper does, and I find it weirdly endearing that she has picked up this habit from him, either from environment or genetics.

"Izzy," I say. "I have to run an errand. I'll be back in about two hours."

"Okay," she says without looking up.

"Could you keep an eye on your sister for me?"

"Sure, Mom."

"Thanks, sweetie. You're the best."

Izzy has always been the easier child. I fixed her little problem, and she was *grateful*. She didn't run to her bedroom and sob for hours because Coach Pike got arrested.

I stop at Lexi's door next. She still has her door closed, and I knock gently. She doesn't answer, so I knock again.

"Go away," Lexi mumbles. It sounds like her face is stuffed into a bunch of pillows, which it may very well be.

"I'm going out for a bit," I say. "I just wanted to let you know."

"Okay," she says through the door. "Try not to kill anyone."

I stifle a smile. She has no idea.

There is one very big problem I need to fix, and after I do that, maybe I'll be able to sleep through the night again. After nearly half a century of life, I've realized that the only person who is truly looking out for my best interests is myself.

CHAPTER 53

The trip takes about an hour and change, driving up I-95 north through the South Shore. It will be longer on the way back, but if I can be finished before rush hour, it might not be too bad. If I get stuck in rush-hour traffic, it will take an eternity.

But I'm not in a hurry.

I haven't made this trip in the entire time I've been living on the South Shore. We're far enough from Cambridge that there's no reason to. And although Cooper doesn't know why I left MIT, he senses there's a reason I don't want to go back, and he has never suggested it.

But today, I am on the highway, headed in the direction of Cambridge. Except I'm not going to the MIT campus. I'm going to an off-campus house. One that I never thought I would return to.

Zeta Pi. The fraternity house that has haunted my dreams since that night during my freshman year.

I've gotten so good at pretending that the night that

ruined my life never happened. But over the last year, I can't stop thinking about it. It's become an obsession for me. I feel like I'm losing my mind.

I need to do this. I will never feel at peace while this house is still standing.

It's just after three o'clock when I pull up in front of the large house on the border between Brookline and Cambridge. There's a parking spot just down the street, and I snag it before anyone else can or before I change my mind. I kill the engine and then sit there in the car, summoning up all my courage.

I'm braver than I was when I was nineteen. I'm stronger too. I can do this.

So I grab my purse and get out of the car.

The house looks different than I remember. It's smaller, for starters. When I walked in there the night of that party all those years ago, it seemed gigantic. But now it doesn't seem so much bigger than any other on the street. It's made out of grayish-brown bricks with white columns lining the entrance. The doors are a stark white color, and there's a sign over the entrance with the words ZETA PI in calligraphy with the Greek letters beneath. There are five steps to the front door, and my legs feel heavy as I climb them.

When I reach the door, I press my index finger into the doorbell. The chimes ring throughout the house. And I wait.

The door is eventually opened by a clean-cut young man wearing a navy MIT T-shirt and a pair of blue jeans. His hair hangs a bit in his eyes the same way Hutch's did on the night I can't forget. I hate the kid instantly.

"Hey," the boy says. "Can I help you?"

"I hope so," I say in a chipper voice. "My name is Nicole Quint, and I'm writing an article for the *Cambridge Chronicle* about MIT fraternities. Would it be okay if I came in to chat a bit?"

The *Chronicle* is a weekly paper that mostly does puff pieces and definitely no hard-hitting journalism. I had been slightly concerned the boy might quiz me on the article before letting me in, and I had prepared answers on the way over, but instead, his face creases into an eager smile.

"Sure!" He steps aside to let me enter the frat house. "Come on in!"

I smile up at him as I enter the house where I experienced the worst night of my life. "Thank you very much."

CHAPTER 54

COOPER

The day moves slowly.

It seems like five o'clock will never come. Mrs. McCauley often leaves as early as three o'clock on Fridays, but maybe because of the missing money, she is staying later, so there's no chance of sneaking out.

Worse, she keeps stealing looks at me like she doesn't trust me. At one point, she followed me into the break room and stared at me while I heated up my Cup Noodles in the microwave. I had planned to eat in the break room, but I ended up taking the food back to my office and closing the door behind me.

It's about half past three when my phone starts ringing on my desk. When I see Lexi's name on the screen, I feel a jolt of surprise, followed by worry. Lexi *never* calls me. Her generation doesn't seem to make many calls in general, but I can't even remember the last time she placed a call to me in particular. If she needed anything, she'd almost certainly call Debbie before me.

Then again, Debbie has been acting very strangely lately. Maybe Lexi feels uncomfortable reaching out to her with a problem. I know the feeling.

I reach for my phone and click on the green button to take the call. "Lexi?"

"Dad?" There's a tremor in her voice. "Where are you?"

That's a strange question. It's three o'clock on a Friday afternoon. Where does she think I'd be? "I'm at work. Why?"

"Do…do you think you can come home? Like, now?"

I look down at my watch, knowing that it's way too early to leave with Mrs. McCauley keeping watch. "Is it an emergency?"

"Kind of." She sounds much younger than her seventeen years. My kids are both teenagers, but they sound like babies on the phone. "I think there's something wrong with Mom."

What?

I clear my throat, trying not to jump to conclusions. Debbie and I have always taken a united front when it comes to parenting. I don't want to betray her. "What do you mean?"

"It's just a bunch of things that have happened," she says. "And it's all…it's making us think Mom has, like, gone all vigilante."

"Gone all *vigilante*?"

"So Izzy got kicked off the soccer team," she says, "and then the very next day, Coach Pike gets *arrested*."

I suck in a breath, not wanting to admit my own suspicions about that night. "Well, I'm sure it was a coincidence."

"Yeah," she says, "but then last night, I was telling Mom about some…problems I was having with Zane. And then this morning, he…he drove his car into the school." Her voice breaks. "He's in the hospital now."

I nearly choke. "He *what*?"

"She didn't tell you?" Lexi blinks her suddenly damp eyes in surprise. "It happened this morning. She had to pick me and Izzy up from school."

No, Debbie didn't happen to mention that our daughter's boyfriend was in a serious car wreck. Apparently, it didn't seem important enough to tell me about.

Christ, what happened to us?

"And then," Lexi continues.

Oh God, there's *more*?

"I had to print this thing out for school, and my printer wasn't working. So I went downstairs to use Mom's desktop. And she had this document open on the screen, and it was…really weird."

"What do you mean by 'really weird'?"

"Um, I think you better come home and take a look, Dad."

I get a sick feeling in the pit of my stomach. I'm not sure if I even want to know. But it's pretty clear I'm not going to get any work done.

"Where's your mother?" I ask.

"I don't know," Lexi admits. "She said she was going on an errand, and that was, like, an hour and a half ago. She's not back yet."

An *errand*? Like the *errands* she went on the last two nights?

I open the Findly app on my phone to see where she went. But when I click on it, the last known location for

Debbie updated two hours ago. She must've turned off location sharing.

She doesn't want me to know where she went, and that scares the shit out of me.

"I'll be home in a minute," I tell Lexi. "Don't worry. Everything's going to be fine."

I can lie to my children too, apparently.

CHAPTER 55

I drive twenty miles over the speed limit all the way home.

I don't know what is in this document on Debbie's computer, but I can't pretend anymore that there isn't something seriously wrong with my wife. I agree with Lexi—it seems like Debbie is getting vigilante justice on everybody in her life who has wronged her or her family.

And I'm worried that I might have made the list.

I park at a weird angle in the driveway, but I don't bother to correct it. I leap out of my car and head for the front door. I've barely got my key in the lock before Lexi yanks it open.

Both Lexi and Izzy are waiting for me with identical expressions of concern on their faces. Not just concern but something else. Like they're counting on me to fix everything wrong in our lives. They haven't looked at me that way since they were little.

And clearly, there's still no sign of Debbie. I checked

my phone to see if her location popped up before I started driving home, but no luck.

What could she be doing? I suspect this document on her computer will be another disturbing piece of the puzzle.

"I don't know what she did to Zane," Lexi says to me as I shut the door behind me. "But I know it was something."

"How do you know?"

"Because she basically told me." She squeezes her white fists together. "When we got home from school, she told me she 'fixed' my problem." A few tears squeeze out from her brown eyes, which I now notice are bloodshot. "But I never wanted her to do that! I never wanted Zane to get *hurt.*"

I look over at Izzy next, who says, "I'm also worried about Mom. But I'm okay with Coach Pike being in jail. He was a dick."

Good to know.

"Let me take a look at the computer," I say, trying to sound collected.

Debbie's computer is in the living room. Both the girls have laptops, but Debbie wanted to buy a desktop, with a whole complicated explanation about how she felt you could get more power for a similar price. I don't argue with Debbie when it comes to technology, so she went ahead and bought one.

I sit down in the ergonomic chair in front of the computer. I move the mouse, and the screen jumps to life. A message prompts me for a password, and I look up at Lexi.

"It's the date of Izzy's birthday, then mine," Lexi tells me.

Well, shit. I look up at her helplessly.

"Dad!" Lexi cries.

"Okay, okay."

I do know this. I'm supposed to be good with numbers, but somehow, I can never seem to keep birthdays straight. Finally, I type in 1523, and thank God I get in, because I'm pretty sure neither of them would've spoken to me for the next week if I got it wrong.

There's a folder titled "Dear Debbie" on the desktop. I click on it, and it's filled with Word documents. I click on one of them. It appears to be a letter addressed to Dear Debbie, followed by her reply.

"It's just her column," I say. "What's the problem?"

"It's her column," Lexi confirms, "but read her answers to the letters. They are really, really weird."

I look at the question posted on the screen.

Dear Debbie,

Oh, I do so love to knit. There's just something so peaceful about sitting in the rocking chair on my porch with my yarn and needles, a cool glass of iced tea at my side. My daughter loves the little gifts I make for my grandbabies, and all my friends appreciate the scarves I gift them for holidays. But my husband just doesn't see the charm in it.

Last winter I knitted him a lovely blue scarf that was as soft and warm as could be, but that man didn't even wear it once! Not even to humor me! But he'll wear department store scarves like they're made of gold. I'm not one to kick up a fuss, but it would warm my heart to see him happily wearing one of my homemade gifts.

Any suggestions to convince my husband that my homemade scarf, knitted with love, is as good—if not better—than the one he bought in the store?

Knitting Nancy

Dear Knitting Nancy,

The next time the two of you are going out together on a chilly day, why not suggest that he wear your scarf? If he's reluctant, you can get it out and wrap it around his neck yourself. If you wrap it tightly enough, he probably won't be able to take it off. And if you wrap it even tighter, he won't be able to complain anymore. Feel free to wrap that scarf as tightly around his neck as needed!

Debbie

My mouth drops open. I admit, I don't read Debbie's column every single week, but I'm fairly sure I've never seen anything like *this* printed in it. Usually her advice involves getting out stains or suggestions for a movie night. It's pretty tame.

It doesn't usually involve strangulation.

Clearly, this was never published. This is a draft she wrote and saved on her hard drive, except I'm not sure why. Did she respond to Knitting Nancy personally? Are the two of them currently swapping advice on asphyxiation?

"I read most of the files," Lexi tells me. "Like eighty percent of them are instructions on how to kill your husband." She pauses. "Did you do something to piss Mom off?"

Shit.

"No," I lie.

"Dad, do you think Mom has lost her mind?" Izzy asks in a small voice.

"I…I don't know." At the crestfallen look on her face, I quickly add, "I'm sure she's fine. She's just going through a hard time."

I click on the files one by one. It doesn't get better. It gets *worse*, in fact. Debbie has come up with a *lot* of creative ways to advise women to kill their husbands.

I reach for my phone. I check the Findly app again, but it still has no updates since she left the house. I click on her name in my contacts and wait as the phone rings. And rings.

"Is she answering?" Izzy asks me.

"Does it *sound* like I'm talking to someone?" Immediately, I regret snapping. This isn't Izzy's fault. "No, she's not picking up."

Her face falls.

The call goes to voicemail, and I leave a message: "Debbie? It's me. It's Cooper." Why do I think she won't know who "me" is? But right now, I truly don't know what's going through her head. "I really need to talk to you. I found… Anyway, please call me as soon as you get this. Please." I take a deep breath. "And don't…don't do anything stupid."

I hang up, and both the girls are hovering behind me at the computer, staring at me with alarm. I probably should have played it cooler for the phone message and reserved the panic for texts. But I can't help it. What the *hell* is Debbie doing? Where is she?

"Maybe you should see where Mom went earlier?" Lexi suggests.

I shake my head. "What do you mean?"

"Like, in the Findly app she made," she says. "Check where she went yesterday and the day before."

"Wait, I thought you could only see her current location?"

"Oh, Dad," Lexi sighs. "You are *such* a boomer."

What? I don't have time to figure out her Gen Z insult. I thrust my phone in her direction. "Show me what you mean."

Lexi takes my phone and shows me that if you click on the icon of Debbie's face, there are three dots that pop up. She clicks on them, and it brings up a series of locations.

"See?" she says. "It shows everywhere she's been for the last week if she has stopped there for at least ten minutes."

Holy crap. I didn't know the app could do that. My wife is very talented.

I scroll through the list of places she visited before turning off her location sharing. Most of them are easily recognizable and not concerning. There's the school. The plant store. The grocery store. Titan Fitness. That house in Weymouth where Robert Pike lives. The Hingham Shipyard.

And then two other locations that don't fit into any of those categories.

Oh shit. Oh no.

"Dad?" Lexi says when she sees the look on my face.

I bring up the list of my contacts on my phone and click on one of my favorites. I say a prayer to myself that I'll hear someone pick up on the other end of the line, but it's not a surprise when it goes to voicemail. Even so, I call one more time for good measure.

This is very bad.

I stand up abruptly from the chair, and it rolls several feet out of the way, crashing into our sofa. "I have to go."

Lexi and Izzy exchange looks. "Go where?" Lexi asks.

"I'll be home as soon as I can." I pat my pockets to confirm my keys and phone are there. "And if your mom calls or comes home, call me right away."

· "Dad, where are you going?" Lexi presses me.

I can't tell them though. What I suspect is too awful for words.

"I'll be back soon" is all I can say.

I can only pray that I've got it all wrong.

CHAPTER 56

DEBBIE

The boy steps aside to let me enter the fraternity house. He has an open, friendly expression on his face, because he has no idea what I'm planning to do. If he knew, he wouldn't let me past the front door. Actually, he'd probably be calling the police.

"My name is Lennox," he tells me. "I'm the president of the fraternity."

"Is Lennox your first name or last name?"

He laughs. He seems sweet and earnest, but so did Hutch. "First name. My last name is Newberry."

"Like the comic store."

He nods. "No relation."

I look around the small space of the living area. It contains a few ratty sofas that look like they came from the curb and a coffee table with books stacked on it. The top one is labeled *Statistical Thermodynamics*. This place looked so different on that night that changed my life. If somebody transported me here and didn't tell me where I was, I never would've known. I suppose it looks different when it's nighttime, filled with loud music and the stink of alcohol and cigarettes in the air.

"So what's the article about?" he asks me.

"It's just a profile of fraternity life," I explain. "We picked Zeta Pi randomly, and we just want to know what it's like to live here."

I expect him to remark on the fact that it sounds like a very boring article, but instead he nods like this is completely reasonable.

"Do you want a tour?" Lennox offers.

I hesitate. I do want a tour. That's part of the reason I'm here, but part of me is scared that I might get triggered, remembering what happened to me that night. The last thing I want is to have a panic attack in this frat house.

But I came here for a purpose. And I'm not leaving until my work is done.

"I'd love a tour," I tell him.

Lennox smiles eagerly, gesturing around the room we're standing in. "This is our living area," he says. "We spend a lot of time hanging out here, mostly talking. We have our meetings in the basement."

"Is the basement where you have parties?" I ask, trying to keep the edge out of my voice.

If Lennox notices the subtone, he doesn't let on. "Yeah. It's a big open space so it's perfect for parties. We don't get *too* wild though. It's MIT after all."

He laughs at his own joke, but I don't join him.

"All the fraternity brothers here are friends," he tells me. "Some are obviously closer than others, but I consider every member of Zeta Pi to be my brother. We look out for each other."

"And if one of you did something wrong, for example"—I poise my pen at the notepad I cleverly grabbed at a drugstore on the way over here—"would all the brothers be held accountable?"

He takes a moment to think over that question. "Yes, I think we are. Every member of Zeta Pi represents all of us. If one of us does something wrong, that's a reflection on the entire fraternity."

I wonder if the other brothers knew what Hutch was up to. I highly doubt it was the first time he did something like that. He was so smooth. In retrospect, it was all very rehearsed.

If one of us does something wrong, that's a reflection on the entire fraternity. If the other brothers knew Hutch was doing something wrong, they would have covered it up. They wouldn't want his actions to reflect badly on all of them. A fraternity could have their charter revoked over something like that.

Lennox takes me around the first floor of the house. He shows me the kitchen and a little backyard area. It's all interminably dull, but I pretend to be enthralled by everything he shows me. The tour of the ground floor ends at the base of a flight of stairs.

"Most of our members live in the house," he explains. "Do you want to see the rooms? They will likely be pretty empty since everyone is in class now."

I would rather eat glass, but I know that I have to go with him. I can't do this if I don't. "That would be great, thanks."

I follow Lennox up the stairs to the second floor with a feeling of doom in the pit of my stomach. The last time I climbed these same stairs, it was about twenty-five years ago. I didn't know what was about to happen and that my whole life was about to change.

"So like I said," he continues at the top of the stairs, completely oblivious, "most of our members live in the house. We have bunk beds, so it's a little tight, but it's worth it to be able to live with your brothers. Would you like to see one of the rooms?"

"Yes," I squeak out.

He takes me down the hallway, and the first room on the left is already cracked open. He pushes the door the rest of the way open to reveal a small room with a bunk bed and two desks. In a way, it looks like a standard college dorm room. Nothing special.

But it's nearly identical to the room I was in that night. So much so that my head starts to spin.

Please stop!

Don't worry. This will be over in a minute.

My heart starts to race. I feel suddenly lightheaded—there's a very distinct possibility I might faint. Lennox is droning on about the course load at MIT and how he still has PTSD from his operating systems class last semester. "I can't even go in that building anymore," he jokes.

I take deep breaths, trying to get myself under control. This is just a college frat house room. Nothing more. It can't hurt me anymore.

You can do this, Debbie. You're stronger than you were when you were nineteen.

"Hey." Lennox stops his monologue when the pad of paper falls from my fingers, splaying out on the floor. "Are you okay? You look kind of pale."

"Fine." I gulp in another breath as I bend down to

251

pick up the pad of my chicken scratch. "I skipped lunch. Stupid me."

He smiles sympathetically. "We can wrap things up if you want. Really, the only thing left to see is the basement. We can skip that though, if you'd like."

"No." I square my shoulders. The lightheaded feeling has passed, and my sense of resolve has returned. I have come this far, and I'm not about to turn back. "Let's finish the tour."

I take one more look around the room. It looks like any other college frat house room, but one thing catches my attention: the lighter on one of the two desks. I hadn't necessarily expected to see one, but now that I have, I know that this will be the room that I must return to.

Lennox leads me back out of the room, but before I leave, I casually drop my purse on the desk closest to the door. He doesn't see me do it, but when the tour ends, I will explain to him that I accidentally left it behind, and he'll let me come back up here to retrieve it.

That's when I will burn down Zeta Pi.

Today, I will end this.

CHAPTER 57

COOPER

Debbie went to Ken Bryant's house.

I don't know why, but Debbie was at Ken's house yesterday. Findly doesn't say the exact time she was there, but I recognize the address. I'm trying to think of a benign reason why she could've been at the home of my soon-to-be former boss who is supposedly on a fishing trip right now.

I can't think of any.

My daughters are looking at me with concern as I head back out the front door and climb into my car. I want to reassure them that everything is going to be okay, but with each passing moment, I feel less and less sure that this is the case.

But it could be fine. Maybe Debbie just went there to talk to Ken about the job and asked him to consider letting me stay. I'm sure that's all it was.

Actually, no, I'm not sure of that at all.

Ken lives in a nice house in Hingham, about a

ten-minute drive from our place. He has kids, although they're both now in college. He's also married, although he rarely talks about his wife, and I get the feeling they may have separated at some point. So it's entirely possible that Ken now lives alone in that big house.

When I get there, the house looks quiet. The lights all appear to be out, and there's no car in his driveway, but that doesn't mean he doesn't have one parked in the garage. At the very least, it doesn't appear that there are any signs of life.

I park on the street and get out of my car, holding my breath the whole time. The most likely explanation for the dark house is that Ken is on a fishing trip. Debbie probably came here to plead my case, discovered he wasn't home, and then left.

But Lexi told me that the app only records addresses that she stopped at for more than ten minutes. So if Ken wasn't home, what was she doing for ten whole minutes?

I stop at the front door and ring the doorbell. The chimes echo within the house, but when the sound dies down, it's completely quiet. It's clear that nobody is going to come to answer the door.

I know from when I watered Ken's plants for him that he hides a key outside the house. A lot of people do that in our neighborhood, but Debbie won't let us. She insists that they're too easy to find and somebody could sneak into our home without difficulty. As I'm checking under the potted plants near his front porch and discover a little bronze key, I have to agree with her.

I return to the front door, this time armed with a key. As I'm fitting it into the lock, I question what I'm doing. I am basically breaking into my boss's house. He didn't tell me to water his plants, and he most certainly did not give me permission to enter his home. Even though I have a key, this is breaking and entering.

But after seeing this location in Debbie's history, I can't leave here without checking the house. I have probable cause to enter, although I realize that, legally, that excuse only applies to the police.

Like the outside of his house, the inside of Ken's house is eerily quiet. The lights are out, and it's so silent, you could hear a pin drop. There's still enough daylight left for me to be able to look around at his living room, which is a lot nicer than mine. He can afford all the best furniture and a television that looks about twice the size of mine.

"Ken!" I call out.

Unsurprisingly, there's no answer.

I don't know what I expected to find here. My boss's dead body lying bludgeoned in the middle of the living room? He's clearly not here. He's probably fishing, just like he said he was.

As for Debbie, I don't know what she was doing here, but she clearly didn't come here to trash the place. The living room is immaculate.

For the first time since I saw this address on the screen of my phone, I feel myself relaxing. Okay, Debbie has been acting strangely lately, and we seem to be temporarily unable to locate her. But she didn't *hurt* anyone. She hasn't completely gone off the deep end.

Everything is going to be fine.

And I would have kept on believing that. I would have turned around and gone home, secure in the knowledge that all was hunky-dory at Ken Bryant's house, except at that very moment, I hear a phone ringing.

And it's not a landline. It's a very distinctive cell phone ring. It's coming from the direction of the sofa.

I approach the leather sofa in the corner of the room, which seems to be the source of the ringing sound. It's only when I get closer that I see there is a phone nearly concealed by one of the couch cushions. I pick it up and find Mrs. McCauley's name flashing on the screen.

After another second, the call goes to voicemail. The lock screen alerts me to multiple missed messages and voicemails, mostly from Mrs. McCauley, that have arrived over the last two days.

Would Ken have gone on a fishing trip without his cell phone? I suppose it's possible. Maybe he wanted to unplug for a few days. But to be honest, that doesn't sound like Ken. He is *never* without his phone. And even if he did decide to leave his phone behind, wouldn't he have plugged it in to charge?

There's something wrong here.

My gaze falls on the stairwell to the second floor. I had planned to leave without investigating further, but now my curiosity is piqued. I'm already in the house. I need to check out the second floor.

I place Ken's phone on the coffee table and head in the direction of the stairwell.

CHAPTER 58

DEBBIE

I've never committed arson before.

I've never even thought about it. I get anxious when I have the flame too high on the stove. I don't even like to barbecue steaks, much less an entire frat house.

I thought putting things right with Zane would make me feel better. I thought it would ease the pressure that's been building up in my head. But nothing was fixed. I'm glad I was able to help my daughter with her problem, but my own problems were still there. The house where my life fell apart was quite literally *still there*.

And then the idea occurred to me that I could burn down Zeta Pi. I could light up that house and let it burn to the ground.

It brought me a sense of peace like something I hadn't felt in over twenty-five years.

I don't want anyone to get hurt. That's why I came here in the middle of the afternoon, when most of the students are likely to be in class. Part of me feels like the boys at this fraternity deserve whatever is coming to them, but I don't know that for sure. Hutch graduated a long time ago, and so did any of his brothers who were protecting him. I don't want to kill anyone innocent.

Nestled within my purse is a cigarette taped to a book of matches. Before I leave the fraternity house, I will tell Lennox that I forgot my purse upstairs. I'll run to get it, use the lighter on the desk to light the cigarette, and place it in the bed of the boy who owns the lighter. That's the best chance to make it look like an accident.

I'll also lay the cigarette and matches on a couple of pieces of paper. I had some in my purse just in case, but I also saw a few scraps of paper on the desk, and if I use those, it will be more authentic. As the cigarette burns down, it will ignite the matches, and they will in turn ignite the paper, and that will ignite the bedsheets. At that point, the fire will spread quickly.

I'll be long gone by then.

Lennox leads me back to the first floor, and then he opens the door to the basement. He referred to this as the room where they have their meetings, but it's clearly also the room where they have their parties. I would recognize that even if I hadn't been to a party in this very room.

"As you can see, it's a wide-open space." He gestures at a few couches pushed against the wall, and there's even a makeshift stage at the front of the room. "We host a few coffee shop nights here with an open mic. It's pretty fun."

"Sounds fun," I say, barely listening.

He tilts his head. "Do you want to get any photos or anything?"

I don't want to seem suspicious. He's giving me the entire tour, and it does probably seem weird that I'm not taking any pictures. "Definitely," I say. "I'm getting the article written first, but our photographer will be in touch next week for a shoot."

Lennox accepts this explanation without question. "Oh great."

I look around the room again, and there are several posters mounted on the walls. My eyes fall on the poster nearest to me. In big block letters, it says, DO NOT LEAVE YOUR DRINK UNATTENDED.

Lennox sees me staring at the poster. "We have that up for parties," he explains.

I arch an eyebrow. "Oh?"

"Nationwide, the risk of sexual assault is higher at fraternity and sorority parties." To my surprise, he seems very eager to talk about this touchy subject. I would have thought a frat brother would avoid it like the plague. "We take it *very* seriously here. We don't have punch bowls, and we encourage female guests to drink from cans or bottles that haven't been opened yet. And during parties, we close off the upper floors, so nobody's getting up to the bedrooms. All partygoers are in a place where we can see them."

"But you can't prevent sexual assault entirely," I point out.

"Maybe not." Lennox's eyes flash. "But I'm president of Zeta Pi, and nothing like that is going to happen in this house while I am in charge. If I ever suspected that one of our brothers was trying to roofie a girl or take advantage, we'd investigate. Anyone who did that…they would be *gone.*"

He sounds like he means it. Of course, he thinks I'm a reporter and all this is going in an article. What is he supposed to say? *Our members roofie girls all the time! It's so fun!* It's hard to imagine much has changed since I was a student here. Boys are still boys.

But he does have that poster on the wall. And he brought it up without me even having to ask, with solid rules in place that sound…well, *real*. He sounded furious at the idea of any kind of sexual assault happening under this roof.

"Anyway," Lennox says, "that concludes the grand tour. I don't think there's anything else to show you, but I'm happy to answer any questions if you'd like."

"No," I say, "I've seen enough."

We return to the first floor, and he escorts me to the exit. He offers me an endearing grin. "I'd love to see the article when it comes out," he says. "Will you send us a copy?"

"Absolutely," I say. "I'll send it to Zeta Pi, care of Lennox Newberry, like the comic store."

He laughs. "You got it."

Then we're at the front door. It's now or never. I came here for justice, and this could be my only shot.

"Oh shoot." I look down at my right arm and shake my head. "Silly me—I forgot my purse upstairs. I think I put it down on a desk when I started feeling a little loopy."

"Whoops," Lennox says. "You better go get it. Do you need me to show you upstairs again?"

What a *gentleman*. But that won't be necessary. "No. I know exactly where I left it. I'll just be two minutes."

"Okay," he says without even a trace of suspicion. "I've got a ton of studying to do for my thermodynamics exam on Monday, so I'm just gonna be on the sofa over here getting back to it."

Lennox plops down on the sofa, grabbing the heavy textbook and a pack of highlighters. He doesn't seem the slightest bit concerned with me anymore. After all, I look completely innocent. I probably remind him of his mother.

He's not even looking at me as I climb the stairs to the second floor.

CHAPTER 59

COOPER

I climb the stairs to the second floor.

I've never been on the second floor of Ken's house. In fact, I've only been here twice before, both times to water his plants when he wasn't around. He doesn't entertain, at least not for coworkers, and I suspect not at all. I've never met his wife, and he's never met Debbie.

When I get to the top of the stairs, I am presented with five doors, one of which is slightly ajar. The others are closed. I start with the one that is open, and I quickly discover this is a bathroom. I flick on the lights, and it's empty. No blood in the sink, no dead bodies lying in the bathtub—just a normal, ordinary bathroom that doesn't look like it's been used recently. Maybe Ken really did just go out of town for a few days and leave his phone behind.

I work my way down the hallway after that. I check the first room, which is a small room with a twin bed inside and posters on the wall of a band I've never heard of called Glass Animals. I assume this is the room of one of his children who has gone to college. The next room I check also has a teenage vibe to it, and I quickly move on.

The next room contains a neatly made double bed and a small dresser. If I had to guess, this is a guest room. It doesn't look like anybody has lived in this room in a long time. Ken isn't one to entertain.

There's only one more. Based on the last three rooms I checked, this must be the master bedroom. If I look in there and it's empty, I can feel comfortable saying that wherever Ken is, he is not in this house.

(Actually, there's still the attic. But I'm not going up *there* unless I hear screams or something.)

I turn the knob of the last door with my right hand. I notice immediately that this room is darker than the others, because all the curtains have been drawn. There's nothing intrinsically suspicious about it, but I am filled with a sudden sensation of dread. I push the door the rest of the way open.

And I fall to my knees.

I thought that if I saw something truly horrible, I would scream. But at this moment, there are no sounds coming out of my mouth. I can only stare at the motionless body of my boss lying on the bed, his eyes cracked open, his jaw slack, and a bullet hole in the center of his forehead.

He's dead. And he's probably been dead for a while. At least since yesterday morning, when he didn't show up for work.

I can't seem to make myself get back on my feet. A wave of nausea washes over me, and it takes everything I have not to throw up. I put my head between my legs, taking big gulps of air.

Ken is dead. Somebody shot him. Somebody murdered him.

And I can't forget the reason I'm here in the first place. Because my phone told me that Debbie had been here.

But that doesn't mean Debbie was responsible for this. It seems like Ken might've been going through a divorce, based on the complete absence of his spouse and some comments I heard from Mrs. McCauley. *She* could be the one responsible. Or…a burglar! A burglar could have shot him. *Anything* would make more sense than Debbie murdering Ken because he wouldn't promote me. She doesn't even own a gun.

Okay, I've got to calm down. I've got to pull myself together and call the police to tell them what happened.

And then, just as I'm reaching for my phone, another thought occurs to me. One that stops me in my tracks.

It's true that Debbie doesn't own a gun. But *I've* got one. It's registered in my name. And my fingerprints are all over it.

I suck in a breath.

I thought that Debbie might have come here to ask Ken to give me my job back. And I thought there was a chance that when he refused, she got angry and did something terrible. But now that I'm thinking more clearly, I realize that given the guy was shot in his bedroom, it seems unlikely that Debbie was having a conversation with him that went awry. If Debbie *is* responsible for this, her motivations were very different from what I originally thought.

Shit.

I've got to get out of here. I've got to check my garage.

CHAPTER 60

DEBBIE

I speed down I-95 south in the direction of home, a pop station blasting on the radio. I spent more time than I anticipated at the fraternity house, but I have completed my task, and now I'm ready for the next step in my healing.

I have to teach someone a lesson he will never forget.

I turned my phone off when I got close to the frat house because I didn't want there to be any chance someone could prove I was there at the time of the fire. When I turned it back on after leaving, there were dozens of phone and text messages from Cooper. He's frantic to reach me. The last one was in all caps.

DEBBIE PLEASE CALL ME!!! I'M SO SORRY FOR EVERYTHING!!!!!

Hmm, a little late for that, isn't it? But fine. He's so, so *sorry*. I'll deal with him soon enough.

A few minutes after I get on the highway, my dash

screen announces a call coming in from Harley. It's sort of a coincidence, because I had been planning to call her myself, so this saves me the trouble.

"Hi, Harley," I say.

"Debbie!" She's likely at home, based on the lack of noise in the background. "I know it's kind of last minute, but do you have any interest in coming over for dinner tonight?"

I smile. Cooper and the kids can call out for pizza tonight. "That sounds great. Are you cooking?"

"Absolutely! Any *allergies*?"

I laugh. "No, I'll eat anything you make."

"Great! Can you be here by six?"

With the amount of traffic on the road, that sounds about right. It's going to be a slow drive back to the South Shore. "Sure."

"Wonderful! I can't wait!"

I'll just bet.

That girl has some nerve. She really thinks that I don't have any idea what she's doing. When I first met her, I thought she was "cool," and I was stupidly excited to make a new friend. I thought maybe after all these years, I found somebody I could confide in.

How could I have been so wrong?

Harley isn't my friend. She is a terrible person.

I glance at the glove compartment of the car, which contains the gun I've been carrying around for the last couple of days since I took it from its hiding place. Whenever I touch it, I put on a pair of leather gloves, careful to keep my fingerprints from rubbing off on it and careful to preserve the prints that are already on it.

Tonight will be the last time I use the gun. The next time someone picks it up, it will be evidence.

CHAPTER 61

COOPER

I need to get out of Ken's house as quickly as I can.

He's got a fence encircling his property, so hopefully the neighbors did not see me. It's about five o'clock, close to dinnertime, and people probably aren't paying much attention to this house anyway. They're focused on getting home to their own families.

I consider wiping down anything I might have touched in the house. I can't remember what I touched though. I definitely touched the doorknob and the front door, but that could be easily explained. He's my boss after all. It's not suspicious that I would have been in his house.

There's his phone though. I would have trouble explaining why my fingerprints are on that.

I find his phone where I left it on the coffee table. I want to get out of here, but I've got to wipe this down, or else it's going to look really bad for me. I go into his kitchen and grab a paper towel. This shouldn't take long.

Unfortunately, wiping fingerprints off a phone proves

to be more difficult than I thought. If I had gloves, it would be easy, but attempting to wipe it down without touching it *more* during the process seems impossible. I am tempted to search his kitchen to see if he has any rubber gloves I can borrow, but what if I got fingerprints on *that*?

I do the best I can. I wipe one side, then I hold it around the edges to flip it onto the other side and wipe it down while it's lying on the coffee table. I can't guarantee there isn't a partial print left behind, but I'm wasting too much time. I've got to get out of here—now.

I think about slipping out the back, but that seems like it could be worse. Someone sneaking out the back could be more suspicious to the neighbors. Better to just walk out the front door as casually as I can. It's dinnertime, and a person entering or leaving a neighbor's house shouldn't attract much attention.

But as I'm going out the front door, I notice something I hadn't seen when I came in. Something that makes me realize I shouldn't have been quite as concerned about the neighbors.

There's a door cam.

A camera is mounted over the door, which captured me entering the house and now leaving. I was worried about the neighbors, but this camera will tell the police everything they need to know. I am beginning to realize how screwed I am.

But wait. Ken must've been shot at least a day ago. The police will match up the camera feed with the time I'm here, and they will recognize that it does not coincide with the time of his death. Maybe this will be fine. I can pretend that I came in here to water his plants, and I never went upstairs.

Again, a voice in the back of my head is telling me that I should just call the police and let them deal with it. And I will.

But first I have to get home and check my garage.

I walk as briskly as I can over to my car and jump into the driver's seat. I grasp the steering wheel with both hands, taking deep breaths to calm myself down. I need to get a hold of myself. I'm not going to make the situation better if I get in a car crash.

I think about Coach Pike, who dared to kick Izzy off the soccer team, and now he's in jail. Then I think about Lexi's boyfriend, Zane, who is lying in a hospital bed with a broken neck.

I reach into my pocket for my phone. I send off a text message, then I start driving.

CHAPTER 62

HARLEY

Debbie will be here soon.

I'm cooking spaghetti for dinner. I have a feeling she's not going to be very hungry, but I have to make something. That's what a good hostess does after all.

Tonight, I'm going to tell Debbie everything.

I'm sick of sneaking around with Cooper. I prefer more *mature* men, and it just so happens that a large chunk of them are already married. Over the last decade, the only one who was ever willing to leave his wife for me was Edgar, and *that* was a huge bust. I can't stand it anymore. When you're the other woman, you're always second-best. Even if they pretend they like you better than their wives, you're always just their dirty little secret.

Well, I'm sick of being a dirty little secret.

Debbie needs to know that her husband has been messing around behind her back. It might seem cruel to spill the beans, especially since she thinks of me as her friend, but really, it's cruel not to. She deserves the truth.

For months now, Cooper has been telling me that he doesn't love her anymore. He says they're like strangers and barely talk. He admitted that he no longer finds her attractive, and he has no interest in having sex with her anymore. He said they haven't had sex in years.

He's grateful to me for coming into his life. He says it every time we're together. His kids are almost grown, so there's no reason for him to stay with Debbie. He needs to leave her and start fresh with me.

But none of this will happen if Debbie remains in the dark. She needs to understand that her marriage is over.

And I will be the one to tell her.

As I stir the pot of spaghetti, I wonder how she'll take it. Will she cry? Am I going to have to *comfort* her while she cries? Oh God, I really don't want to.

I'd prefer if she got mad. Maybe threw a few things. I'm more comfortable with anger than sadness.

In the end though, she will have to accept everything. And Cooper will be grateful to me for ripping off the Band-Aid.

I leave the sauce to simmer and return to the living room. I left my phone on the sofa, and I see a new text message on the screen. I hope it isn't Debbie canceling. Obviously, it isn't necessary to tell her tonight, but I got myself all psyched up for it. It'll be disappointing if we don't get to do this.

But when I get to my phone, it's not Debbie after all. The text message is from Cooper.

We need to talk.

Hmm, what does *that* mean?

We need to talk. Is that a good type of talk, like he wants to take things to the next level and leave his wife? Or is it the bad type of talk? *I really, really like you, but this just isn't working for me anymore. I can't keep sneaking around like this.*

Ugh, I *hate* that kind of talk.

I type back a message to him:

You're still coming for dinner, right?

The conversation with Debbie is going to be difficult, and she might not believe me. She might think I'm making the whole thing up or at least exaggerating. But if Cooper is here, then that will force the issue. When Cooper shows up at the door, she will understand everything immediately. She'll probably kick him out on the spot. And whatever he wants to talk about will suddenly become moot.

I smile at the thought.

Yes. I'll be there at 6:15.
See you then.

CHAPTER 63

COOPER

When I get home, I'm tempted to go right for the garage. But first, I need to check on the girls.

To my surprise, they're sitting together on the sofa, talking quietly. It's nice to see them leaning on each other in a difficult time. I'm glad they have each other, because there could be a day when that's all they have.

That day could come sooner than expected.

Both of them jump to their feet when they see me. Lexi's eyes are still swollen like she's been crying intermittently the whole time I've been gone.

"Did you talk to Mom?" Lexi asks.

I shake my head. Not for lack of trying. I have been texting and calling Debbie nonstop. She's not answering.

"Not yet," I say. "I just… I need to check something in the garage."

"What?" Izzy asks.

I can't tell her. I can't even begin to let my two daughters know what I suspect. "I'll be right back," is my answer.

The garage is empty, because Debbie has her car and I'm parked in the driveway. I have a worktable in the garage, although I don't use it that much because I'm not exactly handy. I do try to fix things around the house to save money on our repair bills, but it's not my greatest skill. Everyone has things they're good at. I'm good with numbers, and Debbie is good at everything else.

I crouch down below my worktable. Debbie bought a six-pack yesterday for reasons I still don't understand, and the only one still left in the pack is on the floor. For a moment, I'm tempted to grab that beer and crack it open. I have never needed a drink more in my entire life.

But no. I can't. I have to stay clearheaded.

There is a toolbox down there too, and I lift it off the object it's on top of, which is covered in a blanket. I pull off the blanket to reveal a small gun safe.

Like I said, Debbie adamantly did not want to buy a gun. She pointed out that you're more likely to shoot a member of your family than a burglar, and I pointed out that I'm not naive and that I would take precautions. In the end, she couldn't stop me. The gun is in my name, and she just had to deal with it.

One of the precautions I took was keeping the gun in our garage, inside a gun safe. So far, I have only taken it out to go to the firing range. There hasn't been a burglary in a while, so I considered getting rid of it, just to ease Debbie's anxiety. But I enjoy firing it on the occasional weekend.

The gun safe is small enough that I can pick it up off the floor and lay it on the worktable. It opens with a four-digit combination that I chose because I knew I'd remember it—our wedding anniversary—and my hands are shaking so badly that I'm having trouble punching it in. I finally hear the click that means the safe is unlocked. I pull it open and...

It's empty. Just as I feared.

I stare down at the empty gun safe, realizing that my worst nightmares are true. I wasn't sure what was going on until this minute, but I know now.

Ken Bryant and I had an argument, and I quit in a fit of anger.

There is a *lot* of money missing from the company, and all signs point to it being an inside job.

Ken has been murdered. He was shot in the head.

The murder weapon is almost certainly my gun, registered in my name.

The gun is now missing, but I suspect that it will eventually resurface, covered in my fingerprints. Not to mention all the fingerprints I surely left behind at Ken's house.

Holy shit. Debbie is framing me for the murder of my boss.

"Dad?"

I look up, quickly closing the lid of the gun safe. Izzy is standing at the doorway of the garage, a troubled expression on her pale face. She steps into the garage hesitantly.

If I go to prison for murder, how often will I see my daughter? Not very much. It's not like Debbie will bring her to see me.

"Hey, Iz," I say around a lump forming in my throat.

"Dad," she says. "What's going on? I'm really worried about Mom."

"Yeah." I don't know what to say to reassure her, but I know that's what I need to do. That's my job as her dad.

I'm supposed to make her feel safe. "She's going to be okay."

"Where *is* she?"

I can only shake my head. "I'm sorry, honey. I'm trying my best to find her."

"I know," she says quietly.

The two of us just stand there for a moment in the garage. I'm trying to think of the right thing to say, but my mind is blank. I'm so bad at this. If Debbie were here, she'd know the right thing to say.

"Izzy?"

"Yeah, Dad?"

I try to smile, but I know it's crooked. "I don't want you to worry, Iz. I love you very much."

She frowns, because that isn't something I say very often. I do love her very much, but I just don't think to say it. But I need to say it right now.

In case it's my last chance.

Her face crumples slightly. "Mom is going to be okay, right?"

She is so worried about Debbie. I feel like I've been a good father—or at least done the best I could—but she's been their whole world. I don't want to lose her. If it comes down to me or Debbie…well, they should have her. Even if she's a little off right now, their lives would be destroyed without her.

"Mom is going to be fine." I grab my phone from my pocket and look at the screen one last time. "I have to run out again. I need to… I might know where to find your mother." I shove my phone back in my pocket. "Will you and Lexi be able to get some food in the house?"

Izzy nods slowly. "Yeah. Mom went to the grocery store yesterday. There's lots of food."

Of course she did. Debbie always makes sure our household functions like a well-oiled machine.

"I'll be back soon," I promise her.

I hope I don't have to break that promise.

CHAPTER 64

HARLEY

Debbie is prompt. I have to give her that.

She shows up at exactly six o'clock. She's well dressed in a cream-colored blouse paired with a light pink skirt and chunky heels. She looks ready to go to a business meeting, except that her hair has come slightly undone from the bun she must've tied it into earlier today. It's falling in tendrils around her face, and not cute, stylish tendrils. She's too old to look so disheveled—she can't pull it off.

"Hi, Debbie," I say brightly.

"Hi, Harley." She smiles warmly at me. "Sorry I didn't bring anything. I've been on the road."

"No worries."

I lean in for a brief hug, and while she hugs me back, she seems stiff. We've gotten in the habit of hugging at the beginning or end of seeing each other, but it feels different this time. It feels like she doesn't want to touch me.

Is it possible that she knows?

No. She doesn't know. She wouldn't come here and smile at me if she knew I was sleeping with her husband. Who would do that?

"Is there anything I can do to help in the kitchen?" she asks me.

I almost suggest that she help me chop the salad, but then I think better of giving her a knife. "No, I've got it under control."

She follows me to the kitchen so I can tend to my pasta and finish up with the vegetables. She stands there for a moment, watching me.

"That's a lot of food," she comments.

"Actually," I say, "I invited another guest to join us. Someone I'd like you to meet."

"Really?" She looks intrigued as she leans against the kitchen counter. "Who is it?"

"It's my boyfriend."

Her eyebrows shoot up. "Harley! I didn't know you were seeing someone. Who is he?"

"He's a great guy," I say honestly. "I met him at the gym, and we just connected. Like, soulmates, you know? He's a bit older than me, but he's really hot." I wink at her. "We can't keep our hands off each other when we're together."

"Wow." She blinks at me. "That's so fantastic. How long have you been seeing him?"

"A few months, but it feels like it's getting serious. He told me he's falling in love with me."

"Oh my gosh," she says. "That's so great. I'm so happy for you."

"I'm glad to hear you feel that way."

She adjusts her purse, which is still hanging off her

shoulder, even though she's been here several minutes. I don't know why she doesn't put it down. "What does your dream guy do for a living?"

"He's an accountant."

"Oh!" She looks surprised. "Like Cooper."

"Right," I say meaningfully. "Like Cooper."

I let that hang in the air for a moment. *An older guy who does the same job as your husband. Hint, hint.*

"Well," she says, "I'm excited to meet him."

I rummage around in the refrigerator, coming up with a bottle of oil and vinegar salad dressing. I tried to find the miso ranch at the supermarket, but no luck. "Is this okay?"

"Sure, whatever is fine."

I unscrew the bottle of dressing and release a few dollops of it onto the salad. They land wetly. "There *is* one thing about my boyfriend that isn't entirely ideal."

"Oh?"

I take a deep breath, watching her expression. "He's... he's married."

"Oh." She puts her hand on her chest. "Separated?"

"No, he's still with his wife."

"Oh!" she says again, this time with a hint of judgment in her voice. "Well, that's not good."

"But it's barely a marriage." I still have my eyes on her face, watching for signs of recognition. "They don't even sleep together anymore. They barely talk." *Sound familiar, Debbie?* "He says he would have left her years ago, but she's, you know, emotionally fragile."

If Debbie recognizes that I'm talking about her marriage, she doesn't show it.

"He could be lying," she says diplomatically.

"I don't think he is."

280

"Men lie." She drums her fingernails on the kitchen counter. "Men do terrible things."

There's an ominous look in her eyes, and for a moment, I think maybe she does know. Maybe she knows everything, and maybe she's known for a long time.

Slowly, I move the knife I was using to chop the salad out of the way. I swallow a lump in my throat and attempt to smile, but my lips feel rubbery. Maybe this whole thing was a mistake. Maybe confronting Debra Mullen with her cheating husband was not such a great idea.

But then the doorbell rings, and it's too late to turn back.

"That must be him," I say in what sounds like an abnormally high-pitched voice.

I push past Debbie, walking in the direction of the front door. She follows at my heels, and as my heart speeds up, all my reservations vanish. This is it. This is what I've been waiting for. One way or another, we are going to rip off this Band-Aid.

When I pull open the door, Cooper is standing there in the doorway. He's wearing a dress shirt from work that day, although he has sweat dotting the collar slightly, which makes me think he came directly from the gym. But that's okay—I love him all hot and sweaty.

"Hi, Cooper," I say in a husky voice that makes it clear what our relationship is.

He starts to reply, but then his gaze moves past me, over my shoulder, and falls on Debbie. All the blood drains from his face, and he takes a step back.

"What are *you* doing here?" he gasps.

A smile touches Debbie's lips, although she still has that dark look in her eyes that sends a chill down my spine.

"Hello, Jesse," she says.

CHAPTER 65

COOPER

I've got to find Debbie.

I have run out of ideas to find her, and I've been blowing up her phone with text messages and voicemails for hours now. So I'm driving to the final place I can think of to look.

Except I don't actually know where I'm going. There was one address on the list of places Debbie had been in the last week that wasn't familiar to me. It's an address in Rockland. I don't know anybody who lives in Rockland. I have no idea what this place is, but it's the only clue I have left.

So I'm going.

The sun has dropped precipitously in the sky, and the streets are growing dark. I'm following the GPS as the roads curve and turn. And as I follow the directions from my phone, I think about what I'm going to say to Debbie if and when I find her.

First, I'm going to tell her how much I love her.

Because I do. Even after all this, I still love her. She's the only woman I have ever loved or will ever love.

So there's that. And hopefully that's worth something.

My phone starts ringing, and it's the worst possible timing. It's *her* again. I am in no state to deal with this right now, but I need to take the call, at least to let her know I'm not showing up tonight.

The voice on the other end of the line pipes out of the speakers in my car: "Cooper?"

"Cherese," I say. "Hey."

"Everything okay?" Her voice is scratchy from forty years of smoking. "You sound…off."

No kidding. "I'm fine."

"Have you been drinking?"

I flinch, hating that she had to ask. But it's her job—she's my sponsor. "*No.*"

"Cooper…"

"I swear. I haven't been drinking."

Does she believe me? I hope so. I've been lying to Debbie for the duration of our marriage, but I try not to lie to Cherese. It's the only way I can hope to get better.

"Are you going to the meeting tonight?" she asks me.

"I can't. I'm busy." That's an understatement. "I… I'll go tomorrow."

"You promise?"

"I promise." As long as I'm not in jail tomorrow. "I have to go now."

Cherese sounds like she's not sure if she believes me, but there's no way I'm going to tell her about the day I've had today. Not now—not ever. She accepts that I'm not about to get toasted at this moment and allows me to end the call, although she'll surely call back later. She's not the

283

first sponsor I've had, but she might be the most attentive. She has been calling me constantly since I fell off the wagon to make sure I'm not tempted to start drinking again. And I'm glad she hasn't leaned on me too hard to tell Debbie the truth.

So yeah, I'm a shit. How could I fail to tell the woman I love that I've been an alcoholic since before we even met? How could I conceal such an important part of who I am?

I was ashamed. And I swear, I thought I had it conquered, and Debbie never *needed* to know. But that was no excuse.

I found out about my problem when I was in college. All my friends used to drink, but I realized it was different for me. I never knew when to stop. I started drinking every night, even before I was twenty-one and could get it legally. I had a fake ID, and when it was confiscated, I got another fake ID. I got fired from my job flipping burgers when I showed up to work drunk, but I still didn't take it seriously. It wasn't until I ended up with a DUI that I realized I had a problem.

I got it under control though. I started going to AA meetings, and I gave up alcohol entirely. I was proud of myself, and when I met Debbie, I truly thought I had left it all behind me. I didn't think I needed to lay that piece of baggage on her when it was firmly in the past.

Except it wasn't actually in the past. During our marriage, I have fallen off the wagon three times. And each time, I have come very close to telling her, but I didn't. I would call my sponsor to confess my sins, turn off location sharing, sneak off to the AA meetings, and get myself back under control all on my own.

I know. It's ridiculous. I *obviously* should have told her. But before we were married, I was scared that if I told her, she would lose respect for me and dump me. And then after we were married, I realized it was too late, and she would be furious with me for lying to her.

A few weeks ago, I fell off the wagon again. It was the stress of knowing that I was going to be asking for the partnership and knowing in my heart that he would say no. I didn't realize he'd let me quit, but when that happened, the financial stress only made things worse. I wanted to talk to Debbie and confess everything, but she'd become so strangely distant over the last six months. When I polished off the white wine above our refrigerator and replaced it with tap water until I could grab another bottle, I knew I had to start going to meetings again. I couldn't even resist the random six-pack of beer I found in the kitchen.

I should've just told her from the start. I should have been honest, and maybe if I had, she would've been honest with me.

Now, as I drive to Rockland, my foot pressing as hard on the gas as I dare, I make a promise to myself that the moment I see her, I'm going to tell her everything. No more secrets. Whatever she's done, we're going to figure it out.

Christ, I hope it's not too late.

CHAPTER 66

DEBBIE

Harley looks stunned. It's fun to watch.

She thought that she was going to shock me by bringing my husband here and revealing that she was his lover. But it didn't go quite as she expected.

I have to hand it to Jesse—telling Harley that his name was Cooper Mullen was a smart move. Cooper was already in the system at the gym because he used it too. Also, as a technophobe, he didn't have any social media presence online. Any search she did would fail to turn up a photo or any information. It kept Jesse's wife—actually quite a nice woman who doesn't deserve any of this—from discovering what her husband was up to. I have no doubt this was not his first rodeo.

Cooper hasn't been entirely honest with me, but one thing he would never do is cheat on me. He has many faults, but he does love me, and he is very, very loyal.

I hope he doesn't find out what I will be doing here tonight.

"Jesse?" Harley repeats in confusion. Her eyes, heavily lined with mascara, are huge. "Who's Jesse?"

Jesse squirms. Harley has likely seen *my* Cooper when he's been working out at the gym, and I'm sure she finds Jesse more attractive than my husband, but I've always found Jesse's looks to be slimy. I could be biased though.

"Look, Harley," he stammers. "There are a few things that…that I might not have been entirely honest with you about."

I burst out laughing. I can't help myself. It's entertaining watching him try to squirm his way out of this one.

Jesse shoots me a look, then he turns back to Harley. He's desperate to explain himself, but not because he wants to continue things with Harley. I'm fairly certain he came here to end things with her tonight. But now that she knows his name, he doesn't want her approaching his wife.

"Your name isn't Cooper Mullen?" Harley asks incredulously.

He shakes his head slowly as he takes a step toward her. "No. I'm sorry. Cooper is… He's that other guy that I come to the gym with all the time. He and I… We work together."

"Oh my *God*." Harley shoves him hard enough that he stumbles backward. "Here I thought that you *loved* me and you might want to spend your life with me, and all along, you didn't even tell me your real name, you *piece of shit*."

Jesse opens his mouth to protest, but then he sways on his feet. He presses his fingertips against his temple and squeezes his eyes shut for a moment. "I think I need to sit down."

"You need to get out," Harley retorts.

But Jesse isn't listening to her. He pushes past her in the direction of the sofa, and he collapses onto it. He doesn't look like he can get up again.

He must have been chugging from his water bottle the whole way home from the gym. The opium that I mixed into that water is working nicely.

Jesse's eyelids are starting to sag. The adrenaline of the encounter may have helped a little bit, but it's wearing off.

"Don't close your eyes!" Harley shrieks at him as she shakes his shoulder. "You've been lying to me this whole time! How could you do that to me?"

I can't believe I ever thought Harley was cool. The pink streak in her hair misled me. Or maybe it was the way she genuinely seemed interested in what I had to say, although now I realize she was just picking my brain for details about my husband. I didn't start to put it all together until I found that T-shirt at her house. When I smelled it, I knew immediately who it belonged to.

Then I went to the gym and talked to Cindy, who was extremely eager to share information about her philandering coworker. She was very, very helpful. After that, I knew everything I needed to know.

"Cooper!" Harley snaps. "Or...Jesse. Or whatever your name is. *Are you listening to me?*"

He's looking at her, but he's not seeing her. The drugs in his system have taken hold, and I'd say in another few minutes, he'll be unconscious. This conversation will seem like a dream later, if he remembers it at all.

Now is the time to make my move.

I reach into the purse slung over my shoulder and first take out my pair of leather gloves. After I pull them onto my hands, I take out the Glock I've been carrying. I shot it once when I put a bullet between Ken Bryant's eyes. Now I'm going to use it a second time.

"Harley," I say.

Harley interrupts her tirade against Jesse and turns to look at me. When she sees the gun in my hand, she inhales sharply.

"Debbie?" she says. "What are you doing?"

In a way, Harley is innocent. She never did anything to me directly. She did think she was sleeping with my husband, but she wasn't. I have no beef with her.

But she's a terrible person. She used me. And she has destroyed countless marriages without any remorse. I hate to use her as a pawn, but she would do the same to me. It's no big loss.

"Sorry, Harley," I say.

Then I point the gun at her forehead and pull the trigger.

The gunshot kills her instantly. Her body drops to the floor, and a pool of blood forms around the back of her head. Her eyes are open, staring at the ceiling. I'm glad she let me know that her upstairs neighbors were out of town, because I would be worried about the noise. But as it is, we're all alone out here on this dead-end street.

I look over at Jesse, whose head is lolling on the sofa. He is now unconscious, and even the report of the gunshot wasn't enough to bring him back. I had thought I might need to give him another shot of opium, which I've got handy in my purse, but he drank enough that it wasn't needed.

It's better he's asleep. He almost certainly won't remember a thing from what went on in this apartment, and it's safer for me that way.

But I wish he could know. I wish he knew that it was *his* gun that I used to shoot Harley. The one I took from his house a few days ago. (The key was *under the doormat*, if you can believe that. Barely even a challenge.) I was smart enough to turn off my location sharing for that little heist. I didn't want there to be any clues that I was the one who took that gun.

Especially when the police match the bullet from this gun with the one that killed Ken Bryant. Although I'm not too worried. The paper trail between Jesse and that offshore bank account with all the money that's been stolen from the company will provide ample motive for the murder. I even sent him that text message from Ken's phone, asking him to water the plants so he would be caught on the door cam. That camera at Ken's door proved very useful, especially since I was able to delete the footage of my own arrival at his door. It took me less than sixty seconds to eliminate any evidence of my guilt.

Nobody will suspect me. Jesse and I hardly know each other. Why would I frame a virtual stranger for murder? Why would I kill his girlfriend right in front of him?

"You deserve this," I whisper to the sleeping man on the sofa. "*Hutch.*"

For a split second, Jesse's eyelids flicker. Did he hear me? Part of me hopes he did. Even though it would incriminate me, part of me wants him to know who I am and why I'm doing this. Of course, he hasn't recognized me yet. It was a long time ago, and we both look a lot different. Plus, I am damn near positive that I was not his only victim. I was just one in a long line of faceless, nameless coeds.

But I had no trouble recognizing *him*. The second I

290

laid eyes on Jesse when Cooper arranged that double date with him and his wife, I immediately recognized that face. And that cologne—the same one he wore in college, the same one that was clinging to that T-shirt. It still haunts me. Those olfactory associations are so powerful.

He held out his hand to me, a grin playing on his lips. *It's so nice to meet you, Debbie. Cooper talks about you all the time.*

I took his hand because it would have given me away if I didn't. His skin felt like it was scalding me. When I finally pulled away, my palm was damp. I had to excuse myself to run to the bathroom at the restaurant, where I breathed through the worst panic attack I'd had since college.

Pull yourself together, Debbie, I told myself. *You can't let him know it's you.*

I pulled myself together. I came out of the bathroom, smiled up at the man who wrecked my future, and pretended I was having a great time, although after the second time my shaky hands knocked over my drink and had to be cleaned up, I thought the waitress and I were going to have words. That night, I went home and screamed into my pillow until my throat was hoarse.

The next day, I dug into the slush pile of emailed letters addressed to Dear Debbie. For once, I decided to tell people the *real* way to solve their problems. Everyone knows you don't get your family to sit down for breakfast by asking "pretty please." Of course, Garrett never would have printed those replies, so I saved all of them in a file on my desktop.

That was about eight months ago, and in that time, I've composed dozens of emails to women who had been taking abuse for far too long, just like I have. But I'm not a hypocrite. I couldn't send any of those messages until I paid back the man who ruined my life.

Please stop!

Don't worry. This will be over in a minute.

I couldn't burn down Zeta Pi. I grabbed my purse from where I left it in the bedroom, then I went downstairs and left the frat with the cigarette and matches still in my purse. In my head, it had seemed like a good idea, but once I was there and talking to that nice kid, I couldn't go through with it. Besides, it wasn't their fault what happened all those years ago. It wasn't fair to blame them.

There was only one person who was to blame for that night.

Jesse Hutchinson's eyes flutter shut. There is more than enough evidence to tie him to Ken Bryant's murder and now to the murder/suicide that will soon be discovered at this apartment when I call the police and ask them to check on my friend whose jealous boyfriend was threatening her. When Jesse is gone, I will finally be able to move past this. I will finally be at peace.

Don't worry. This will be over in a minute.

CHAPTER 67

COOPER

The address is not exact, which means that I'm basically driving around a small area in Rockland, keeping my eye out for Debbie's car. This is getting more and more challenging as the sun drops in the sky.

And of course, I have no reason to believe she's actually here. She has turned off location sharing, which means she could be anywhere. But this is the last address that she's been to recently that is unfamiliar to me. So I've got to check it out.

It's my only hope to find her.

I've been driving around the general area for about twenty minutes when I come across a dead-end street. There are two houses on the street, one of which looks completely abandoned. The other one looks like somebody does live there, but all the windows are dark. It doesn't seem like anyone is home.

I almost turn around, but then I notice it. There are cars parked here. Around the side of the second house.

And one of them looks familiar.

I can't get that close in my car, so I park and start walking toward the end of the street. The house is definitely dark, but I want to get a better look at that car. Is it possible that it belongs to Debbie?

As I get closer, I can see that it's a blue Subaru Outback, just like Debbie's. But that doesn't mean it's necessarily hers. It's parked next to another car, which also seems weirdly familiar, but I can't place it at the moment.

I stare at the license plate of the Subaru. Is that Debbie's plate number? Christ, I don't know. It's difficult for me to remember my kids' birthdays; license plate numbers are out of my wheelhouse. It does look familiar though.

I peer through the window of the car, hoping to see her purse or anything that looks like it belongs to her. Debbie doesn't leave much inside her car—she's very neat—but I do see a pair of sunglasses in the cupholder and recall how she always leaves them there. I remember, because I always want to put my Big Gulp there after Izzy's soccer games, and it's always occupied by Debbie's sunglasses.

This is Debbie's car. But where's Debbie?

I walk back to the front of the house. All the windows on both floors are dark. It really looks like nobody is home. But if nobody is home, why would Debbie be here? Why would Debbie *ever* have been here?

I go to the front door of the house and press my finger against the doorbell, holding my breath. I don't know why she'd be here, but maybe if I come clean with her, she'll come clean with me.

Except nothing happens when I ring the doorbell. It must be broken.

I knock on the door, loud enough that at least anybody on the first floor would hear. I don't hear any movement behind the door, so I knock again.

Still nothing.

All at once, I am banging on the door with both fists. I know Debbie is here. That's her damn car outside, and there's nowhere else she could be. I need to talk to her *right now*. I need to figure out a way to make this right, because I can't lose her. I *can't*.

I've been so stupid. I should have come clean with her about everything. I didn't want her to lose respect for me, but nothing is worse than lying.

"Debbie!" I'm shouting now. "Debbie! Please come out! I need to talk to you!"

There's still no sound from behind the door. But she's here. She *must* be.

"Debbie!" I'm shouting loud enough that my voice is growing raspy. "Debbie! I love you!"

I think I'm too late.

CHAPTER 68

DEBBIE

Jesse is out cold.

The gun is in my gloved hand, but I can't just shoot him, as much as I would enjoy that. Killing Jesse will be therapeutic for me in a way that years of therapy could never be. But I have to be smart about this. I have gone to a lot of trouble to frame Jesse for multiple murders, and I can't do anything that will lead the police to suspect that a third party was involved in what happened here today.

That means Jesse needs to shoot himself with his own hand.

The coroner will know the difference between somebody shot from several feet away and a suicide. Plus, there needs to be gunshot residue on Jesse's right hand. The only way that can happen is if he is holding the gun.

I have to get up close and personal with him, which is the last thing I want to do. I sit down beside him on the sofa, and I can smell that horrible cologne. The last time I was this close to him, he was on top of me.

·But he can't hurt me anymore. He's unconscious. And very soon, he's going to be dead.

He can't hurt you.

I repeat those words to myself over and over as I wrap his fingers around the handle of the gun. I point the barrel at his throat, aimed in the direction of his brains. One bullet should do it. One bullet, and this will all be over.

I place Jesse's index finger on the trigger. I get ready to pull.

"Debbie!"

I freeze, my hand on Jesse's, at the sound of the voice yelling my name. It takes me a second to realize that the voice belongs to my husband. For some reason, Cooper is out there, calling my name.

Oh my God, what is he doing here?

He must have seen this location in my history from when I visited Harley earlier in the week, even though I was careful to turn off my phone for this particular excursion. I didn't even realize he knew where to look for that. He's probably been driving around everywhere I've been in the last week, searching for me.

"Debbie! Debbie!"

Why did he come here? Why couldn't he have just waited at home until I was done with everything I had to do?

"Debbie! Debbie, I love you! Please!"

His words tug at me. I look down at the man lying unconscious on the sofa. I have spent the last eight months thinking about how he ruined my life. I had thought I was over it, but when I saw him, my hate and anxiety and shame over what happened to me grew with each passing day until I couldn't bear it any longer.

But that's unfair. My life isn't ruined. My life is good in many ways. Yes, I didn't end up with the career that I'd hoped to have. But I have two wonderful daughters. And I have a husband who loves me enough to drive around the South Shore in the middle of the night searching for me.

I have a lot.

But I can't just abandon my entire plan. Two people are dead. And if I walk away right now, I'm going to take the blame for everything. I don't have a choice anymore.

I put my right index finger over Jesse's, and I pull the trigger.

CHAPTER 69

When I exit Harley's front door, I peel off my leather gloves and put them in my purse. The gun has been left behind, as planned.

I come around the side of the house, where Cooper has stopped screaming my name and is trying to look in one of the windows. Actually, he looks like he's about to break in. He's got a suspiciously large rock in his right hand, which he is raising in the air. I better put a quick stop to this.

"Cooper?"

He whirls around, arm still raised. His eyes widen when he sees me, and the rock falls from his right hand. He doesn't say a word, but he runs over and throws his arms around me.

"Debbie," he murmurs into my neck. "Jesus, I was so worried."

At first, he is hugging me while I stand there stiffly. But after a few seconds, I realize I'm hugging him back.

And then we're clinging to each other. It takes a good several minutes before we pull away.

"I was so worried," he says. "I thought I heard a gunshot."

He absolutely did. But the bullet in question is lodged in the ceiling of Harley's apartment.

Jesse is still alive.

"What was that sound?" he presses me.

"I didn't hear anything," I say. "Maybe it was a car backfiring?"

He looks like he doesn't quite believe me, but he doesn't push it. "What are you doing here?"

"A friend of mine lives here." It's the truth for once. "She has the basement apartment with the entrance in the back. I came to see her, but I guess she forgot because she's not answering her door."

"Oh."

He seems to believe me. There's no reason he shouldn't. He doesn't know Harley, except from in passing at the gym, and has no reason to think I'd do anything to harm this stranger.

"So, uh…" I glance at our cars, trying not to think about that crime scene behind us. Does Cooper recognize Jesse's car? He hasn't mentioned it. "Should we go?"

"Not yet." He grabs both my hands in his and squeezes tight. "I need you to know something, Debbie."

"Okay…"

He takes a deep breath and squares his shoulders. "I have a drinking problem."

I blink at him. It's not what I expected him to say. "What?"

He falters, like he's not sure if he should continue,

but then he plows forward. "It's more than just a drinking problem. I...I'm an alcoholic. I've been sneaking off to AA meetings without telling you."

"For how long?"

"I've known since college."

"Since *college*? And you never *told* me?"

"I know." He hangs his head. "I'm sorry, Debbie. I'm *so* sorry. I was...I was ashamed, and that's why I kept it from you. I should have told you the truth from the start, but you're always so perfect and amazing and...and I didn't want you to think less of me."

He manages to raise his eyes to meet mine. He should have told me sooner, but I also understand why he didn't. I can't throw stones. And now?

It's my turn.

"I was raped in college," I say. "That's why I dropped out."

His jaw drops open. He stares at me for several seconds—too long—until I almost wish I hadn't told him. But just when I'm about to try to figure out a way to take it back ("Ha-ha, wasn't that a funny joke?"), he reaches over and pulls me into another tight hug. There are no words, only his warm, comforting body pressed against mine.

When he finally pulls away, his eyes are slightly damp. "I think," he says, "we need couples therapy."

A laugh bubbles out of me. *No freaking kidding.*

"There's something I need to ask you though." He rubs the back of his neck. "And I need you to tell me the truth."

"Okay..."

His brows scrunch together. "Do you promise to tell me the truth?"

"I promise," I say, hoping it's a promise I can keep.

"Did you shoot Ken Bryant with my gun?"

I flinch. He must have gone over to Ken's house. He must've seen him lying dead with the bullet wound in his head. He thinks I might have killed him, but instead of calling the police, he ran to find me.

"I swear on our children's lives"—I place a hand on my chest—"I did not shoot Ken Bryant with your gun."

And it's true.

I used Jesse's gun.

"Thank God." He believes me. His body goes limp with relief. "I was worried that…well…" He heaves a sigh. "In that case, we better call the police when we get back home."

I nod slowly.

"Also," he adds, "my gun is missing from the safe. Do you know what happened to it?"

That's another softball that I can answer truthfully. "I got rid of it."

"You *got rid* of it?"

I put my hands on my hips. "I told you, you're more likely to shoot a family member than an intruder."

Cooper just shakes his head. It's something we'll have to talk out in therapy. And I have a feeling after tonight that he won't be eager to have a gun in the house.

"Okay," he says. "Let's go home."

He doesn't have to ask me a second time.

EPILOGUE

COOPER

I'm making breakfast this morning.

It's nothing special. Just a couple of pieces of toast smeared with jam, paired with a bowl of cereal. I'm eating Debbie's fiber cereal, because it's actually sort of grown on me, believe it or not.

I would say my newfound love of fiber cereal is probably the thing that has changed *least* about our lives in the last year.

For starters, after Ken's murder, I founded my own accounting firm, and it has flourished. I've now got a staff of half a dozen people, and we even got a favorable write-up in the *Boston Globe*. I never thought of myself as much of a businessman, but apparently, I'm better at it than I thought. I guess Debbie was right.

I still can't believe Ken was murdered. Even worse, that my friend Jesse was the one who killed him. I refused to believe it at first, but the evidence kept mounting to the point where it was undeniable. Jesse stole money from the company, and when Ken found out, Jesse shot him.

And that's not even the worst of it.

Jesse was having an affair with this trainer from the gym named Harley. I had seen her around several times before and remembered the pink streak in her hair. Debbie was friendly with her too, although I hadn't really realized it at the time. I had seen Jesse talking to Harley a few times, and I had to admit, I did notice the low voices they used when they talked. But I never really thought he was having an affair, and with everything else going on in my life, I didn't give it another thought. I mean, yes, I'm aware that plenty of men have affairs, but to me, it's unthinkable.

Apparently, Harley was putting pressure on Jesse to leave his wife. She was threatening to rat him out if he didn't do what she wanted. So he went to her house with the same gun he used to shoot Ken, and he killed her.

I later discovered that random address where I found Debbie was Harley's apartment. Debbie explained to me that when she went over there to see Harley, she didn't answer the door. Because, as it turned out, she was dead.

Debbie was the one who finally called the police, saying she was concerned about Harley's boyfriend, although she had never met him before. The police arrived at Harley's apartment and caught Jesse trying to scrub the place of his fingerprints while Harley lay dead on the living room floor.

He was arrested immediately.

The evidence was overwhelming, and he was essentially caught in the act. His trial took place last month, and when he asked me to be a character witness, I had to decline. Jesse was my friend, but there was no doubt in my mind that he killed our boss and his mistress. The jury agreed. He was found guilty of two counts of first-degree murder and received two consecutive life sentences. He'll spend the rest of his life in prison.

But other than the nasty business with the trial, our lives have been great. Lexi and Debbie became a lot closer after that whole business with Zane, and it seems like a bit of a miracle that they don't fight anymore the way they used to. Debbie cried for a week after Lexi moved out to go to college, even though she stayed local and has already been home to do laundry. She got into a great school, by the way. I don't want to brag or anything, but it rhymes with Schmarvard.

Debbie's just happy that Lexi has nothing to do with her old boyfriend, Zane. After his accident, I heard about charges against him—something to do with illegal photos he was passing around—and now that he's out of the hospital, he may be in serious legal trouble. I saw him just once, at the grocery store with his mother, using a wheelchair that he operated with his mouth. I didn't say hello.

And Izzy is kicking ass on the soccer team. As usual. Debbie and I attended every game last year.

Debbie is having some of her own career success too, and I'm really freaking proud of her. She's been writing all these apps for her phone that we have been using for years, and one of them really blew up. It's called Punish Your Husband, where a wife can assign some potential punishments (the most popular being cleaning the bathroom) to her husband for misdeeds like forgetting a birthday or anniversary. Wives apparently find it hilarious to come up with more and more creative punishments.

A couple of months ago, Debbie sold Punish Your

Husband. I'm not gonna say how much it sold for, but it's enough to pay for Lexi's entire tuition at Schmarvard. Debbie has been working on some new projects, and she seems a lot happier overall.

Debbie explained to me that the file of threatening advice on her computer was a way for her to deal with the trauma of what happened to her. Now that she's in therapy to help her deal with it, she revisited all those emails and rewrote her advice. Even though she's no longer Dear Debbie, she answered every single one of those emails, and she's been counseling a lot of women with their problems. What can I say? My wife gives great advice.

As for me and Debbie, that's a complicated one.

We've been seeing a couples therapist. Obviously. We have both been keeping huge secrets from each other, and I feel simultaneously guilty that I didn't tell her mine and guilty that she didn't feel comfortable telling me hers. Debbie was sexually assaulted. The thought of it makes me so angry, I can't even think straight. How could somebody do that to her? To *anyone*?

I'm glad she doesn't know the name of the guy who did it, because if she did, I would be tempted to find him and beat him to death with my bare hands.

But we're going to have an empty nest in only two years, and I want to make sure Debbie and I are okay. So every two weeks, we've been seeing the couples therapist. We never skip, no matter what. Nothing is more important than working on our marriage.

Just as I am popping my whole wheat bread out of the toaster, Debbie comes into our kitchen, dressed in her gym clothes. Our therapist said we need to get better at saying what we're thinking, so I decide to practice that right now.

"Hey," I say, "you look really sexy in those leggings."

Debbie rolls her eyes, but she smiles. "You don't look so bad yourself, Mullen." Her gaze flicks over my chest. "You even tied your own tie perfectly."

"I watched a video online," I say proudly.

"*You?* Watched a video *online?*"

I laugh because she has a point. It doesn't sound like something I would do. But I've actually been spending a little bit more time on the internet, building our business. I've built up my company's website, including putting my picture on it. I discovered that Jesse had been telling Harley that he was me to hide his identity, and he could only do that because there were zero pictures of me anywhere on the internet.

"You know," I say teasingly, "I don't have to be at work for another hour. Just saying..."

"Don't tempt me," she retorts. "If I don't go to the gym now, I'm never going to go."

Since my former workout buddy Jesse is serving two life sentences for murder, I've joined Debbie a few times at Titan, but I don't have time for that right now. "How about if I take you to dinner tonight? Izzy has that sleepover, right?"

She grins at me. "It's a date."

She comes over to give me a kiss before she leaves. A year ago, I thought I had lost her, but now it seems like we are closer than we have ever been. I hate all the pain that we have been through, but there's a reason for everything.

In the end, it worked out for all of us.

JESSE

Nights in prison are the worst.

At home, I had a memory foam mattress with a pillow that contoured to the shape of my head and neck. I had a special hypoallergenic down comforter. I couldn't sleep without it.

Now I am lying on a thin mattress that is probably an inch or two thick at most. I do have a pillow, but it definitely doesn't contour to the shape of anything. Like my mattress, it feels more like a board than a pillow. And then there's the scrawny blanket, which I think I'm allergic to, based on the bumpy rash that has sprung up on every part of my skin that has been touched by the thin material.

If I sleep, which I sometimes do out of sheer exhaustion, half the time I get wrenched out of my slumber by the sounds of the guy on the top bunk snoring like a chainsaw. I've never heard anyone snore that loud before. I've also never seen anyone with that many tattoos on his body.

There are four of us in this small cell. My bunkmate is called Geho, which I think is his last name. Nobody uses first names here. It's like back in college, when everyone used to call me Hutch, except it's not anything like college.

I was transferred to this maximum-security prison last week, which is where I will be spending the rest of my life. I shouldn't be here. I *really* shouldn't be here. Maximum-security prison is not for somebody like me. The other men here are hardened criminals like Geho—they are terrifying. Someone like me should be at one of those minimum-security prisons that looks more like a resort.

But really, I shouldn't be here at all. Because I didn't kill anyone.

I woke up at Harley's apartment, not entirely sure how I got there, and she was dead on the floor from a bullet wound. The gun—my gun—was in my right hand, but I didn't shoot her. Yes, I know how that sounds. And I know there was gunshot residue on my hand. But I didn't want to kill Harley. Yes, I was looking to end our relationship, but I didn't want her dead. I don't even remember bringing my damn gun to her house. Why would I have done that?

I made a grave mistake though. When I woke up and found Harley murdered, I immediately tried to scrub down the apartment before leaving to get rid of any trace of my presence. The police caught me doing it, and it looked…bad. From that moment, I was their only suspect.

It didn't help that I had no damn clue what happened. That sounded unbelievable to them. Saying it now, I understand why.

And then, to my complete shock, they accused me of killing Ken Bryant too. I thought it was a joke at first. I didn't even know he was dead, and I certainly didn't kill him. But the bullet in his head matched my gun. They found footage of me entering and leaving his house, even though I tried to tell them I was just watering the plants like he asked me to, although those text messages had mysteriously vanished from my phone. Then they said I stole money from him, and that was the last nail in the coffin.

They tried to offer me a deal for pleading guilty, and my lawyer encouraged me to take it. Second-degree murder charges for both Harley and Ken. It meant that

I could be eligible for parole in thirty years. But what the hell good was that? I'm forty-seven years old. I decided to roll the dice with a trial, knowing that I was innocent.

I lost my gamble. I'm serving two consecutive life sentences, and I will die in prison. I'm just lucky they don't have the death penalty in Massachusetts.

Geho shifts in the bunk above mine, and the springs let out a loud groan. As if the snoring wasn't bad enough, every movement in the bed echoes through the cell. I feel like I'm losing my mind, and I've only been here for a week. The idea of spending the rest of my life here…

I don't deserve any of this. My wife filed for divorce a few months after my arrest, which means she's not going to be visiting me anytime soon. This was not my first affair, and she was not even the tiniest bit understanding. She wasn't that amazing as a wife, which is why I was with Harley in the first place, but after a year without being close to a woman, I would give anything for a conjugal visit. My kids hate me too for what I did to the family. I'm alone.

It would be different if I were guilty, like the other men here. Geho actually brags about the guy he stabbed in the neck. But I'm not a bad guy. Yes, I cheated on my wife. A lot of guys have done that. It's not a capital offense.

Admittedly, I did some things in college that were less than admirable. Sometimes at parties, I'd talk to a girl and offer to get her a drink. I had these ground-up sedatives, and I used to mix them into drinks—jungle juice, rum and Coke, it didn't matter. Between that and the alcohol, they would be pretty out of it. Then I'd take them to my room, and they didn't protest too much.

It wasn't even a big deal though. Most of them barely remembered it. Or if they did, I bet they enjoyed it.

I finally start to drift off, but then I suddenly jolt awake. And when I do, I can't believe my eyes. Geho and my other two cellmates are standing over me. Each of them has a sock gripped in one hand, with something weighing down the other end. A bar of soap? My stomach churns. The skeleton face etched on Geho's bald skull is barely visible in the dim light of the cell.

"What's going on?" I choke out.

"Keep your mouth shut," Geho hisses at me, "and maybe you'll get through this alive."

Even though he gave me a warning, I sputter, "But what did I do?"

Geho responds with a swift punch to my mouth. Instantly, I taste blood. And then a moment later, I feel one of my teeth floating around my mouth.

"This is for Misty Cardon," he tells me. "Her brother is in Block D, and I owe him a favor."

Misty Cardon…

That's a name I haven't heard in over twenty years and hoped to never hear again. Misty was a girl from Wellesley who I had a great time with until she blew the whole thing out of proportion. I couldn't believe it when she called me up the next day, ranting about rape. It wasn't rape, but when I tried to explain it to her, she didn't want to hear it. She finally agreed to meet with me, and let's just say I took care of that situation.

So technically, even though I pled innocent in my trial, I couldn't say I never killed anyone. But nobody found out about Misty. The police asked me a few questions, but it never went any further. I was very, very careful. That's why it didn't make any sense that I'd be so sloppy in killing Ken and Harley, but I couldn't exactly say that in my defense.

I hold up my hands to shield my face. "Please... don't..."

My pleas are met with a sock slamming into my right side. And then a second blow, this one even harder. I feel my ribs cracking, but the pummeling shows no sign of stopping. Where are the guards? Why aren't they stopping this?

One of the socks hits me in the jaw, and the pain is blinding. That's not a bar of soap. It's something much worse. A rock? A combination lock? I can't even imagine. Every time one of them slams into me, it's like a burst of unspeakable agony.

"Please..." I appeal to them one final time as I cling to the brink of consciousness. "Please stop."

Through the blood dripping into my swelling eyes, I can barely make out Geho's face, grinning down at me.

"Don't worry," he says. "This will be over in a minute."

DEBBIE

I feel good after Cooper and I make dinner plans for tonight. He's trying so hard to be a good husband. Everything we went through was hard, but it's made our marriage so much stronger.

Our therapist keeps telling us that we need to be honest. And I am trying to be honest. But there are some things that I can never tell him.

I can never tell him that I killed his boss, for instance.

I can't tell him that his former best friend, who will be spending the rest of his life in a maximum-security prison, is innocent. At least he's innocent of killing Ken and Harley.

Cooper doesn't know that Jesse is the one who raped me. Given how furious he was when I told him what happened, I think he'd agree Jesse got what he deserved, but I didn't want to make him party to what I had done. There was a tense period when I wasn't sure how the trial would go, and I was worried Jesse might remember there was a woman in Harley's apartment just before he passed out. I wanted to make sure Cooper could credibly plead ignorance. If someone was going to jail, it should be me and me alone.

I drive to Titan Fitness to get in a workout before I start my morning. I've got a meeting with a company that is looking into having me develop a new dating app for them. It's going to be a challenge. I love a challenge, especially with the financial resources they will be putting at my disposal. It feels like my brain is finally getting the stimulation it deserves.

When I get to the gym, Cindy is at the front desk. She flashes me a broad smile. "Hi, Debbie."

"Hi, Cindy."

She winks at me. "I put a towel on the elliptical machine by the window so nobody else would use it."

I grin at her. "You're the best, Cindy."

As she looks at me, her smile falters slightly. "It's the least I can do."

Cindy Bryant believes with all her heart that she owes me everything. Nearly two years ago, she wrote me a letter at Dear Debbie describing the financial abuse by her husband. When I begged her to leave him and told her to contact me, she did exactly that. But it turned out we were more connected than we thought.

I did everything I could to help her. I found her a place to live. I helped her find this job at Titan Fitness. She was doing so well, but her husband, Ken, was making the divorce miserable for her. He was using every trick in the book to deprive her of any financial resources, and he was trying to turn their children against her. He even eventually got me fired, never realizing "Dear Debbie" was the wife of his employee.

I couldn't let him get away with it. I had to help Cindy. And that's why I decided to put a bullet in his head and blame it all on Jesse Hutchinson.

I made sure to do it at a time when she had an alibi. And she helped me too. On the night before Harley was shot, she overheard Harley and Jesse's plans to meet and filled me in. Then on the evening in question, while he was in the gym shower, she spiked his water bottle with the opium I gave her. What can I say? I was inspired by what Jesse did to me all those years ago.

"How is Cooper?" she asks me.

"Great," I tell her. "The business is going well. And he's been really sweet lately. We're going out for a date tonight."

"Fun." Cindy grins at me. "You and Cooper should double with me and Ajay sometime."

Cindy has been dating a really nice guy recently. They're taking it slow, but I met him once, and I can tell he's going to treat her right. Even so, a double date might be tempting fate. There's too much we don't want our men to know. "Maybe sometime," I say evasively.

"I'm glad Cooper is treating you well," Cindy says, "because if he's not..."

We exchange a meaningful look. "Same," I say.

Cooper has been really good to me. But I'm not too worried. Cindy and I will look out for each other.

Nobody will take advantage of me ever again.

THE END

Read on for a sneak peek of Freida's next thriller, *Want to Know a Secret?*

CHAPTER 1

From: Unknown number
Want to know a secret?
Your son isn't where you think he is.

As you can see, I've now got a tray of delicious, ooey-gooey fudge brownies, fresh from the oven!"

I use my oven mitts to hold up my tray of brownies to the expensive digital camera mounted on the tripod in my kitchen. I tilt the tray slightly, so viewers will be able to see the brownies. They look delicious, if I do say so myself.

"Now for a taste." I pick up the carving knife on the kitchen table. I cut myself a nice big square of choco-latey goodness and take a careful bite. When I first started doing this, I recorded myself eating treats multiple times, trying to figure out the right formula for not looking like a slob while I stuffed confections in my mouth. "*Mmm. So good!*"

Truth be told, I overbaked them by about five minutes. They taste a bit dry. But nobody watching will know it. That's the great thing about video.

I lay down the rest of the brownie. I only ever take one bite and that's it. Nobody wants to watch me gorge myself on their computer screen. "And there you have it, folks! My secret recipe for the most delicious brownies you'll ever eat." As long as you don't overbake them. "If you enjoyed watching *April's Sweet Secrets*, please subscribe to my YouTube channel."

And now I wave at the camera, my eyes connecting with the lens. "Good night, Mom!"

That's how I end every episode.

My show is called *April's Sweet Secrets*. My secrets are my hook. In every episode, I tell viewers a few "secret tips" to get their sweet treats to taste better than anyone else's. Want to know the secret to delicious brownies? The secret is melting good-quality dark chocolate in with the cocoa powder.

I shut down the camera and detach the microphone. It's only after the recording has stopped that my shoulders relax. Even though I'm not recording live, I feel tense when I'm on the screen in front of my thousands of subscribers. Even after five years of doing this.

And now there's the question of what to do with all the brownies. A huge tray of them, sitting there, taunting me. They may be slightly overbaked, but they're still delicious, and I would love to stuff myself with two or three of them (or five). Unfortunately, I can't afford to eat even one. That's the ironic part—my career is teaching people to put together the most delicious treats, but I'm not allowed to touch them aside from that one bite on screen. I have to look good for the camera.

317

I'll put aside a few for my seven-year-old son, Bobby—he's playing out in the backyard, and he'll come back inside soon, hungry for snacks. He deserves a treat for not having interrupted me even once during the filming. It's something of a world's record!

And I'll bring the rest of the tray to Carrie Schaeffer later today. She's going through that horrible divorce, and I know she'll appreciate them.

I head out to the living room, where I stashed my cell phone during the recording. My phone is a distraction that I can't have anywhere near me when I'm making these videos. Nobody wants to watch a video of somebody sneaking looks at text messages on their phone—it's *so* unprofessional. And sure enough, I've got several waiting for me.

The first text is from Julie, who lives two houses down from us and is my absolute best friend. She has two sons: Leo, who is Bobby's age, and Tristan, who is a couple of years older. She's a little intense, but that's only because she used to be an attorney in her previous life. You know, Before Kids (BK).

Are you coming to the PTA meeting on Tuesday?

She has asked me that question no less than five thousand times. And the answer is always the same. Yes. *Yes*, I'm coming. I have come to every single PTA meeting in the entire time we have known each other. But I know if I don't answer this one time, she'll get snippy. So I quickly reply:

Yes, I'll be there!

> Can you come twenty minutes early to help me set
> up the tables and chairs?

I groan. I knew I was going to get roped into that. But it's very hard to say no to Julie. And she means well. She's amazing as president of the PTA.

> Sure! No problem!

I notice another unread text message, this one from an unknown number. Undoubtedly, it's a spam text message. Or maybe it's from a fan who somehow got my cell phone number. Every once in a while, my number seems to get out there, despite my best efforts to keep it secret. I've had to change it twice. I click on the message to view it:

> Want to know a secret? Your son isn't where you
> think he is.

I stare at the message on the screen. *What?*

A cold, sick feeling comes over me. Bobby is in the backyard. We have a fenced-in backyard, and he and I have an agreement that when I'm filming one of my videos, he's got to either stay out there or in his room. But about half the time, he finds a reason to interrupt me. I was feeling proud of him that he didn't interrupt me this time.

This has got to be a prank. But even so, I'll go check on him.

My legs feel a little wobbly as I step onto the back porch and scan the grass, which is in dire need of trimming. I look around the yard, my eyes darting between the two trees and the little swing set that Bobby has nearly outgrown. I don't see him. Maybe he's hiding behind a tree or something. That kid loves to hide.

"Bobby!" I call out.

My only answer is a slight rustling of leaves.

"April?"

I whirl around, my heart pounding. My husband, Elliot, is standing behind me, dressed in an Armani suit. It's Sunday, but of course, he's on his way to work. I wouldn't expect anything different from my workaholic husband. It used to drive me out of my mind, but I've learned to accept it.

"I'm on my way out," he says. "Just wanted to let you know."

"Wait." There's a slightly hysterical edge to my voice. "I don't see Bobby in the backyard."

Elliot straightens out his tie. It's his red power tie. He must have something important going on today. I remember the first time I saw him in that tie nine years ago, I swooned. I actually *swooned*. I had never met anyone like Elliot Masterson before. He was one of the most handsome and charismatic men I'd ever met. There was something in the back of my head, even then, telling me this man would be my husband and the father of my child someday.

But right now, I can't appreciate how good he looks in his suit and tie. All I can think about is who sent me this text message and where my son is.

"Are you sure he's not out there?" he asks.

"Yes!" I fish around in my pocket for my phone. "And look at this text message someone sent me!"

Elliot takes my phone and reads the text as he rubs at his scalp. It's very smooth—he must have shaved this morning. That's right—my husband shaves his head. He started doing it about four years ago, and I screamed and pulled out my can of mace when he came into the living room with his newly shorn head for the first time. I thought he was going to burgle me—he looked like a completely different person, and I hated it. But after a few weeks, I came around. The shaved head is sexy, virile, and admittedly better than his badly receding hairline.

"It's probably just a prank," he says, although there's a slight tremor in his voice.

"Why would somebody play a prank like that on me?"

"I don't know! You're a public figure. People know you. Maybe somebody's cookies didn't come out right, and they're angry at you."

He's right that I have become a public figure lately. Everybody in our Long Island town seems to know who I am, thanks to my YouTube show. And truth be told, I have received a few creepy text messages over the years from viewers who tracked down my number. But nothing ever came of it.

"Maybe he's upstairs?" Elliot suggests.

It's possible. But I've been in the kitchen for the last hour, and he would have had to go past me to get back in the house. I would have seen that. So he must still be outside.

"He could be hiding…" I say. Bobby is at an age where he thinks it's hilarious to hide somewhere and jump out and startle me at an inopportune moment. *Haha, I scareded you!* If he wasn't so darn cute, I would be furious.

Right now, it would not be cute.

"I'll go check upstairs," Elliot says.

"I'll check the side of the house."

I go out into the backyard, tugging at the bright red

blouse that suddenly feels too hot. On camera, I always wear bright solid colors. Usually, I change shortly after I finish making my video, but there's no time for that now. I feel my ballet flats squishing against the damp grass. "Bobby!" I call again.

No answer. But that doesn't mean anything. If he's hiding, of course he's not going to give away his location.

I stop for a moment and listen. Even though he's good at hiding, he is still only seven. At this point, he's probably giggling to himself. So I listen for giggling. Or crunching of leaves. But I don't hear any.

I get another sting of panic in my chest.

I venture further out into the backyard. I look along the side of the house, where we keep our garbage cans. It's a perfect hiding place for a little boy—I'm hoping to find him crouched behind one of the bins. At this point, he's giving me enough of a scare that I will definitely have to scold him: *Mommy was really scared! Next time, don't hide like that!*

I look behind the bins. Nothing.

Then my eyes fall on the gate to the backyard. It's the only way to get in or out of the backyard without going through the house.

The gate is wide open.

With a shaking hand, I pull my phone out of my pocket. I bring up the text message one more time:

Your son isn't where you think he is.

My hands are shaking so much, it's an effort to respond: *Who are you? Where is he?*

I stand there, watching the screen. Waiting.

But there's no reply.

READING GROUP GUIDE

1. Why do you think the novel opens with a *Dear Debbie* draft in chapter one? What do these drafts add to the story?

2. Do you think Debbie is a good mother? A good wife? Why did she do what she did?

3. Has there ever been a time when you felt fed up with those around you and wanted petty revenge? What is the pettiest thing you have done out of frustration?

4. What did you make of the buzzing in Debbie's head? When did it show up? Why did it appear?

5. Characters find many ways to cope with frustration in the novel, both healthy (working out) and unhealthy (revenge). What are some of the ways you try to cope

with negative feelings? Do you think those ways are healthy or unhealthy?

6. What did you think of Harley's character and her choices? Did you agree with them? Were you surprised about what happened to her in the end?

7. Debbie and her daughters have complicated relationships. Why do you think that is? Did that change by the end of the novel?

8. Would you consider any of the characters to be unreliable narrators? Why? Why not?

9. What did you think of the relationship between Cooper and Debbie? Did it seem like a happy one? Did your perspective change by the end of the novel?

10. Would you take advice from Debbie? Who do you usually go to for advice?

11. Debbie got revenge on a lot of people. Did they deserve it? Who did or did not? Why?

ACKNOWLEDGMENTS

My daughter is the biggest Melanie Martinez fan.

I really like her music too. But at my age, I'm no longer capable of the same sort of hero worship bestowed on a popular singer by a tween girl. My daughter is *obsessed*. And that's how I found myself planted in a front row seat at a Melanie Martinez concert at TD Garden.

Melanie is an incredible performer. My daughter and her friend got out of their seats and were hanging over the railing to get the best view, recording every moment on their iPhones instead of just watching it with their eyeballs. I knew all the songs and loved the performance, but I felt in a different universe from the young people in the audience. And when I looked around me, I saw the same pattern: the excited and energetic teens/tweens standing with their phones in the air, and the tired-looking mothers sitting patiently in their seats. When I looked at those mothers, I could see my own reflected wish that I could be watching this performance from the comfort of my own home rather than in a sticky seat with lines for the ladies' room that stretched around the crowded stadium.

That was the moment when I first came up with Debbie—the middle-aged housewife struggling through life. Who would do anything for her family.

On that note, I want to thank Melanie Martinez for inspiring both my daughter and myself in completely different ways. I only hope her subsequent concerts will be equally fruitful, since I see many more in my future.

(Also, I found a secret bathroom and told as many of my middle-aged mom cohorts as I could.)

I already dedicated this book to my mother, but I want to thank her for instilling in me a deep love of a satisfying revenge story. She loved this one.

I need to give an extra big thank-you to my agent, Christina Hogrebe, who believed in this book so much from the moment she read it. There's nothing more inspiring than someone who believes in you. The entire JRA team has been incredible—it's amazing to have so many people working hard on my behalf.

Thank you to Sourcebooks and especially my editor, Jenna Jankowski, for the most detailed and insightful feedback I could imagine. Mandy Chahal is a publicist extraordinaire—I genuinely don't know how she does what she does, but I'm so grateful. And thank you to all the editors and cover designers and all the people behind the scenes who made this book come together.

Thank you to my many beta readers: Jenna, Maura, Beth, Rebecca, and Pam, who provided some amazing feedback. Thank you to Val for the help with proofreading.

Thank you to Tara for the insightful sensitivity read. That feedback was so incredibly helpful.

Of course, I have to thank all the moderators of my Facebook group—Emily, Daniel, Nancy, Carrie, and Nikki—who help me with social media so that I have more time to write!

I always have to give a huge thank-you to my readers, both online and the ones who don't even own a computer. I am so grateful for your support!

And last but not least, I have to thank my kids, who thankfully both allow me to speak to them in the morning again. Well, sometimes.

ABOUT THE AUTHOR

#1 *New York Times*, *USA Today*, *Washington Post*, *Publishers Weekly*, and *Sunday Times* internationally bestselling author Freida McFadden is a physician specializing in brain injury. Freida is the winner of both the International Thriller Writer Award for Best Paperback Original and the Goodreads Choice Award for Best Thriller. Her novels have been translated into more than forty languages. Freida lives with her family and gray cat in a centuries-old three-story home overlooking the ocean.